# MEAN BONES

## MICHAEL SANTOS

D1153786

BAD CAT PRESS

This book is a work of fiction. The characters, incidents, and dialogue are creations of the author's imagination and are not to be construed as real. Any resemblance to actual events or people, living or dead, is pure coincidence.

ISBN 978-1-7327100-5-4 (Paperback)

*For my parents, who raised me right, so that I haven't turned out like my characters.*

# MEAN BONES

by Michael Santos

## CHAPTER ONE

Earl Tucker Lee was arrested in Cabarrus County for felony speeding, doing 120 in a stolen Camaro and drunk as a skunk while he did it.

He'd led deputies on a forty-minute chase up and down 85, toward the Mecklenburg County line. When they finally managed to box him in, they brought him out of the muscle car at gunpoint, yelled for him to lay his ass on the ground, and pulled his records in their computer system. Saw he had a fugitive warrant, outstanding drug and gun charges from his days pushing Oxy and heroin from Wilkesboro to Asheville. Tucker Lee had run with a group of criminals back then, a family of shit-kicking, drug-dealing good ol' boys called the Deegans, and had been a wanted man for some time.

He stayed the night in the Cabarrus jail, got printed,

and had a fresh mug shot taken—he was a good forty pounds heavier than in his last one, ten years ago. Had lost some hair, too, but his round face and coarse brown beard remained the same. He wore glasses now and told the officers with a grin, "Hey, I might've been drunk and speeding, but least I had on my corrective lenses, uh?"

They didn't find it funny.

The next morning, he learned a man would be coming that evening to take him back to Charlotte, where he'd be in federal custody, a result of being wanted by DEA and ATF. Shit, he was famous.

That afternoon, he called one of the Deegans' other associates, a fella whose name he didn't know and wouldn't have said anyway, what with the police monitoring the call. They talked about Tucker Lee's situation and how he was to be transported to the city. The associate said not to worry, the Deegans knew a guy who'd get him sprung, and to just sit tight, boy, until he arrived. Tucker Lee asked, Well, how would the person know where he'd be at, when he didn't even know? Again, they said not to trouble himself with the details. The police listening in assumed that meant an attorney would be coming by and didn't pay it any mind, thinking they wouldn't have to deal with Tucker Lee or his lawyer once the federals had him.

Tucker Lee understood what the guy meant.

He sat in his cell, wondering what kind of man the

feds would send to pick him up. Asked a guard about it and got no answer, but kept pressing just to have something to do, somebody to at least talk *at*. Wasn't it out of Charlotte police's jurisdiction to come here? So, probably not them. Maybe a county unit would take him, uh? He'd get another ride in the back of one of their radio cars? Or somebody with Highway? They had jurisdiction in the whole state, right?

He got his answer late that night, around eleven, after waiting all damn day. A slim fella, late twenties or early thirties, skin and bone with some muscle, pale skin, and dark hair signed for him. This fella had a star on his belt and carried a holstered Glock 22. A deputy United States marshal, he told Tucker Lee, though he didn't share his name just yet. He said he was with the Hornet's Nest Fugitive Task Force. The fella was real soft-spoken, like he was so sure of himself, there wasn't no need to raise his voice to convey a point. Hell, it was more intimidating, the way he made you really listen to catch every word out of his mouth.

One curious thing about him, he wore all black— black suit, black button-down, black tie.

Tucker Lee said, "You're dressed for a funeral."

The marshal, in that same soft voice, said, "Yours, if you try anything."

Well, at least the man was cool. He'd need to be. The Deegans would have *some*thing in store for him, some plan to spring Tucker Lee, and God only knew what they'd do to the marshal in the process.

Now Tucker Lee rode behind the passenger's seat of a black Chevy Tahoe, with cuffs on his wrists and this United States marshal behind the wheel, cruising down 85, the same stretch from his joyride in the Camaro. Every minute or two, the marshal would glance in the mirror to check on him. One hand on the Tahoe's wheel, the other on his holster.

Tucker Lee said, "Why you moving me so late at night?"

"Oh, there are lots of people eager to see you, and it was a busy day at the office. CMPD, Drug Enforcement, ATF. Nighttime's just as good for transport duty. Better, when you consider there's less traffic." He was looking in the mirror again. "You realize how bad you're wanted? Those drug charges? I'm surprised you been able to run this long." And smiled at him with warm but steely eyes and white teeth that seemed to glow in the dark. Or maybe they just stood out next to the fella's black clothes.

"Why're you dressed like that?"

"You know, we really don't need to get acquainted."

The fella's accent was interesting. A North Carolina boy, for sure, but what part of the state? He had crisp pronunciation, like he'd spent too much time in the big city and it'd rubbed off on him. But the voice had some of the Blue Ridge Mountains in it, an old-school South kind of sound that came out in a slight drawl, dropping a word here and there, taking his sentences slow and steady like a mountain creek.

"I'm only conversating," Tucker Lee said, "with a fellow western North Carolinian. Am I right?"

The marshal gave him a Cheshire cat grin. "Here I thought nobody could tell anymore. Not after working in the Queen City a couple years."

"Maybe some people can't. But I hear your background in your speech."

"Wilkes County, huh? I read it in your file."

"Born and bred. Worked in a poultry plant in the '80s. You're probably too young to remember when we had textiles and furniture and mirrors all being made in the county. And meat, yeah, the huge poultry companies supplying kitchen tables everywhere."

Tucker Lee was in his early sixties now, and shit, he missed those days.

"I might not have as many years as you," the marshal said, "but I know what you mean. Talking about when Wilkes had an economy."

"That's a fact. Before fucking NAFTA had all the factories closing their doors, moving overseas. Hard to make a decent living with them, near impossible without them." He laughed to show how clever he was.

The marshal nodded. "I'm a North Wilkesboro kid,

but I was lucky, going into public service. Government'll never shut *its* doors."

Tucker Lee stretched his legs under the passenger's seat, enjoying his interaction with another Wilkes native. It was as good a way as any to pass the time until he got sprung, and the marshal maybe got killed. Talking to a dead man dressed for a funeral, how about that?

"So, you left and moved to Charlotte?"

"Started with Highway Patrol," the marshal said, willing to get acquainted now, maybe because they were from the same place. "Climbed the ranks and eventually got hired by the Marshals Service. Charlotte's got the largest federal court in the Western District, so that's where you'll find me."

"You like it, hunting down assholes such as myself?"

"It's the purest form of law enforcement. I'd do it for free."

They were silent for a time, Tucker Lee looking out his window at the streetlamps they passed, light and shadow falling over the car in an alternating, lulling rhythm.

Then he saw two white crosses on the side of the road, a wreath of flowers hanging on each of them.

"You see that? Always makes me sad, thinking of people losing each other like that. Their lives destroyed, blink of an eye."

The marshal was serious now. "Says a man makes his living with drugs, getting folks addicted."

"I already told you, I'm an asshole. Don't mean I'm a completely terrible person, does it?"

"I don't particularly care what kind of person you are. I've got nothing against you, you understand? It's just, you're my current fugitive, and after you there'll be another. But you have to know I don't look kindly on what you did to get those warrants. You talk about it being tough up in Wilkes? Act like you wish it was better?"

"But I do, really I do. If we could just go back to the old days..."

"Yeah, you say that. Then you sell your shit to people so down on their luck, a quick high is how they stand to keep living. And then they get hooked, and you make more money, and they wonder why the hell everything's falling apart around them. You think that's better?"

"When the system's rigged against the working man, why can't the working man go outside the system, uh? We all got to get by."

The marshal shook his head. "What you just said, now you understand why I'd do my job for nothing."

Tucker Lee hesitated a moment, thinking about that, resenting this fella's self-righteous bullshit, like the star on his belt made him superior. Then said, "Well, least we'll always have Wilkes in common. Don't matter what side we're on, there's *always* that." Trying to make the fella see he'd forever be a man from the county, regardless of how much time he spent down in the city, with its wealth and industry and people in a routine of living large.

"Tell me something," the marshal said, looking di-rect into the mirror with piercing eyes, but still speaking in his soft way, "when you were dealing Oxy and heroin and the like, you ran for the Deegans?"

Tucker Lee frowned and would've crossed his arms, except for the handcuffs. "Ain't you have to read me my rights before questioning me?"

"I ain't questioning you," the marshal said, his accent getting thicker the longer they spoke together—Tucker Lee was proud of that. "I'm just curious, is all, whether they're still in business."

"You know them?"

"I did, once upon a time."

"Yeah, they're still in business," Tucker Lee said. "So I'm told."

"Who's in charge, the old man?"

"Joseph? Naw, he took ill, moved to assisted living to spend his final days with his money. Luther, his boy, he's got the reins. Again, so I'm told. I wouldn't know anything about it now."

"Uh-huh," the marshal said, staring straight ahead and clenching his jaw, like the subject bothered him.

But then why bring it up?

Tucker Lee said, "Are the marshals going after the Deegans?"

That'd be some nice information to give Luther and Joe, a little thank-you for getting him out of custody.

The marshal didn't answer him, and they were quiet again, approaching the Charlotte city limits now, the tall pines that had lined the highway giving way to office buildings, vehicle rental lots, and healthcare offices, all dark and shut down for the night. Traffic had picked up but still flowed, and they kept on at the speed limit. Tucker Lee wanted to ask how fast this government Tahoe could do. Maybe 120, like he'd done in the Camaro? But he decided not to push his luck with this fella who wore all black.

"You never answered my question," Tucker Lee said, still in the mood to talk.

"Which one? There've been several."

"Why you dress the way you do."

The marshal shifted in his seat and a small smile tugged at the corners of his mouth. "I told you I did well with Highway Patrol? I was the meanest pursuit man they had."

"Shit, they could've used you the other night. Took them forever, close to an hour, to catch me."

"I'd have stopped you quick." Saying it in that cool, soft-spoken voice and with a slight nod of his head. "See, before then, I raced late-model stock cars, when I was a teen."

"No kidding?"

"At quarter-mile asphalt ovals across the state. All the

big ones, Hickory, Wake, Tri-County, Orange County. Even won a championship. Had my sights set on racing North Wilkesboro one day, before it closed in '96."

"I used to love that track," Tucker Lee said. "I went to the last race. Gordon won it."

"Don't tell me you liked him?"

"Hell no, I pulled for Earnhardt."

The marshal's smile widened. "You're right, you're not a completely terrible person. Anyway, what I loved back then, I loved the chase. When there was a guy in front of me, but I had the faster car and knew it. I'd ride in his tire tracks and pull up to his bumper, give him a bump to get him loose. Then pull beside him and race, wheel-to-wheel under the lights. He'd get a run out of the corners, I'd dive it in and brake hard." He shrugged. "I think that's why I became a marshal. I'm still all about the chase."

"What was your number?"

"Three. I drove a black number three, same as Earnhardt. You can see why I was a fan."

It made Tucker Lee pause, something about the fella's story not sitting right now.

"And I had the same aggressive style as Earnhardt, too, after watching him on television every weekend. People would see my black hood in their mirror and move aside, not wanting to *get* moved. So, when I told my colleagues about all this, they gave me my nickname, 'The Intimidator,' just like Dale. Saying I should use the same strategy with fugitives. Intimidate them, pursue them like I used to race people, never letting up. And that's why I wear all black. Funny thing is, I'm known for it now. And it works. They see me coming, they know they can give up, or I'll make them."

Tucker Lee's mouth had gone dry. Yeah, he knew who this was.

"What's your name, Marshal?"

"Shay Harlowe."

"Shit," Tucker Lee said, and sat up fast, causing Shay Harlowe to pull his Glock from its holster. "I remember you. And your daddy."

"Sit back," Harlowe said, his tone ice-cold. When Tucker Lee had complied, the marshal said, "What about my daddy?" His face showing interest.

"I knew him. Before he got shot. How old were you when it happened?"

"Seventeen. I'd just won my championship. Week later, two deputies knock on the door, saying he was dead. Shot where he stood, in the garage we rented down the street for the car, and nobody could figure why it'd happened."

"They never found his killer either, uh?"

"Not yet." The marshal squinted at him in the mirror. "If you knew him, how come I don't recall meeting you? He used to introduce me to all his friends, showing me off to them: Look at my boy, the racer."

"I wasn't his friend."

"What were you to him?"

Tucker Lee leaned forward again. "I'm the fella who shot him."

∗ ∗ ∗

"You're bullshitting me," Shay said, believing it to be a joke, a bad one, this prisoner having some fun with his captor.

After all, this man was from the county, and there wasn't a soul there who hadn't heard the news of his father's murder at the time. It had been in the papers. It had been the only thing people talked about, except around Shay. He remembered the stares he used to get as he passed, the hushed voices speaking about the shooting, like they'd expected Shay to fall apart any minute under the weight of his daddy's death. But he didn't fall apart and didn't need them sheltering him. What he did, he abandoned his racing career and became a lawman, looking for justice or revenge, one.

Maybe this Earl Tucker Lee knew who Shay was and wanted to get in his head, mess with him some, and this was how he'd chosen to do it. It was a poor choice.

"I'm not," Tucker Lee said. "And I can prove it to you. I can tell you why he was killed."

Shay didn't say anything, letting the man talk, waiting to see what the angle would be. Could it be true, that this prisoner was the one fugitive Shay had always wanted to find? If it was, Shay had a mind to stop on the side of the road, shoot him, and claim an escape attempt or assault on a federal officer, say he'd pulled his gun in self-defense.

But knew he couldn't give in to those thoughts, even if revenge would be more satisfying than justice.

"In exchange," Tucker Lee said, "I want you to get me a deal, 'cause there's information you'll want, I mean officially, in what I'm gonna tell you. Can you do that?"

Now Shay did pull over, put the car in park, and twisted around in his seat to face Tucker Lee.

Stuck a finger in the man's face and said in his even tone, "Know this, if you're the man who killed my daddy, if this isn't a load of horseshit, I will see to it you rot, you understand? Deal or no, I'll make sure your life is over, even if I can't end it myself."

Tucker Lee nodded and gave a cautious smile, almost apologetic. "It was back when I was running with the Deegans." Shay squinted. "You know they're into more than pills and dope. Like loans. Okay? I give you something to use against them, you help me with the judge, prosecutors, anybody that'll listen?"

"I'll see what I can do."

"I need a guarantee."

"I can't give you one. So what you're gonna do, either start talking, or we'll continue the drive, and you won't speak again until we get there."

Tucker Lee screwed up his face, like he was considering his options. Shay stared him down, showing he was serious.

Then Tucker Lee sighed. "You had a good season that year, lot of wins, I remember it, and the title. Now, I've never raced, but I'd bet putting that good a car on the track, week in, week out, must've cost your daddy a damn fortune, even with sponsors. Got to a point he needed cash to keep you going."

"He told me the winnings always covered the expenses."

"Maybe for each single race. But for the season, all the work he was doing on your ride? Naw, he ran dry. And he knew right where to get more. Made a deal with the Deegans, saying you were gonna win the title and he'd give Joseph the championship money to pay down the loan. And that would've covered it, too. Except the first deal wasn't enough to keep you winning. How else you think a small, one-car team beats the big boys, otherwise? He came back, couple months later, asked for more, and it began adding up. Said he'd find the money, but he had to know he wouldn't be able to do it. Your daddy, though, he would've done *any*thing for you. I admired that."

It explained some things Shay had never been able to figure out back then. Why his family never did anything with the winnings, his daddy saying they'd put it all into savings. Savings? Seventeen-year-old Shay had never understood it. Then there was the man who came to their house a few times, causing his father to look real nervous and then talk to the visitor in private, away from Shay. Now he tried to remember if that visitor might've been Tucker Lee, but couldn't recall the face. Then there was the way his parents had started fighting at the kitchen table every night, while Shay listened from upstairs. He could hear the tone, not the words. After years of happy marriage, something had them going at it —like his father getting mixed up with criminals and their dirty money.

All for his sake.

"After giving your daddy two or three second chances to pay up, Joseph called me and explained the problem," Tucker Lee said. "I want you to know, I fought like hell to talk him out of it. Told him, what about Harlowe's son? His wife? Can't you give them a little more time? If he's dead, you won't ever get that money back. But you can't talk Joseph out of nothing, and your daddy had used up his sympathy."

Shay hadn't shifted his gaze once this whole time. Still didn't, as he said, "How did you do it?"

"We knew he worked late at the garage, like you said. The trick was picking a night when you weren't in there with him. Top of not wanting to leave a witness, I didn't want you to get hurt. Or see it happen, you being a kid."

"Well, thanks for looking out for me," Shay said with venom.

"I confronted him, let him see who it was. He was

aware who sent me. I gave him a final chance. If he had money with him, anything, give it to me, I'd take it to Joseph, and I'd lobby for his life. But it didn't end peaceably."

"He knew why you were there?"

"Oh yeah. He did a dumb thing, taking those loans. But he was smart."

"What'd he say? His last words, did he say anything to you?"

"He looked me in the eye, told me, 'This'll settle it, and don't you touch my family.' Then called me a son of a bitch for good measure. The last thing *I* said? Told him I was sorry, but I didn't have a choice. I meant it."

Shay smiled, seeing his father's gaunt face in a snarl, the tan, sun-wrinkled skin creasing around his eyes as he squinted to show he was tough, and heard his old man's soft voice saying those words.

Now Shay gave Tucker Lee the same treatment. "Sure you did," he said. "What I'm wondering, why you telling me this? Why confess to me?"

"I want the deal," Tucker Lee said. "And ... I'm gonna save your life, tonight."

"Excuse me?"

"There's somebody set up down the road, waiting on us, taking advantage of the late hour, no one around. A person the Deegans sent to spring me. Okay? Gonna kill you and bust me out of custody."

"They're fixing to do that right now?"

Tucker Lee gave a slow nod. "They don't want a guy knows as much as me in a position to spill, like I just done."

Shay stared down the stretch of dark highway, traffic thinned to a trickle now. They had reached a series of exits leading to the industrial areas around Uptown, a concentric circle of utilities, railroad tracks, and lower-population land between the city center and all the neighborhoods and towns beyond. It would be an ideal location for an ambush, Shay had to admit, especially at this time of night.

"Why not let them do it?" Shay said. "I'm dead, you're free."

Tucker Lee had an earnest look in his eye. "I don't want to see another Wilkes County Harlowe die 'cause of me."

"Or," Shay said, using his even tone to cut through the man's bullshit remorse, "you understand the score. Whoever the Deegans sent, they'll kill you, too. That'd be the only way to make sure you can't snitch on them. We're both familiar with how far they'll go, huh?" Tucker Lee didn't have anything to say to that. "So, you want me to save you, that it? Then get you a deal, get you sitting pretty with the law. After what you done to me and my family?"

"I'm trying to do right by you now."

"I'd just as soon let them shoot you, you understand? You won't get pity from me, nor forgiveness. Was a time,

I had in mind to chase you down and put a bullet in you myself. Now I can't, I'd lose my star and worse. But if the Deegans want to take care of it for me, that'd be fine."

Shay took a second to compose himself again, wiping his mouth with the back of his hand. Then said, "Thing is, I don't intend to let another Wilkes County Harlowe die tonight either."

"What do you propose we do, then? Call for backup and hope your friends at Highway Patrol drive fast as you?"

It gave Shay an idea, one that didn't entail backup. He started the car and took them up an exit ramp, to get off the highway and find a better place for it all to go down.

"Mr. Lee, how you think you'd look in all black?"

\* \* \*

THEY STAYED in position on the side of the road, two lanes running north and south into the city, lots of trees and overgrowth, a car passing only every few minutes.

Shay was fixing it so whoever the Deegans had sent would come to him. He wasn't about to drive headlong into an ambush. If they wanted Tucker Lee as bad as he imagined they did, their button man would still make the first move.

Tucker Lee was in the driver's seat now, hands cuffed to the steering wheel, fingers tapping on the gray leather.

Wearing Shay's suit, which was too small for him but would be convincing enough from a distance. Shay occupied Lee's former position behind the passenger's seat. He had on the man's green North Carolina DOC jumper. Shay recognized the outfit color coding from his previous prisoner-transport assignments. Red for death row inmates, brown for close security, and green for low-level offenders like Mr. Lee.

Except Earl Tucker Lee wasn't low-level to him.

Shay had his Glock 22 pointed at his fugitive but kept his gaze centered on the road ahead. Waiting, scanning each passing car to see if it stopped or circled back on them. None did.

Until a silver Ford Escape, the model year at least half a decade old, a headlight out, pulled to the shoulder in the opposite lane, about forty yards down, across the 85 overpass between it and the Tahoe. The driver killed the sole working light and sat there. Shay could feel the person's eyes on them, especially on Tucker Lee in the black suit of clothes.

Tucker Lee must've felt it, too. He squirmed in his seat and looked at Shay in the rearview.

Saying, "Your plan here, it's gonna work, right?"

"Not sure. We'll see how it plays out soon enough."

"What do you mean, you're not sure? Why the hell're we even trying this, if you're not sure?"

" 'Cause I'm the one with the gun and the star, and this is how I say it's gonna be."

"Way I see it, *I'm* in a bad spot, them thinking I'm you."

Shay gave the man his Cheshire cat grin again. "Yeah, I better know what I'm doing, huh?"

"This ain't a time to be fucking with each other," Tucker Lee said, his voice higher and panicked. "You probably hate me for what I done, I get that, but c'mon now, you got to tell me you're gonna work this out. Ain't it your job to keep me safe?"

Shay shrugged. "Look, the fact they haven't come over already, it means they're reevaluating. The way it was set up, they expected us to come to them. Now we've changed that."

"You think they'll give up?"

"Maybe."

"Decide it ain't worth the risk now?"

"It's a possibility."

Tucker Lee seemed to relax, letting out a long breath and leaning against the headrest. "Okay, yeah, yeah, that's what they're doing all right."

Shay let the man feel at ease a moment before saying, "On the other hand, I can't imagine they want to return to the Deegans empty-handed." Paused for emphasis and said, "Can you?"

Tucker Lee's wide eyes were back in the mirror. "What do you mean?"

"After all," Shay said, "*you* didn't want to, huh?"

* * *

ANOTHER FIVE MINUTES passed before the Escape crept forward, still on the shoulder and right up against the railing. It halted about twenty yards away, now on the same side of the overpass as them, and the driver shut off the engine.

Shay squinted to see the person in the dark. He could make out the driver, a male, getting out of the SUV with what looked like a pistol in his hand. Wearing cargo pants and a hoodie over a ball cap. He crossed the road and was now closing in on the Tahoe.

Tucker Lee jangled the cuffs like he wanted to run. "Are you gonna do something? Shit, Marshal, you got to do *some*thing."

What Shay did, he ducked down in the back seat, making sure his body was out of the firing line but still raised up enough to see over the dash. He watched as the triggerman aimed the pistol. Heard Tucker Lee yell for him to shoot the guy, shoot him quick, and then saw two flashes as a pair of bullets pierced the windshield, Tucker Lee slouching behind the wheel, the man silent now.

The shooter approached real slow, keeping the gun pointed at the limp figure of Tucker Lee dressed like a marshal.

Then stopped at the hood of the Tahoe and shouted, "Earl, you there?" A high, rough voice with a thick accent.

Shay said, "Yeah, c'mon and get me out." Putting as much Wilkes County into his speech as he could.

The shooter came to the back door on the driver's side, and Shay shot him, making sure his single round from the Glock put the man down without killing him.

Shay stepped out and walked around the front of the car so he could get a look at Tucker Lee's body, two holes in the prisoner's chest, blood turning Shay's black shirt even darker. He kept the Glock on the shooter as he drew up to him and kicked aside the pistol, a .45 Colt.

The shooter writhed on the ground, holding his shoulder, grunting and groaning and hissing, like making that much noise would ease the pain any.

"You're not Earl."

"No shit," Shay said. "Now listen, I'm gonna get EMS out here for you, and then you're gonna be taken into custody."

"Why didn't you kill me?"

"So you can relay a message to whoever hired you. Luther, the old man, I don't care who, long as they get it, you understand?"

"Man, call that ambulance, I'm bleeding out."

"Do you understand?"

"Yeah, I understand, come on, man."

"What you're gonna say when you call them from the hospital or the prison infirmary, wherever you end up," Shay said in his soft-spoken way, "you're gonna let them know that Deputy U.S. Marshal Shay Harlowe is coming for them. If they say they don't remember me, tell them don't worry, they will real soon."

"I'll do that, I'll do all that, okay? Now get me some fucking help, man, I'm dying."

"No, you ain't. And I'm not done."

"The hell else is there?"

"Tell them their best bet is to start running. But even still," he said, "I'll chase them down."

## CHAPTER TWO

CLINT PURDY GREW CHRISTMAS TREES ON TWENTY
acres of land near the border of Ashe and Wilkes coun-
ties. And 3,000 marijuana plants, hidden in grow houses
and a drying shed he tucked away among the rows of
balsam and Fraser firs that covered his rolling fields.

Today he wheeled his white van, with Purdy Farms
printed on the side in big red letters framed by holly leaf
graphics, over the grass trail that cut through the trees to
his house. Saw a champagne Jeep Wrangler kicking up
dust on the dirt drive that fed in front of the place, and
Clint knew who it belonged to.

Victoria Beaumont.

Flipping her long red hair at him, as he parked his van
and went over, Vickie in her early thirties and still fine
like wine in her black blouse and blue jeans. Sometimes
when she came to see him, she wore her red polo shirt

and name tag from the drugstore where she worked in Wilkesboro.

She looked at him sideways and said, "I've been meaning to ask you, why don't you ever wear a shirt?"

Clint always went bare-chested to show off his tattoo, what he was proudest of in life besides his farm. On his thirtieth birthday, eight years ago, he'd gotten a naked woman put onto his belly. She had gigantic breasts, and what was really cool about it? Her inked left nipple lined up perfect with his real one. He just loved how she got heads to turn, people doing double takes, staring on the sidewalk or in traffic while they processed what they were seeing, and then either getting offended or pointing and grinning. Some folk with higher sensibilities would often tell him to cover that shit, man, it was indecent. But he never did.

Well, except for when he was in church.

What he said to Vickie, he told her, "She got to keep her color." Pointing at his belly woman. "I like 'em good and sunned."

Vickie shook her head, not passing judgment but getting a kick out of him. Then pulled an orange pill bottle from her pocket and shook it, letting him hear the satisfying *clack* of one hundred round tablets of Oxy hitting the plastic.

"No," Vickie said with a smirk, "you like them pharmed up." He reached for the bottle, but she put it behind her back and hiked her eyebrows at him. "Not until I get mine."

Clint adjusted the straw hat he wore over his long brown hair. He waved for her to follow him through the gate of his white picket fence that was missing some posts, onto the wraparound porch with two picnic benches he'd stolen from two different parks several years ago, and inside to the kitchen. The home built of sturdy old wood, its gray paint and green trim chipping, the roof streaked with age, and the pine floors creaky. His barn, which had been there as long as the house, looked about the same. But the faux log cabin across the dirt drive was in real good shape. Clint had built it on a deck-between trailer, adorned it with Christmas lights and artificial wreaths, and would haul the whole thing to Charlotte, Winston-Salem, and Raleigh, where he'd sell his trees on lots during the holidays. Beyond the house were the hazy hills of the Blue Ridge Mountains, the leaves starting to change in early October.

Now he opened the bread box on his kitchen counter and grabbed two bags of his best reefer from behind the rye. A blend of his own invention, low cannabidiol and high THC, made you real energized. And horny, which was why he called it "Purdy Woman," implying when you smoked it, you should get you one and have a good romp.

He wanted to partake with Vickie, but she'd never gone for the idea. Not once, each of the four times he'd suggested it.

She folded the plastic bags and hid them in her purse. Saying, "Saw on the news, this old drug-runner from here got shot. While in federal custody. Some nut tried to ambush the U.S. marshal he was with."

"Heard that too."

"It made me think of you, Clint."

"Me? I didn't have nothing to do with that."

"I bet you knew the guy, though."

Clint shifted his weight and crossed his arms, covering his tattoo woman's face. "And I bet you got a reason for bringing it up."

"Get me a drink and I'll tell you."

He liked her style, the cool demeanor she had.

Clint took a bottle of Jim Beam from the cabinet above the bread box and poured glasses. Downed his, while she sipped on hers.

"You figure," he said, "I grow reefer, that guy used to *run* reefer and narcotics, so we must be connected."

"I remember how it was, when I was a girl in Cricket. Joseph Deegan, public enemy number one, if you believed the police. He and his network, like the guy who got shot? They were who you went to if you were, say, a teenager looking to get high in the back of your boyfriend's pickup on a Friday night."

"You know that old fart's still pumping blood? Deegan, I mean. Not doing diddly-shit now. But he's still around. And influential, I'd guess."

"I didn't think he'd make it to old age. At least, not as a free man."

"His son's taken over." Clint filled his glass and held it, deciding he better change the subject before Vickie asked him more about the Deegans. "Your folks still down in Cricket these days?"

"Mama died after two strokes, and Daddy's gone out to the coast. Carolina Beach, has a condo a few blocks from the water. What he's into now, pretty much just fishing and reading about fishing and watching fishing on TV. And forgetting I exist."

"You piss him off?"

"I think it was the second time I got arrested that did it, yeah. The first was when my boyfriend and I got caught with pot in the back of his pickup." She smiled. "We broke it off after that. *His* daddy was running for sheriff, and how would it have looked, his son getting mixed up with me, a bad influence and overall delinquent?"

"Hell, I can't imagine you with a cop for a father-in-law anyways."

"The second arrest," she said, after another sip of bourbon, "was on suspicion of dealing pills."

"They weren't wrong."

"But they had no proof."

Clint grinned. "Still weren't wrong. I get it, though, I been hassled by them county cops too. Coming by, wanting to check into rumors I'm cultivating herb. Took me to the station in Wilkesboro, oh, two months ago. A DEA federal was there too, in this nice suit. Winking at me, he says, 'How you doing, Mr. Purdy?' like an asshole, like he ain't there to ruin my life. Me and half a dozen Mexicans I got tending my trees, we all got pulled in for questioning. Told 'em I'm not guilty and accused 'em of profiling my guys."

"You *are* farming it."

"Bet your sweet ass I am. My family, we been on this land three generations. I hope I'd have learned *some*thing by now. Never needed to work for anybody but myself. That's what I told them police. They caught me at a bad time, just about to harvest and ship the year's inventory. Gonna be a busy two, three months, all right. 'See,' I said. I told 'em, 'what we do, we hand-cut each tree, shake 'em to get rid of the debris, bale 'em nice and tight, and then I take my tractor, this big green monster of a thing, and we rest 'em under those natural pines growing on the edge of my fields. Then they sit there 'til November, when they go bye-bye.' I let 'em know how busy I was and how inconvenienced they'd made me."

"Did they care?"

"No, but I didn't get charged, now did I?"

Vickie topped off her glass without finishing what he'd already given her. This lady had a weird way of drinking. And of living, but Clint wasn't one to judge. He just wondered what her angle was. Normally, she'd come for her weed and take off, not inclined to spend extra time with him. So what else did she want this visit?

"What happens," she said, "if you ever have to go on the lam? You know, say they come after you and they're serious about it."

"Like they weren't serious before, with Mr. DEA Asshole asking how I was?"

"You know what I mean. Would you leave your land behind?"

"Not sure," Clint said. "What if I did, what would happen to it?"

"They'd seize it, probably."

"Then hell no," he said, gulping down another shot and slamming the glass on the Formica counter for emphasis. "Let 'em kill me right on this spot before I'll see 'em take the farm from me."

"You could burn it," she said, smirking, like she was trying to get him riled up. "Like the Russians did to the Nazis in World War II? Or like the end of *Pineapple Express*."

"Saying I could burn all the reefer, like they did in the movie? James Franco and ... who was that other fella?"

"Seth Rogan."

"That's right. He plays the same stoner character in everything he does, I can't remember one from the other no more."

"So, would you torch your own farm to keep the police from seizing it all?"

Clint said, "Maybe. It'd be an in-the-moment decision."

She took another dainty sip, and he caught her staring at his tattoo again.

"Don't offend you, does it?"

She shook her head. "It's funny, in a deft way."

"How about," he said, his drink giving him confidence, "you and I sample some of that Purdy Woman real quick, have some fun?"

"Don't you have work to do?"

"Nothing that can't wait two minutes."

Vickie poked his chest, right between the inked lady's eyes. "I'll say this, your tat got my attention the day we met."

"At the apple festival in Wilkesboro last year."

"I thought it was funny then, too. Just glimpsed it through the crowd and knew I had to see who this was."

"Cute redhead—my favorite, so's you know—comes up to me and says hi. I'm in the middle of gnawing on a caramel-dipped Red Delicious and another kind of red delicious appears."

She put a hand on her hip. "Come on, you can give me a better line than that shit."

"It's what I thought, honest to God. And look where that meeting led." He took a step closer to her. "Could lead to even more."

"I'd like it to," she said.

He took that as a green light and moved to grab her around the waist, but she dodged him and laughed.

"Didn't you just say—"

"Not like that, Clint. See, I think you *are* connected to that pill-runner and, by extension, Joseph Deegan."

Now they were coming to it. "What do you care if I am or not?"

"Just tell me. You want to screw my brains out but you can't talk to me?"

Clint licked his lips, getting the last taste of whiskey off them. "You're only teasing me like this 'cause you got an idea for making a play and you need me to help you do it. Must be something heavier than your little setup swiping pills."

"Well, if you're not interested..."

She headed for the front door, her heels making a deep report on the pine floors.

"I am," he said. "But anything that relates to the Deegans? I got to know how much trouble this could get me into."

She gave another one of her smirks, *still* teasing him, knowing each time she did he got closer to saying yes. Came back to him and said, "That guy getting shot has me thinking."

"You're always thinking."

"The way it used to be? That doesn't have to be the way it is now."

"You're losing me already."

"You grow for them, right? You're the Deegans' main weed supplier?"

Clint frowned, disappointed it was that obvious. "Maybe so."

"With how much you produce, how could you not be? Who else in the county could you be selling that much to? And God knows they're the only ones with the network to distribute it, unless those Mexicans you mentioned are connected."

"You assume that just 'cause of their heritage? Not very tolerant of you. When you went to college, they didn't teach you to respect other cultures in all those snowflake classes you took?"

"Cut the shit, Clint, and tell me if I'm right."

"Maybe you are. I'm still waiting to hear why the hell I should keep listening."

She looked into his eyes. "If it were me, and I saw that marijuana was losing its spot as the top drug on the market *and* that the Deegans' hold on that market was weakening, too? I'd be considering the future. Asking myself, Who's going to make all that money, now that Joseph's in retirement?"

"I told you, his boy's in charge—Luther. But you're saying I could do it myself?"

"What if somebody got Luther out of the way? Created room for another player to run the pot game? And the pills, the *new* cash cow."

He set his hat on the counter and ran a hand through his hair. "You mean we should take him out?"

"Why not? Other than his last name, what makes him so special?"

"Kill a Deegan—that's a bold fucking idea, you know it? Then again, so's me running the entire drug business."

"Not *you*," Vickie said. "Us."

# CHAPTER THREE

THEY SUSPENDED SHAY, PENDING THE RESULTS OF THE investigation into Tucker Lee's demise and a psychiatric evaluation clearing Deputy Marshal Harlowe for duty.

His doctor was a woman named Amy Barolo, pretty, thirty-three or -four, dark curly hair down to her shoulders, and skin the color of coffee with a lot of cream. Had this been anything other than a punishment for failing to protect his prisoner, he would've cared to learn more about her.

Instead, he sat in a black leather chair across from Amy, his arms crossed, a disinterested look on his face. She was silent in her navy blazer and suit skirt, maybe waiting for him to speak first.

He wasn't going to.

After a minute, she said, "I've treated several law enforcement officers before."

" 'Treat' implies there's something wrong with me," he said, and knew it was a mistake, an opening for her to exploit.

"Do *you* think there is?"

So this was how it was going to be. A personal battle between them over nothing, just so he could get a form signed and be cleared to go back to work.

"I mention those other LEOs," she said, "because I want to give you confidence that I can help."

"With what? I didn't come for any problem. It's a requirement for my job, no more."

"Remind me what branch of law enforcement you're in."

Shay sensed the question was bullshit. She knew exactly what he did, who he was, everything the marshals had no doubt shared with her. Probably had it typed up in the file folder resting on her lap.

"I'm a United States marshal. Well, a deputy, technically."

"What's your main duty, as a marshal?"

Shay cleared his throat. "Catching fugitives."

"Why did you become a marshal?"

"They were hiring at the same time I was applying."

A slight smile tugged at the corners of Amy's mouth. "I mean, why *that* type of officer? As opposed to a detective or, say, an FBI agent?"

Shay shrugged. "I liked the idea of chasing wanted felons who're running for their lives."

" 'Running for their lives.' The way you say that, it makes them sound almost sympathetic. Like they're the good guys and you're the villain."

"That's how they see it, I'm sure. And I don't hate the idea of being a villain to them. You have to understand, we deal with all kinds. Killers, sexual predators, drug traffickers, gangsters, even terrorists. Dangerous people society's better for losing. I'll gladly be their bad guy."

"Where does that come from?"

Amy had a calm, pleasing voice that carried an earnest quality. If you weren't careful, it would lull you into a relaxed state, get you to confide in her. Shay wasn't about to fall for it. No, keep this simple and quick, in and out. Get his clearance without giving away anything to her. But he liked talking about his job. Maybe if he played along now, he could avoid the deeper, more personal subjects she probably planned to discuss later.

"I raced cars as a teen. Then went to Highway Patrol out of college. I guess pursuits have always been a thrill for me."

"How long have you been a marshal?"

"Four years."

"From age twenty-five?"

"Correct."

Shay glanced around the office, a rectangular space with arched windows, a glass-and-iron desk at the far end, and their two chairs with a matching glass-and-iron coffee table between them. Amy's degrees from Georgetown and UNC–Chapel Hill hung on the wall behind her.

She was still focused on him, analyzing him. He was more uncomfortable here, being studied like this, than when he'd been waiting for the Deegans' gunman with Tucker Lee.

Amy must've picked up on what he was looking at, saying, "Where did *you* study?"

"CPCC, right there in Uptown. Two years there, then transferred to UNC–Charlotte. Went for criminal justice and criminology."

"So you knew you wanted a career in law enforcement by the time you were in school."

Shay shrugged again. "By the time I went to UNCC, I'd say."

"Let's go back to your racing days. Why did you quit? I'm not very familiar with that whole world, but it doesn't seem like the kind of thing that's easy to get into. Or give up."

"Money ran out. It's expensive as hell to field a competitive car. And mine was the best. I was good behind the wheel. Won a championship in my final season. But putting on that kind of campaign? It used up the sponsor dollars and everything else we had."

"By *we* you mean your parents were supportive of it?"

"They were behind me the whole way."

"Was it your dream to be a race car driver?"

"Isn't it every boy's, at some point? At least here in the South."

"More than being a marshal?"

"Yeah, that didn't become my goal until college."

She nodded and wrote something in her file. Then looked at him again with that same analytical gleam in her eyes, like she knew she was getting close to the truth about him and was enjoying it. Shay shifted in his seat, wishing he could see her notes. He hadn't divulged anything too sensitive or revealing.

Had he?

And how far would he let this go? He couldn't just walk out. He was stuck here, until this Dr. Barolo decided she was finished with him.

"You're single?" she said.

He couldn't help himself. "You ask all your patients that, or should I feel special?"

"Interesting."

Shay didn't believe any of what he'd said could possibly be *interesting*. But she cocked her head, thinking about *some*thing. Hell, the way she could pick up on tiny details and make them into massive issues was astounding.

"You called yourself a patient. So you *do* think there's a problem I can help you fix."

"It was a joke. You're reading too far into it."

"Never devalue the importance of words, Shay." Using his first name now, probably a sign they were getting too personal. "Many times, our subconscious says more than our conscious mind understands. We only have to listen."

Man, she could really pour it on with the psychiatric jargon. Was it for his benefit or hers? Maybe it was a type of power dynamic going on, and she wanted this tough-guy marshal, a villain to criminals, to see how smart she was. But he didn't think so, because there was still the sense that she was having fun peeling back his layers.

"Back to my question," she said.

"Yes, I'm single. Engaged once, to my girlfriend at UNCC." He decided to explain it, before she shared any other theories about his subconscious with him. "We were too young, too immature to make it. What I think, we both liked the *idea* of marriage but couldn't handle the reality of it."

Idea versus reality—the kind of psychobabble she might go for.

"Why couldn't you handle it?"

"I told you, we were young."

"But what kept *you* from a healthy relationship? In your opinion."

"She was a computer science major. Going for a degree that was sure to get her a stable job, a stable life, all that. Then she falls for an aspiring cop, and her stability goes out the window."

"How?"

"I could get shot, killed. It's a dangerous career."

"So she ended it?"

"I did," Shay said. "I could see it coming, the heartbreak we'd have had later on, so I made the decision to call it off."

"She had the issue, but you ended things."

"Correct."

That got Dr. Barolo's pen moving again.

"Do you worry about getting killed?"

"No."

"Even after the other night, when it nearly happened?"

"I'm still alive. What's to worry about?"

"You didn't want the stable life she did?"

"I'm *doing* what I wanted. It's part of who I am now, and I'm happy with that."

Amy leaned forward and clasped her hands. "Let's say, hypothetically, you met somebody else that you thought of as the love of your life. But she's another 'stable' person. Would you choose her or the job?"

"The hell kind of question is that?"

"Hypothetical."

He hesitated, wondering if his true answer would be the wrong one. "The job."

"So whatever it is you derive from your work as a marshal, *that* is more important to you than anything else, even companionship, one of the most basic human drives."

It wasn't a question or a judgment, either of which he would've preferred.

"I suppose so."

"Then, what, I wonder, Shay, is it that you get from your career that you value so much?"

"I like what I do, is all. If I didn't, I'd go and be something else. Why should it be any more complicated than that, huh?"

"But *why* do you like it?"

"Told you, the pursuit is fun to me."

"The thrill?"

"It's deeper than that. More like fulfilling."

She sighed. "Tell me about your father."

Shit. Here it came.

"What about him?"

"Was he a tough man?"

"Oh yeah. When he needed to be. Didn't take crap from anyone. Had strong values and passed them on. The type who worked hard every day and expected nothing that wasn't earned."

"He believed in right and wrong?"

Shay nodded. "A man of real character."

"Would you call him a *just* person?"

"Always."

"Was he strict with you?"

"He set high expectations. And taught me that there are consequences for every action, some good, some bad, and it's up to each individual to make their choices wisely. You decide for yourself and then deal with the result. It's on *you*," he said, putting a hand to his chest, "it's *your* responsibility to be the kind of person who has good consequences come their way."

Now Amy hesitated before saying, "Would he punish you for failing to meet expectations? What were the bad consequences for you as a kid?"

Shay sat up on the edge of the seat and squinted at her. "Let me stop you there. My daddy never once beat me or threatened physical harm, nothing close to it, you understand? If you're fixing to go down that road, 'Shay's messed up because his old man hit him'? You'd best turn around now. I won't have anybody speaking of him like that."

She and her pen went to work, scribbling away again.

"You obviously have a lot of love for your father. Was he your biggest role model?"

"Still is. I try to be half the man he was."

"Did he ever encourage you to enter law enforcement?"

"No, he wanted me to keep racing. What he saw for my future, I was to climb the ladder up to the professional stock car series. ARCA, NASCAR. He worked hard to get me there, hoping a well-funded pro team would pick me up for a national touring championship."

"But it never happened."

"Like I said, the money wasn't there."

"Where are your parents now?"

"Ma's still in Wilkes County." He paused and rubbed the back of his head. "Daddy passed away."

Did she know about the murder? It had been in all the local papers, most of which were accessible online now. She'd only have to do a little digging to find out the truth about his father's death.

"Sorry to hear that," she said, maybe playing down her familiarity with his story. "Any siblings?"

"I'm an only."

"Close with your mother?"

"I could visit more."

"But it sounds like you bonded more with your father, as you got older."

"It's natural for boys to do that."

She tapped her pen on the file and pursed her lips. "Deputy Harlowe, I'm going to put a question to you that I ask every law enforcement patient who comes in here. I want you to answer it honestly."

He shrugged, thinking that would depend on the question.

"What," she said, "do you fear? It's not death, from what you've already told me. So what does scare you?"

"Nothing."

"Everybody has fears. Most never seek to confront them, because we fear the fear itself."

Hell, how much more of this psychological bull was he going to have to take?

"Snakes?" he said. "Like Indiana Jones. I used to shoot them when I was a kid. Copperheads, mostly, but we'd get all kinds in the mountains. You find them under the dumpster, under the deck, in flower beds."

"Did your father teach you to shoot?"

"He hated guns. My mother showed me how, with this antique shotgun *her* daddy gave her."

"The first time you killed a snake, another living thing, did it bother you?"

"Not in the slightest. It's what you have to do with dangerous pests. The way I looked at it, I was protecting me and mine."

"Dangerous pests—such as killers, sexual predators, drug traffickers, gangsters, and terrorists."

Shay grinned at her, once again marveling at how she could pull a connection between his childhood and his job out of her ass and make it sound credible.

"But I don't necessarily mean a tangible fear," she said. "For some patients, that's a productive area to explore. With you, I don't think you're afraid of getting *physically* hurt."

"I can't wait to hear what you do think."

"My opinion is irrelevant here. I want yours."

"Right now? I'm worried I'm wasting time with you, while there are fugitives out there hurting people. All I want is to get back to work, you understand? Instead of sitting in a chair, listening to you tell me I'm screwed up in the head. Which I don't believe I am."

"Interesting."

"C'mon, will you quit it with that *interesting* shit?"

"What you're saying is that you're afraid of what would happen if you aren't there to stop it."

"Am I supposed to get your meaning?"

"Without you performing your duties as a marshal, something bad will happen to someone else. That's how you see it, at least. And perhaps that's why you're so willing to put your job ahead of other important things, like a future with your fiancée or your childhood dream of racing cars. If you stop to pursue your own life, you're terrified somebody will lose theirs."

Shay stayed quiet, feeling this particular theory resonating inside him. But not about to admit it.

"Why do you put that huge responsibility on your-self? Because it's obviously not reasonable for you to think you can save everyone who's in trouble. So, Deputy, what we'll discuss next time—"

He stood. "Wait. This is a one-visit deal. I come and sit for an hour and then I'm good."

"You said it yourself, you're a patient. And I'm not clearing you until we've had more chances to talk."

"They're paying you by the session, huh?"

She ignored that, which pissed him off. He wanted her to fight back.

All she said was "Next time, I want to explore how you feel about your nickname: The Intimidator. And your father's shooting. Or, as I suspect your subconscious calls it, the first crime you weren't there to stop."

## CHAPTER FOUR

"How have you broken the law before?"

Clint, now wearing a Ratt concert shirt, blinked at her. "Well, ain't that just a peachy question to ask me in a public place."

They sat at a booth in a Wilkesboro bar, one of the historic shops and restaurants lining West Main Street, a forty-minute drive from Clint's farm at the edge of the county. Twenty-*five* minutes, how fast he drove. The evening crowd of locals—workers fresh from their shifts at the chicken plant, retired guys who had been coming here forever with their wives, and families whose roots had been good and put down in Wilkes—created a din of conversation mixed with the clinking of silverware on plates.

Clint felt real nice and happy. Naw, more than that, he was euphoric. Enjoying a fresh dose of the hillbilly heroin Vickie had brought him earlier. He sipped a beer from some fancy microbrewery in Asheville, and waited for the alcohol to heighten the effects of the pills.

Vickie seemed to glow at him across the table, with her red hair that shined in the dim light of the bar, Vickie sipping on a martini—always sipping, sipping, sipping, this lady—and smiling at him, as he smiled back, the two of them having fun conspiring together, Clint having a blast being stoned out of his mind.

She said, "No one can hear us. Like people care enough to pay attention to anybody but themselves anyway."

Clint relaxed, feeling his breaths coming one at a time, which he supposed they always did, but now he was noticing them. In, out, in, out. He let his back collapse against the booth, a wave of comfort washing over his whole body, as he seemed to keep going back and back and back, fusing with the bench now, so comfy that he couldn't tell where he stopped and the cushion began.

"Why you interested in whether I done anything before?" he said, still smiling, thinking he wouldn't be able to frown if he wanted to.

"We should assess our experience levels. Make sure we can take on a guy like Luther Deegan."

"Yeah, now you mention it, how in hell're we gonna do that?"

"I'm working on a plan. But that's why I need a reference point for what we're capable of."

Clint nodded. Meant to do it only once or twice to show he followed her logic, but his head kept going. Up, down, up, down, up, down...

In, out, in, out.

"Careful it doesn't fall off," Vickie said, laughing at him.

"What?"

"Your noggin. Oh man, you're somewhere else right now."

"Surprised *you* didn't sample nothing before we left."

"One of us has to be sane enough to make the drive back."

"Hey," Clint said, "I'm a better driver stoned than sober."

Vickie rolled her eyes, and Clint felt his own do the same, tracing hers and going around and around like laundry on tumble.

"You sell Christmas trees every year, right?" she said. "You go yourself and set up tree lots?"

"Yeah, I take 'em to the main cities in the state, Charlotte, Winston—"

"Sell to nice families," she said, cutting him off, "kids and their parents?"

"They're the best customers, 'cause you give 'em a good experience their first visit, and they'll come back every year, least until the children go to college. At eighty bucks or more per tree, that adds up, especially if you got a location near rich, fancy-pants neighborhoods, where they buy multiple. A Fraser for the living room, a hemlock for the bonus room, and so on."

Vickie scrunched up her nose in a cute way, still making fun of him. "If they could see you now, they'd run *so* fast."

"I behave myself during the season, no smoking. It's only you brings out the worst in me."

"And you love it. So, before you had me, what was the worst thing you did?"

She hiked an eyebrow at him, and he saw a fuzzy caterpillar scurrying across her forehead. Look at it move.

"You mean crime?"

"Yeah, Clint, I have to know."

Clint thought back to his childhood. He'd been a good kid, mostly. Helped on the family farm, learned the ropes so he could take over one day, didn't cause much trouble. Except this once…

"Almost got pulled in for vandalism when I was ten," he said.

"Ten? How much damage can a ten-year-old do?"

"Quite a bit, if he has a jerry can full of gas."

The caterpillar had stopped, maybe resting, out of breath. Did caterpillars *have* lungs?

"See, me and my friends," he said, "we'd sometimes ditch school and go shoot the living daylights out of each other with paintball guns. There were these woods half a mile away, so we'd ride our bikes there, instead of being at our desks when the bell rang. This is all maybe fifteen minutes from the farm. These woods were perfect for our battles. Then one day we see a sign on the curb in front of the trail we'd take into the trees. A developer had bought the land. Wanted to put up a bunch of houses."

Vickie leaned over the table. "Did you burn the sign?"

"Naw, we wanted to send a real message they weren't welcome in our woods. So we waited and we plotted and we schemed."

"And you were *ten?*"

"Kids are smart. I was a scrappy thing, even then."

"Continue, please, what'd you do?"

"We kept up our paintballing for the next month or two, nothing really changing yet. Then the construction crews started coming. Took down trees and laid foundations, all that shit. Now, there was this big bulldozer they had, tires taller'n we were. We got to thinking, How do we break it? That'd be a message to send."

Vickie's eyebrow was up again, the caterpillar getting fidgety. He had to concentrate to keep from getting fixated on it.

"Clint, what are you staring at?"

"Nothing, I'm just remembering. Okay, we started out by taking a bucket of gravel and dropping it into the engine compartment of the 'dozer. We waited a day or two and didn't see it nowhere on the construction site. Shit, thought we'd won. That'd been easy. But it came back. Next step, I got one of the industrial jerry cans from my farm, and we went over late one night and we doused that bitch in gas. Set it on fire with Eddie Mayhew's lighter he carried around so we'd all see him with it. He didn't smoke, he just wanted to be cool."

"Get back to the bulldozer. Did it explode?"

"Naw. We were hoping it would, like in the movies. Gas tank catches and *boom*," he said, spreading his hands on the table to mimic an explosion. "But it did wreck the thing. Charred the cockpit and melted a lot of the components inside, I bet."

Vickie pushed a strand of hair from her face. "You said you almost got pulled in."

"The cops guessed it was kids. They talked to just about every family within a mile or two of the site, including mine. But there was nothing to connect us to it except some paintballs they found, but that didn't give 'em shit."

She sighed. "That's cool and all, but how about something more serious?"

"That was pretty serious, you kidding me? Ten years old, doing that?"

"What I mean is," she said, "it's not like armed robbery or B and E or, you know, the kind of crime that comes with a payday after."

"All right, missy," Clint said, "what have *you* done?"

"Nothing like that," she said. "I haven't even vandalized. Only had those minor drug arrests I told you about.

Slap on the wrist both times, and I don't even consider what I was doing crime, per se. Then I went to college and got a ticket for drinking in public. Wasn't even my fault. What happened, we were at this barcade?"

"A what?"

"A barcade—half bar, half arcade. You get drunk off your ass and play Space Invaders and pinball and racing games and shit. Anyway, I was finishing the night off with a beer, a cooldown, and my friends wanted to leave with these guys we'd met, walk back to their apartment just off campus. We all left so quickly, I didn't pay attention and still had the open bottle. A cop saw us and gave me a ticket."

"That's the worst you've done? Damn, Vickie, then we're good and screwed."

"I was counting on *you* being more experienced in this stuff. I come up with a plan, you execute it."

"Why me? 'Cause I'm a pot grower, I must be an all-around lowlife?"

She shrugged.

"What I can tell you," he said, still riding too high to take offense, "I'm close to Luther. Not personally, I'm talking proximity-wise. And I can get us near enough to size him up, you know, find a weakness, a way to hit him hard. We can pull it off, it'll just take some due diligence on the sumbitch."

"Joseph's in a nursing home in Cricket, I know that. The rumors were flying he was coming, and sure enough he did. Maybe we use *him* to get to Luther. Like predators go for the weakest members of the herd? The young and the super old."

"Now Joe I've had limited contact with. Always sent his boy to do our deals, never showed up himself. Luther don't talk about his daddy, tell you the truth. Bad blood or something between them, but I guess they stick together for the money they're making."

Vickie fixed a precocious grin on her face. "What's Luther like?"

"A real bastard. You'd have to meet him to get the full picture."

"Introduce me. If I can *see* the man, it'll help me figure out how to get him."

"I'll show you where he hangs out. Rest'll be up to you, though, 'cause I can't let him see us together. He's sharp, he'll connect the dots if we ain't careful."

She looked off behind him, the caterpillars on her forehead inching closer together, the skin around them wrinkling as they crawled. "When you say *bastard*..."

"It won't take you no time to see what I mean."

## CHAPTER FIVE

Luther Deegan looked like a pissed-off horned owl. So he'd been told, by somebody who should have run faster.

He was giving his father that expression now, saying, "I'm concerned because you've gone fucking senile, and I have to be the one to pick up the pieces. Take this drug runner, one of your old guys—Earl Tucker Lee. A wanted fugitive, DEA after him for that very line, going to Florida and doctor-shopping for you, bringing the product back. And what does the asshole do? Gets wasted and goes on a joyride in a stolen car, makes the eleven o'clock news and YouTube and everything else. How could he not, a pursuit like that down 85? And what do *you* do about it? Your dementia-ed brain starts to thinking, starts to pondering, starts to wondering if Tucker Lee'll cut a deal and sell us out. Not a bad thought, but here's where you went wrong ... your solution was fucked. Send a *different* guy to go and kill Tucker Lee. It worked, I'll give you that, except now *that* asshole's in custody and liable to snitch. Ambushed a federal marshal in the process, a local boy who knows us, no less. Harlowe, remember the name? We went to Central together, two years apart. You think he's gonna let it drop?"

"Son," Joseph Deegan said, "you best take a breath, before one of my lovely nurses hooks you up to an oxygen tank."

The old man waved his hand and kept walking, the two of them getting some sunshine in the garden of Joseph's assisted-living home outside of Cricket. A three-story condo building with additional hilltop villas, one of which Luther leased for his father to pass the rest of his time on Earth, with premium views of the hazy Blue Ridge Mountains. The kind of place for people who were on their way out, who were self-aware enough to realize they should get the hell out of their family's affairs.

Wouldn't that be nice?

But here was Luther, trying to talk sense into his old man. No, you didn't *talk* to him. You had to *handle* him, the once fearsome Joseph Deegan reduced by age to the capacity of a child. His mind slipping, sure, but with enough lasting cognition to believe he was still as quick as he used to be. Luther would just have to remind his father how things were now.

"I got a call from him," Joseph said, as they strolled through beds of mandevilla, verbenas, and pentas, an artificial stream flowing a few yards to their left, the cool breeze off the hills making the colors sway.

"Who called you?"

"The man I sent, fella named Byron Keith. You wouldn't know him."

"Another from before my time?"

"No, but you forget I still have my contacts. You may be in charge now, son, but I'm not in the ground yet."

"What'd this Keith prick have to say for himself?"

"Phoned from jail and kept it real simple, so the police didn't glean nothing important. He told me he'd met Harlowe, and the marshal was coming to see us."

"You listen to that, it almost sounds like a pleasant thing. He's 'coming to see us.' Shit, and you don't see the issue?"

"There's nothing to connect you and me to what happened with the marshal."

"Unless the asshole talks," Luther said.

"He won't."

Joseph's white beard, round forehead, and reddish skin made him look sickly in the sunlight. As opposed to Luther, who kept his dark hair slicked back into a mullet to match the bushy mustache and thick eyebrows on his tanned face. Wearing a black suit and beige shirt.

He thought again about that owl remark. It was true. The eyebrows and his beaky nose gave him that appearance, and he didn't mind it anymore. In fact, he liked seeing himself that way—a predator that could strike out of nowhere and sink his talons into a weak little mouse, like what his old man had become. Like Joseph had treated him, when Luther had been younger and still learning the business.

He spat on the brick sidewalk. "What makes you so certain? The sentence he'll be facing, not to mention the pressure the federals'll put on him to open his mouth, you *can't* be sure."

"There are thirty thousand reasons guaranteeing his silence," Joseph said, "in a fund for his daughter's schooling. She lives with his ex-wife in Traphill."

"That's quite the expense, just to cover your slip in judgment."

"But it's done. Let that Harlowe boy pursue us if he sees fit to, there's nothing for him here."

"Point is," Luther said, "look what you cost us. And that's only just this one time, never mind whatever future screwups you have in store for me."

Joseph stopped in front of the stream, staring at the red and white fish traveling in the gentle current. Luther waited for the old man to turn and face him again and then delivered that same predatory glare, eyebrows hiked, his nose turned up, anticipating an unpleasant but necessary conversation.

"If you got something to say, son, go on ahead. I don't

have enough time left to waste it pussyfooting around with your games."

Here was the shower of guilt, his father's favorite tactic when he didn't have a real basis for an argument. Luther was numb to the old man's bullshit after years of exposure to it.

"I want you out," Luther said in a flat tone.

"Of what? You already kicked me from my home, locked me up in this place. It's like a prison, Luther, only worse. 'Cause in real prison, the message you get from everybody, the hacks, the others you're in there with, the police who put you there, is that society don't want you. And you can understand that, make peace with it even. You did wrong, and why *would* they want you? But here? It's your family, your own blood, giving you that same treatment. You have any idea how deep that cuts, son?"

"Relinquish any hold you still have on *my* business. The weed, the pills, the personnel who distribute the shit. Everything."

"*Your* business," Joseph said, with a wheezing sigh. "I dedicated myself to leaving you with financial stability, especially after your mother passed. And this is how it ends for me? You could've been working in a chicken plant for fifty years. You could've been left with nothing, one of those who's not able to come back from losing it all in the recession. But you have it good, you know why? 'Cause *I* made it so."

"This is a final warning to stay clear of what's mine. It's not personal, it's not an issue of family."

"*Life* is an issue of family."

"You keep holding on. Why? Is it that you're terrified you'll lose respect if you let go?"

"What would you know of respect, you little shit? The way you speak to your father ... it'd be best if the Lord came for me this very moment."

Luther smiled under his mustache. "You sure it'll be the Lord?" When his old man didn't answer him, he said, "Sever all ties, or I'll do it for you."

"Now you're threatening me."

"You're still quick enough to pick up on *that*, at least."

"Where did I go wrong raising you? Tell me that, so I can pray for forgiveness."

"You raised me fine. Problem is, the apple fell pretty fucking close."

* * *

THE DOOR OPENED, and Shay was looking at a woman who had his jet-black hair, high cheekbones, and brown eyes.

"Hey, Ma."

Gwen Harlowe gave him a hug and invited him inside the classic American bungalow with black shutters and a brick walkup, Shay's childhood home on D Street in North Wilkesboro. Being back, he recalled just how idyllic the small town was. Quaint residences on quiet roads that fed to the main stretch of old-school southern buildings. Churches, storefronts that dated back to the previous century, light posts that never went a single Christmas without wreaths and red bows. A backdrop of rolling hills and Carolina blue sky. Sure, the economy had been hard on it over the years, and there were people going through tough times. But this wasn't a place you ran away from. Never had been.

Except that he had, and as much as he loved every little detail of this town, it hurt like hell to be back, because for him it would never be ideal again, not really. Something was missing, and he'd never get it back.

The house was small and comforting, with a foyer and staircase at the front door, a hallway going straight to the kitchen—the heart of any southern home—and a living room to the right of the dining L, where the Harlowes had spent many happy years. Together—the way it should've been today too.

"You're early," his ma said.

"I drove fast."

"Leftmost lane the whole trip?"

"Beats dealing with everybody merging and exiting."

"You learned that from your daddy. Just set your suitcase in the den. The room upstairs is ready for you. Your daddy, he was something. Cruising at ten, twenty over, and I'd tell him to slow it down. He'd get this cute grin on his face, like the Cheshire cat, and say—"

" 'You don't have to obey the speed limit. You just have to be second fastest of the people *dis*obeying it.' "

"Some fathers teach their sons how to fish or use tools," his ma said. "Warren taught you how to drive like a crazy person."

"It paid off. And he was right, I found that out myself, working Highway. You pull over the offenders who are worth the paperwork and who are easiest to catch first."

They were in the kitchen now, his ma saying, "I haven't started making supper yet, thinking it would take you longer." She smiled and tossed him an apron. "So guess what, kid? You get to help me."

He took off his black suit jacket and draped it over a chair at the table. Then pulled the apron over his head and tightened it, while she put on a pot of chicken broth, Shay waiting for instructions and resuming his childhood role of her sous-chef, another happy memory from the nights when he hadn't been in the garage, with his daddy and the late-model.

"Grab the green beans from the fridge," she said, "second shelf, in a produce bag from Food Lion." As he looked for it, she said, "What are you doing here?"

"I can't come for a visit?"

"You're not on vacation. You never take time off. Pick the ends off the beans for me and split them in half."

"I recall how to do it."

"Good boy. I hope that means you're eating enough green food in Charlotte."

"When I'm not living off the Bojangles down the street from my condo."

"Another lesson from Warren."

"You'll be relieved to know I finally took some. Time off, that is."

"Most people in this state," she said, "go to the beach or a *touristy* mountain town for vacation. But not you?"

"I felt like coming home. The place where, when you have to go there, they have to take you in."

"Robert Frost?"

"See, I paid attention in school."

"Good, I always worried the gas fumes were killing your brain cells."

"They were. That Robert Frost thing is the *only* bit I remember."

"Hurry up and get those beans in the pot."

"Wait," he said, grinning, "who are you?"

His ma feigned offense, putting a hand to her chest. "The lady who, for some reason, has to feed and house you again."

"Only for a few days."

She set three plates on the counter in sequence: flour, egg, and bread crumbs. Then unrolled two cuts of cube steak from brown butcher's paper and dredged them at each station, before plopping them in a pan of hot vegetable oil. The crackling sound and the aroma of fried meat took Shay back to Sunday suppers here in the dining L, when a NASCAR race would be on in the living room, and he and his daddy would wear their matching Dale Earnhardt T-shirts.

"Ooh, I know," she said, a hand on her hip and her eyebrows hiked, teasing him, "you're in trouble."

"Of a kind."

"Everybody runs back to Mama. So, what'd you do?"

"It's nothing bad, really."

"But it is *some*thing."

Shay finished with the green beans and wiped his hands on a towel. "I'm suspended. Not because I did anything wrong, you understand, but there was this shooting, and they have to look into it."

His ma closed her eyes and drew in a deep breath. "Uh-huh."

"I'm fine," he said, and turned around in a circle. "See? No holes. At least, not any more than what came standard."

"Who's *they*?"

"An assistant U.S. Attorney. And my boss, the chief deputy of the district."

"And they told you it'd be *best* if you took a vacation."

"It was a forceful suggestion, you could say. Along with my seeing a therapist."

She cocked her head. "Well, now that's a positive thing."

"I don't need a shrink."

"After what happened to your father, I don't know,

and you were just a boy? God, *I* probably needed one, but I can't imagine what it did to you."

"I was seventeen," Shay said, "old enough to handle it."

His ma turned over the steaks with a pair of tongs. "I think it's great you're talking to somebody. Even if it *is* a punishment." When he scowled, she said, "But you hate it."

"This doctor, she'll take every tiny thing I tell her and she'll turn it into a big deal. Like she has a theory, you ready for this? That your showing me how to shoot snakes out back of this house, that's the reason I became a marshal."

"Seems sensible to me, kid."

"But it's as if she's saying I didn't make my own choices. My past decided my fate for me. Or my *subconscious*."

"How often do you have to see her?"

"Every week for a month. After that, she determines if I need more. All while the US attorney investigates me."

His ma bit her lip. "Did she ask about your daddy?"

"Oh, I bet the whole next session will be dedicated to that topic. Monday, I'll have to put up with all her questions, her pen scribbling away, putting God only knows what in my file."

"Huh, so you came home in between appointments," she said, staring into the pan, deep in thought.

"C'mon, don't you start analyzing me too."

"I can't help it. You call sometimes, but you haven't been up once since you moved to Charlotte."

"I've been busy. I don't take time off, remember?"

"But one session with a psychiatrist, and you're in my kitchen making country fried steak."

"It wasn't the shrink who made me come back."

Shay thinking he needed to get out into the county to gather information on the Deegans, the real reason he was there. But his ma couldn't know about that, not yet.

They placed the steaks on a rack to drain and scooped the green beans with a slotted spoon. When the meat was ready, they sat at the kitchen table, light streaming in from the adjacent window, the two of them eating in silence.

Until Shay said, "Are you still golfing?"

"When I can. The last round I played, I shot an 82. I think the new clubs are working wonders. Cobras, I love them. But there's been other things to do. Repairs to this old place, getting a new roof, and I'm thinking of redoing the backyard. Picture it, a fountain in the middle of a stone path, a hammock to the side so I can read outside in the mornings."

"While I'm staying with you," Shay said, working a piece of steak around in his mouth, "I can lend a hand."

"Don't worry, it's something I want to do myself. A second chance for this home to be happy." She looked down and then said, "So, let's talk about this doctor." The teasing eyebrow going up again. "Is she pretty?"

"You should see her. I think she's Italian."

"How old?"

"About my age, maybe a couple years apart, if there's any difference."

"Do you like her? My vote is red velvet cake for the wedding. When can I expect grandchildren?"

"Calm down."

His ma nudged his arm. "Is she smart?"

"Oh yeah. And seems to have a knack for getting under my skin. Hell, I think she enjoys it."

"That's always a good sign when you meet someone," his ma said. "It's like I told you when you were in middle school and just starting to get an eye for girls. Pick one who's smarter than you, but you can make her laugh. That was me and Warren," she said, and speared a few green beans with her fork. "Loved it when I laughed at his jokes, *especially* the dumbest ones. So, you should probably ask this doctor lady out, don't you think?"

"She's my therapist. I'm sure there's a host of ethical reasons against doing that."

"Who cares?" When Shay gave her an incredulous smile, his ma said, "Listen, you don't live the life I have without developing a simple philosophy: Happiness is worth fudging rules. Not always—there's still right and wrong. But with matters of the heart, we're not on this planet long enough to bother worrying so much. Unless you *have* a special lady and haven't told me."

"I have them off and on," he said, grinning again.

"Okay, so if this smart, pretty doctor interests you, why not take a shot? What could it hurt?"

"Could land me in more trouble at work, for one thing."

His ma stood to take her plate to the sink. "You're already suspended. What more can they do?"

## CHAPTER SIX

Late afternoon, Clint and Vickie took her Jeep to Old NC 16 Road in Cricket, passing ranch homes and woods on their way to a blue-and-white two-story shack with a gravel parking lot and a sign that read "REFORMATION BAR AND GRILL." Three other cars sat out front, one of them a sleek blue Chevy SS.

"That's Luther's ride," Clint said, pointing out the passenger-side window. "He's here, all right. They don't make that model no more, a $44,000 sport sedan nobody wanted. Except Luther, who saw it running in NASCAR. Something you'll find, the man's used to getting what he wants."

"So am I," Vickie said, her red hair in a ponytail now.

She looked good in her jeans and a white tank top. Clint was shirtless again, riding around the hills with his two favorite women.

"The Deegans've had this place a long time. Use it to clean their money. But they make decent burgers too."

"You've actually eaten here? It's a shithole. Like, I'd be afraid of getting sick, end up in the tummy-health aisle of my own drugstore."

"It ain't as bad as it looks. Though it *looks* terrible, I'll grant you that. Most people would get the heebies and keep on driving."

"Intelligent people, like myself."

Clint smirked. "Luther lives here, you believe that? Has a whole apartment on the second floor."

"Does he move product through the restaurant?"

"Drugs? Oh yeah. I don't know how he dispenses the stuff, but he has a setup for it, I'm sure."

"You've met with him here?"

"Lots of times. Whenever there's an issue to discuss about the weed."

"The pills too?"

"He has other people," Clint said, "who handle that. What he'll do, he sends runners down to Florida to go to the pain clinics down *there*."

"Yeah," Vickie said, "because there's not much regulation on them. Not like in the Carolinas."

"Right, so he'll float 'em a thousand or so in cash to cover their travel and the fees to see a doctor who's just a legal drug dealer. These docs'll make 'em do a phony MRI and find some bullshit problem to prescribe the medicine for. Then the runner'll go and repeat the process at a different office."

"That's the trick, they don't monitor who's getting prescribed what or how much."

"After a couple weeks, these guys come back with five hundred to fifteen hundred tablets. Oxy, Percocet, Xanax. In Appalachia, you can sell 'em for way more'n their street value down there. Especially if you control the supply, like Luther does."

Vickie gave him an envious smile. "See, that could all be ours. We wouldn't use this rathole, no chance. But we have my drugstore. I could get all Luther's customers registered there. Find a discreet way to dispense the extra pills to them. I wonder how *he* does it."

"Don't know, never asked," Clint said. "I'll let you handle that side of it. What I'll do, have all his weed dealers come to the farm for business."

"And you're sure they're not loyal to the Deegans?"

"They don't care who's in charge, long as the supply chain's intact. We get rid of Luther, they'll fall in line. They want what I got. Purdy Woman's a big seller."

"It sounds way too simple, doesn't it?"

"Money and drugs—it's the simplest thing in the world until something goes wrong."

Vickie took in a deep breath. "The play is, I go in and do recon."

"Just gonna walk in all casual?"

"One more paying customer. Maybe I ask to speak to the owner."

"You're serious? That's what you'll do if you're hoping to get tossed out on your ass. Customer service ain't a big concern at the Reformation B and G."

"Let me work it out, okay? Once I'm inside, I'll find an opportunity."

"But then what? How do we go from *recon* to overthrowing Luther?"

"I've been thinking. What if we have some fun with him first?"

"Your kind of fun? Shit, I'm worried."

"Shut up, you love it," she said, pushing on his arm. "What I'm saying is, what if we threaten him before we actually take him down? Tell him, Pay us $x$ amount or we kill you, that kind of arrangement."

"So he delivers us the cash but then we still make good on the threat."

"We walk away with his money, plus the room we need to make our move for the county's drug game."

"It's a solid idea, you know it? Just need the right plan to pull it off."

She nodded. "Let me work that out, too."

"What am *I* supposed to do?"

"Keep the engine running."

"Hey, has it occurred to you even once that we really don't know shit?"

"Has that ever stopped you before?"

Clint said, "I guess not."

* * *

IT WAS the kind of place that made you want to take a shower when you left. The brown tile floor was sticky, there were cobwebs in the corners, and two of the five— no, she counted six—neon beer signs were broken. The three rows of four tables were empty, some with half- eaten burgers in plastic baskets still sitting out. A book- shelf lined the side wall by the register, and Vickie wondered what that was for. It was an odd sight in this grody restaurant.

Vickie walked up to the counter, where a man in a sweat-stained Philadelphia Eagles cap and blue T-shirt with cut sleeves wiped away a smudge of something, using a dirty rag. She asked for a burger, and the guy charged her eight bucks for it.

When it was ready, she took the seat closest to the door, giving her a wide view of the dining room—if you could call it that—the register, and a glimpse at a stair- case in the back, adjacent to the kitchen area. There was a strange vibe in here, quiet, lonely, decrepit. Not even music playing from a radio. She took a bite and could hear herself chewing, it was so silent. The burger wasn't bad, but she didn't want to think about how disgusting the grill was.

Then the door opened, and a man in a black suit

and shirt came in. Slim, young, handsome. Dressed for the city in his tailored clothes, not for the country. He glanced at her before the door had shut behind him, like he never entered a room without taking note of every person inside first. She flashed him a quick smile.

Why not?

It got her a nod in return, before the suit strode to the counter, saying, "I'm looking for Luther. I was told he's the owner."

The guy with the rag dropped it next to the register, and then Vickie saw his hands dip below somewhere.

Next thing, the man in black was grinning. "You won't need whatever piece you're holding."

"Says who?"

"I'm only here for a conversation, not to make trouble."

"Says *who*?"

"He knows me. We went to the same high school."

Vickie was interested now, listening to the suit's calm voice with a slight local accent. He was cool, far more than Clint. Serious, though, in a brooding way, like he *took* himself seriously and his dark threads were meant to show people that.

"He ain't here," the man behind the counter said.

Vickie wanted to know more about this visitor asking for Luther Deegan. She decided to interject and see what would happen.

"That's his Chevy out front," she said, getting both of them to look over at her.

"You," the guy in the Eagles cap said to her, "shut the fuck up and eat."

The suit said, "Well, that's hardly service with a smile. Listen, I'm a little pressed for time. Tell Luther that Shay Harlowe's here. If he says he doesn't know me, he's lying. In that case, mention to him I'm a deputy United States marshal now. Means he won't be able to get away from me, you understand?"

"One moment," the guy said, then turned and climbed the staircase.

Shay Harlowe had his eyes on her again, the grin still in place. "You know Luther, too?"

Vickie said, "Not yet."

LUTHER LEANED against the wall by the stairs and listened, as he sipped coffee from the cap of a thermos, the rest of which had gone missing on a hunting trip with his old man, years ago.

He recognized Shay Harlowe's voice, that soft-spoken country tone that sounded more city now, less of a drawl.

The second floor of the restaurant was a hallway with a door on either end. His suite, a modest bedroom and bathroom with a small kitchenette, was to his right. To the left, the office where he conducted meetings with his dealers, runners, and any pill customers who hadn't paid and needed coercing.

Derek Mooney appeared at the top landing in his sleeveless shirt and made a move toward the office. Jumped when he saw Luther standing there in his tan shirt and black sport coat, Luther smiling with brown teeth under the thick mustache.

"Did I startle you?"

"You enjoy that shit," Derek said. "Man down there say he a federal marshal, wants to speak with you."

"I know who he is."

"Yeah, he said that too. What you want me to do about him, run his ass off?"

"You can't," Luther said, and took another pull on his thermos cap. "Even if you blew him away with that gun, more feds would follow him. No, we have to play it smarter."

"You gonna talk to him?"

"Not on your fucking life. Tell him I'm gone. Give me a chance to think about how we handle this. When I *do* confront him, I need to be prepared. A man with a badge has an advantage from the start. You've experienced that yourself."

Derek screwed up his face. "Man, you hiding like a coward. I've never seen you let the law get in your head so bad."

Luther pointed at his number two's chest. "You've never seen Harlowe."

\* \* \*

Vickie and Harlowe didn't say anything to each other as they waited. She munched on her burger and counted herself lucky. Simple recon had turned into so much more. A U.S. marshal was on Luther's tail.

She could feel the plan changing already. Clint would be impatient out there in his truck. But she wasn't going anywhere until this Shay Harlowe left first.

A loud set of footsteps broke the silence, and Harlowe turned to see the guy in the Eagles cap coming down the stairs, the marshal with his hands on his hips, already assuming an aggressive stance.

The guy approached the counter and said, "The man, he ain't in."

"Then who'd you go up there to talk to?" Harlowe said.

"I did you a favor. Went to make sure if he was home or not. Well, he ain't, you got it? Must've taken a taxi or something, left his car."

"You see many taxis in these hills?"

"I don't know what to tell you, Marshal. Except get out."

Harlowe stepped closer to the register and said, "And what's *your* name?"

"Derek motherfucking Mooney, aka the man telling you unless you got a warrant, you got no business in my establishment."

The marshal raised his hands but grinned. "All right, I'll be on my way. But, Derek? It's like I said before. I *will* be back."

He strode through the dining room and gave Vickie another nod. Derek went into the back, and Vickie could hear him cleaning the grill. She took another couple bites of burger before packing up the rest and heading for the door.

Deputy Marshal Shay Harlowe—he'd be perfect.

* * *

CLINT TAPPED his fingers on his door, wondering where in the hell Vickie was. That fella in the suit went in after her and came out sooner. Didn't even have any food, so he must've sat down and eaten in the time it was taking her to do her *recon*. Shit, it was getting dark. He was hungry and had to piss.

Finally, she walked across the gravel lot with a paper to-go bag in her hand. Got in the Jeep and started it, the tires spitting gravel as the car tore out of the lot.

"What took so damn long?"

She rolled down her window and tossed the bag into the twilight.

"Hey, I'd have eaten that," Clint said. "What about all the starving kids in Africa you see on TV?"

"Shut up. I need to think."

"I wish you'd quit that. Meantime, pull into a drive-thru. I'm starving, and Sarah McLachlan ain't making no commercials for my fat ass."

"Did you see that guy in the black suit?"

"Yeah, drove a black Tahoe. A government car, you can tell from the window tint. Swear I've seen him before."

"His name's Shay Harlowe. A U.S. marshal."

"Shit, I'm familiar with the Harlowes. He used to race late-models here. Always in the papers."

Vickie looked over with that same mischievous gleam in her eyes. "Tell me everything you know about him."

## CHAPTER SEVEN

SATURDAY MORNING, SHAY LEFT BEFORE HIS MA WOKE up. He didn't want to deal with her questions about his plans. What he'd be doing, why he was really there.

He couldn't decide whether or not to tell her the truth of his daddy's death. She deserved to know, but would it only make things worse for her? She'd moved on. Redoing the house, staying active. Who was he to come waltzing back home and ruin that for her? Maybe the truth would be worth it, the knowledge that justice of a kind had been done. Then again, maybe it wouldn't.

Tucker Lee's death hadn't satisfied *him*. Otherwise, what was he thinking? Suspended and chasing criminals who weren't even on the marshals' list.

Maybe Amy Barolo had a point about his psyche.

Shay drove back to the Reformation Bar and Grill and parked across the street. Waited there for thirty minutes before a silver 2008 Ford F-150 pulled into the lot—Luther's employee, Derek, wearing his Eagles hat and a gray long-sleeve T-shirt.

Shay wrote down the plate number in a notepad and called an old friend at Highway, asking if he could get a record check on the vehicle.

The trooper told him a Derek Mooney was the RO, the registered owner. White male. Cited twice for speeding, and his sheet showed a prior for assault with a deadly weapon, a Class C felony, meaning Derek had caused serious injury with the intent to kill. That had gotten him five years state time in Georgia, and he'd been out for just over one and a half. During that period, he'd moved from Atlanta to the North Carolina mountains.

Shay had what he needed.

He rolled up behind the truck, Derek still sitting there with his windows down, smoking and listening to Kendrick, tapping ashes onto the gravel. Shay appeared at the fella's door, startling him.

Derek said, "Man, you again? Creepy motherfucker standing there in your suit, like the grim reaper. What are you, FBI?"

"I'm insulted. Marshals Service."

"Thought y'all were just in Texas."

"That's the Rangers."

"What you want with me, *Marshal*? Come to give a poor country man shit?" He turned his cap backwards, as if to make a point.

"I'm here to give you some, yeah. Not because of who *you* are, so much as your boss."

"Luther? Nah, you looking to arrest somebody who deserves it, talk to the man's father, not the man."

"I'd like to. Where can I find him?"

"The hell I should tell you? Get out my way, I gotta get to work."

Derek moved to open his door, but Shay blocked it with his body. Then leaned into the window and spoke in his soft tone, being pleasant as could be.

"Because, Derek—can I call you Derek? We'll be seeing enough of each other, first names ought to be more convenient—because you have a firearm behind that counter in there."

"So? It's for protecting the register, case somebody tries to rob us."

"Smart move," Shay said, nodding. "In fact, I'd probably do the same thing if I had a restaurant way out here."

"Then how about you lay off about it? You a marshal, man, but still a cop, and I know y'all look for any little thing to be a hard-ass. So don't give me none of it, 'cause I *see* what you doing, I *see* you coming a mile away."

Shay squinted. "Difference is, Derek, I'm not a felon. You understand what I'm saying?"

"I'm under*stand*ing you dug up my record."

"Just so you know from the start you can't screw with me."

"*Me* screwing with *you*?" Derek shook his head. "Oh, is that what's going on? Funny, man, that's the best one I heard all week. You doing the Wilkesboro comedy club while you in town?"

Shay passed his card through the window. Derek took it, turning it over in his fingers and staring down at the silver star, like he was making up his mind what to do.

"I want information on your boss. And you're gonna give it to me."

"Nah, I'm good."

"Right now," Shay said, "I can't think of a reason *not* to bust you for that gun. I've witnessed you with it. Wouldn't be hard to get a judge to view that as probable cause to search your place and this truck, find some more weapons. I'm willing to bet you've got them. Could land you back behind the wall for, oh, two to ten years. Previous offender like you, risk to society, I bet the judge goes for ten."

"Bullshit."

"Or," Shay said, giving Mooney a friendly smile, "we can take this in a different direction. Be buddies, assist each other."

"Maybe I don't feel like talking. Maybe all this cool mountain air, it's giving me the sniffles, I'm losing my voice." He gave a couple of fake coughs and a sneeze, right in Shay's face.

"Uh-huh, how about I count to ten, help you decide faster?"

"Coming in here and threatening me for what's not even my damn gun."

"One."

"It's not my gun, you hear me?"

"Two."

Derek beat his hand on the wheel. "Bitch, you listening? I don't own that piece."

"Nine."

"All right, what you want to know?"

Shay said, "Let's start with where Joseph's staying."

"Man, that's public knowledge. A retirement place in Cricket, big luxury community, you can't miss it. What kind of detective are you, you need me to tell you that?"

"A marshal isn't a detective. And I could've asked anybody else, sure, but I wanted *you* to practice talking to me."

"You not from around here, are you?"

"Not anymore. So here's the deal. You're gonna call me with something I can use against Luther in the next twenty-four hours, or I'm gonna come after you instead."

"What if I dump those guns you think I have?"

Shay grinned. "Thing is, Derek, you don't last in the drug trade without being armed. Where there's product, there's money, and you need firearms to keep it safe. There'll be another gun, you'll still be a felon who can't legally possess it. And *I'll* be watching."

"You think you real tough in that cute little black suit, huh? Ever hear, clothes don't make the man?"

"I'll be waiting for your call," Shay said, and slapped the side of the truck. "Until then, you protect that register."

* * *

CLINT SPENT the morning inspecting the trees, as his crew did the final pruning before the holiday shipment would be cut down and prepped. His fir crop looked good and full this year. At eleven, he made his rounds through the grow houses and wooden drying sheds hidden amongst the pines. His reefer crop looked even better and would earn a tasty amount of its own.

He made himself a smoothie of banana, spinach, chard, and frozen berries for lunch. Trying to lose weight, now that he and Vickie were getting closer. But, man, hating every sip of the green sludge juice, all gloppy and cold and full of tiny berry seeds that got between his teeth. The flavor was somewhere between mowed grass and old fruit. He'd gotten the recipe online, and it called for adding nuts too—wasn't this bad enough?

Clint took his drink out to the porch and sat on one of his park benches, soaking in the sunshine and feeling the breeze on his face and chest. Vickie arrived in her Jeep a few minutes later, her hair down today and a little mussed. The kind of woman who was more attractive when she wasn't all put together. She came through the gate and waved at him. Clint thinking, Did he really want to run the drug business, deal with all the shit the Deegans had managed for so long? The money would be sweet, but what if he just stayed right here on this bench and enjoyed the view of the mountains in the distance and kept things as they were? Except for the smoothie—he would ditch that for bourbon.

Vickie stood in front of him, blocking his sun, and said, "You have what I asked for?"

"In the kitchen. There's a box on the counter." She raised an eyebrow, like she expected him to fetch it for her. "Do it yourself, do I look like the chivalrous type?"

She went inside. Came back out a minute later carrying a small cardboard box full of newspaper articles and printed web pages about Shay Harlowe, dating back to the guy's racing days.

"Let me ask you something," he said, as Vickie dropped onto the bench and picked through the papers.

She didn't look up. "Hm?"

"When do you actually work at the drugstore?"

"What do you mean?"

"You been hanging with me so much, how many hours could you be logging there?"

"It's not like I'm the pharmacist."

"Naw, but you want to *play* pharmacist for the whole county with these pain pills."

"Is there a problem, Clint?" Still not looking up, just flipping more pages until she dumped them into the box and pulled out a white Shay Harlowe T-shirt, with a picture of his late-model on the front and a big *3* printed on the back.

"They sold those," Clint said, "during his last year, raising money for the team. What my problem is? I'm feeling way out of control."

She dug down further and retrieved a pile of old newspapers with Harlowe's face on them, the kid's expression a mix of shock and sadness.

"Shit," she said, pointing at the headline, "Warren Harlowe was murdered?"

"Oh yeah, it was huge doings when it happened, what was it, twelve years ago."

"They ever catch who shot him?"

"Nope. Listen, though, what I was saying, I feel like everything's run amok since you came to me with this crazy idea."

"That had to kill Shay." Man, could she shut her trap and listen for even a second? Apparently not, Vickie saying, "I see why he became a cop."

"I don't like our plan, is all, and I want to be included in coming up with our next play."

"I don't like it either," she said, and finally put her eyes on him.

Which had to mean she wanted something. That was the only time she paid him any mind, and he resented the hell out of it.

"Did you ever get to meet Luther last night?"

"No," she said, but didn't seem bothered about that. "Anyway, it's Shay Harlowe I'm interested in now."

"You're gonna get me in a world of a mess, I can see it."

"You have nothing to worry about."

"I have thousands of marijuana plants all up in these hills, and a federal agent's sniffing around. Could land me in prison for the better part of my life. You're right, I'm stressing for nothing."

"I'll wait till you're finished."

"I am," he said, crossing his arms.

How could she be so cavalier about everything? He knew how. *She* was in control here, not him, and it had been that way from the start. He was the one with more to lose, and it irked him that she didn't seem to care.

All he wanted right now? To change that and be the one with the ideas and the power to get them done.

"This marshal shakes things up. And he's not after you or your pot. He's got a hard-on for Luther Deegan."

"So?" Clint said, frowning at his smoothie, the glass still more than half-full.

"We need Luther gone. Why not let Harlowe take care of that for us?"

Clint tapped his fingers on his knee. "Find a way to help the marshal catch him."

"The interesting thing, though, he didn't have a badge or gun last night."

"Maybe he was off duty."

"I don't know, they were talking about how he lives in Charlotte now. What's he doing here?"

"Sounds like whatever his beef with Luther is, it's got to be personal." Clint scratched his head. "There *was* this rumor, back when Warren Harlowe got shot? A Deegan pulled the trigger. But they get blamed for everything. A crime happens, people point fingers at 'em real quick, don't matter if there's evidence or not."

"So we just need to … facilitate Shay's revenge."

"I'd ask how, but you're probably gonna tell me you're *thinking* about it and not share any more'n that."

"Okay," she said, "there's clearly a problem. What is it?"

Her voice was softer now, even a little sympathetic. She touched his arm and leaned toward him.

"I don't feel like we're partners. I been your driver, your errand boy, your researcher getting you all these papers from back in the day. Unless you need something, what am I to you? Hired help."

See how that little speech went over. Maybe *that* would get her.

She took the glass out of his hand and held it up to the light, studying it. "What's in here?"

"Spinach, mango, some other stuff. None of it all that enjoyable."

"Good for you, though."

"That your medical opinion as a drugstore cashier?"

"It's basic nutrition. Like, the stuff they teach you in elementary school."

"Well, at least you got that level of scientific education."

She took on a pouty expression—messing with him, he knew. "What can I say to make you feel better, Clint?"

Time to try again, see if this next line would do the trick.

"Nothing. No more talk. I want to see us take action."

"I'm glad," she said. "Because I have our plan." Paused to set up what she was about to say next. "We're going to *blackmail* Luther. You know how his whole operation works, at least on the reefer side. So, we threaten to give the marshal enough evidence to bring Deegan down unless he pays us."

"You realize that puts my farm, my life, in jeopardy. The trail will lead straight back to me."

"Then give me something to use that won't hurt you. Come up with our leverage, see if you feel more in control."

Clint took the glass and swirled the melting green goop round as he contemplated that. "Okay," he said, "you want to slip into the market occupied by Deegan's pill game, right?"

"Ideally."

"Then we don't use the reefer at all. We figure out

how he's distributing painkillers at the restaurant. And we give *that* to Harlowe."

"But how?"

Clint said, "I'll handle it."

She frowned at him.

Victory.

## CHAPTER EIGHT

THE FIRST THING JOSEPH DEEGAN SAID TO HIM: "ARE you armed?"

"No," Shay said, "I didn't want to tempt myself."

It was a better answer than saying he was suspended.

The two of them were on the back deck of the old crook's retirement villa, the afternoon sun getting closer to the hazy blue horizon of the mountains. The senior Deegan was worse off than Shay had expected. Sickly, pale, hands shaking when he reached for the box of cigarettes in the breast pocket of his maroon robe. Looking at this asshole who had fallen so far, Shay couldn't decide if he should feel bad for him or toss him over the railing, down the rocky ledge, and into the trees below the house's overlook.

"Heard you were back," Joseph Deegan said, his voice weak. "I wondered if I'd see you."

"You know about Earl Tucker Lee?"

"It's a shame he's gone."

"What am I saying? Course you know. Ten to one, *you* ordered the hit."

Joseph Deegan blew smoke into the crisp mountain air, something he'd done for decades, in one way or another. "You didn't come up here to talk about Earl. Otherwise, boy, you wouldn't be alone. And you'd be packing, I am sure of that."

"You wouldn't be a free man anymore."

"I'm not now. I'm already in a prison."

Shay shrugged. "Seems to me you're living large. My condo in the city, it's about a fifth the size of this place. A tower next to the federal courthouse in Uptown. The view, it's skyscrapers, not all this open sky."

"That's your fault for leaving the country," Joseph said.

"Never said I like this better."

"Do you see, my family's thrown me away? Luther, he don't see fit to care for his own father, leaves me on the doorstep of strangers, never visits, 'cept to remind me I'm an old man who should do him a favor and die. End his inconvenience. After everything I did for the boy, that's how he feels? Sinful. I told him, I hope the Lord gives him his wish. I'd be ready, any day."

"Does this pity party work on him? 'Cause it's doing nothing for me."

"Shame Luther and you never got to being friends. You'd have done him good."

"His problem, he couldn't help who his daddy was. Still can't."

Joseph screwed up his face. "Neither can you, boy, you just don't know it."

Shay ignored the remark. "You should see him in his little restaurant out on Old NC 16."

"That rathole he calls his 'place.' I never conducted business in such a dump."

"Nobody inside, you can just tell it's a front for *some*thing. But there's Luther, holding court with his right-hand man."

"The con from Atlanta."

"From your tone, I'm guessing you two don't get along."

"He works for Luther, not me. Luther and me don't get on, and so his man and I don't either." Joseph played with his lighter. "They ever found out about these smokes, they'd chuck 'em into the bush. Give me a reprimanding. That why *you're* here? Give me grief about what happened years ago? That's the only reason anybody comes to see me anymore."

"You live your life striving to be the biggest shithead around. Then you're sur*prised* when people are glad to see you gone?"

"I'm not that man now, as you can plainly tell."

"I can. Luther's the one filling that role. Trying his damnedest, at least."

"Big shoes to fill," Joseph said, giving Shay a smile full of pride. "I think it's hard for him, living up to all I've done. Feeling like he has to measure up."

Shay ran a hand down his black tie, smoothing it out. "What happens to guys like you, somebody else wants to be the head dog. I see it all the time, the boss has a target on his back from the day he takes over. Clock starts ticking, and eventually he gets replaced."

"You've seen that?"

"What's fascinating," Shay said, "is how consistent it is among criminals. Doesn't matter if we're talking street gangs in L.A., mob families in New England, or shit-kickers like you, here in the hills. You were always going to lose your power. And it'll happen to Luther too."

"I remember," Joseph said, staring at the wisps rising from his cigarette, "when it was me waiting for my shot."

"Was your daddy in charge? Grandpa Deegan?"

"No, my daddy was a small-time 'shine runner, back when this county was full of them. I'd drive for him, fast enough to give even late-model champ Shay Harlowe a race. It was a culture thing as much as a moneymaker. A way of life that's been forgotten now."

"Replaced by marijuana and then by pills," Shay said, hiking an eyebrow, seeing if the man would take the bait.

He didn't, Joseph saying, "Another family had the

county by the balls. I was in their crew before long, never finished high school. That's another difference between me and my son. He's educated. So smart, the only thing he don't know is he's a fool. Has no work ethic. Would rather *think* about something than accomplish it. I never got a diploma, but ... there wasn't a job I couldn't learn and do. Now you got kids, you give them a fancy piece of paper, they think they're qualified, but they still don't know shit, not really."

"Is this the part where you blame society for your sins?"

"Hell no. I made my own choices. I took charge of my own life. Made money my way, didn't duck responsibility."

"When you took over, was it clean?"

"You say you've seen it. Is it ever clean?"

Shay said, "But blood money buys a nice retirement villa, doesn't it?"

"I have no complaints about my path," Joseph said, stomping out his cigarette with his slipper. "For years, it was the best whiskey, the best food, women, cars. I *lived* a life."

"While others died for it," Shay said, hoping to provoke him. When Joseph didn't respond, he said, "Luther tells me your mind's slipping."

"He wishes. My son, he wants to justify forgetting about me. It's like I told you, ducking responsibility. Never owning his choices. But he'll find you can't forget about family so easy."

"No, you can't."

Now Joseph turned to him, his eyes heavy. "You're going after my son?" Shay nodded.

" 'Cause of me?"

"He has to be put down, before he repeats your mistakes. We were never friends, he and I, but we were in history class together. Both have a desire to learn from the past."

"Don't punish him to get even with me."

"It's not personal, you understand? He's a piece of shit and I'm law enforcement. Like a cat and a mouse—it's what we do, it's in our nature."

"How about with me?"

Shay hesitated, letting his silence speak for him as he looked out at the hills and decided what it was he wanted from the man. He hadn't expected a civil conversation. But then again, Joseph Deegan was in no condition for a fight.

"Still haven't landed on what's to be done about you," Shay said.

"I won't ask you to forgive me. Only the Lord can do that."

"Tell me one thing," Shay said. "Why did my daddy come to *you*?"

"I loaned people money when the banks refused. No questions asked. See, the banks, they build their tall towers in Charlotte—you drive by 'em every day—spend millions and millions on themselves, but when the little man comes asking for help? There's none to be found. That's where I stepped in."

"The banks don't shoot people."

"Every client of mine got the same terms. If they couldn't pay it back, there'd be trouble. I never forced no one to take nothing."

"But why did he go to you? Why not anybody else?"

Joseph took another smoke from the box, saying as he lit it, "That wasn't the first deal we'd made together."

Shay narrowed his eyes. "What?"

"When he and Gwen bought your house, he needed money. Same with the garage for your late-model. Always paid back the loans. Warren was a man of his word."

"Was that all?"

"Just be sure, boy, you really want to hear this. My advice, let your memory of your daddy alone."

"I'm here to talk. Go on, or I might change my mind about being so friendly."

Joseph took another long drag and coughed out the smoke. "When you were a boy, there was another woman. Lived in Traphill, and your daddy was mad for her."

Shay gritted his teeth. "When was this?"

"You were ... twelve? About then."

"My daddy loved my ma."

"Yes, he did. But a man can feel that way about more'n one woman."

"Who was she?"

"Debra Lofland. And she fell for Warren in return. They were at it for six months. Your daddy never shared the details, never a man to dishonor his lover by spreading rumors about it. But he was happy, I could tell, the few times I saw him."

"You expect me to believe this?"

"What reason have I got to lie? Keeping secrets is for men who ain't dying."

"How did you factor into it?"

"Debra wanted Warren to leave your mother. She threatened to go to your house, knock on the door, and confess the whole thing to Gwen. Force your daddy's hand and destroy his marriage. Warren came to me, asking if I could stop her."

"You didn't..."

"Kill her? Was no need to go that far. And your daddy would've never stood for that. I paid her a good bit to leave North Carolina. She refused."

"But she *did* go?"

"Only after I sent Earl to strongly suggest she take the offer. Warren didn't want her hurt, but he needed her gone."

Shay looked down at his shoes, then back at Joseph, reading the old man's expression, searching those tired eyes for hints of bullshit and finding none.

"He was a good man, Shay. Don't let this change your view of him. But nobody's a saint."

"It's all true?"

"We just try to find joy where we can. He found it in that woman. For better or worse, he was happy. But he never let it get back to you. That's a loving father you had. Look at you. Turned out all right, a marshal, living in the big city."

"You don't know a lick about me," Shay said, standing and straightening his black suit jacket, ready to walk out of there. "And you took him away. You have no idea how what you did changed me."

"It was business, and he understood the risks taking that money."

"Understand this," Shay said, "a Deegan is gonna pay for what happened. Tucker Lee isn't enough. So if I can't get *you*, it'll be your son."

"I failed Luther, and now he's failing himself."

"You talk about taking responsibility? Where do you think he learned how to be the way he is? We're our fathers' sons, him and me, and *that's* the truth."

"Maybe so. But I don't have a mean bone in my body, not no more."

"Well," Shay said, "I still have enough mean bones for the both of us."

\* \* \*

"That marshal come back? Harlowe?"

"Nah, he ain't been by. Why, you expecting him to?"

Luther poured himself a fresh mug of coffee and eyed

Derek wiping down tables, Derek different today, on edge. "Oh, I expect he'll do more than that."

"What's y'all's problem with each other?"

Luther held his cup in front of him and paced behind the counter. "I think he's under the impression my old man had *his* old man shot, twelve years ago."

"It true?" Derek pausing his work and looking over, the dishrag hanging from his hand.

"While you're at it," Luther said, spitting from under his mustache, "wipe that judgmental smirk off your face. Yes, it probably happened. My father's pill runner, Tucker Lee, likely told him about it, and so here comes that prick Shay to piss in *my* cereal for what my daddy did."

"You had nothing to do with it, right?"

"Tell that to Harlowe," Luther said, taking a seat at the table Derek had just finished. "I'm in charge. *I'm* the new Joseph Deegan, and he knows that."

"We could pop him," Derek said, the smirk gone.

"Kill a fed? That's a hornet's nest you do not want to poke."

"What we gonna do then?" Derek dropped the rag and put his hands in his pockets. Tapping his foot like a nervous wreck, like his mind was tied up in a knot.

"He *did* come by," Luther said.

"Was this morning."

"And he asked you to snitch on me."

"Threatened to haul me in on felony possession of that shotgun you got here."

"What'd you say?"

"Told him I wasn't gonna sell you out."

"Did you really?"

"Yeah, what's he gonna do? All he got on me is that old assault charge."

"I been meaning to ask, how'd you come by that?"

"I drove a cab in Atlanta," Derek said. "Yellow shit with the phone number on the side, all the same digit to make it easy to remember. Used to work the airport, the hotels. One day, this dude gets in, I take him near across the city to a strip club, and he owes me forty. Comes time to pay, he puts a gun on me and takes off."

"And *you* got charged?"

"Police didn't like how I chased him down with the baseball bat I kept in the trunk. Beat his ass almost to death, took his gun, and shot him in the knee. Got my forty out his wallet, lot of it in singles."

"Huh," Luther said, his owl eyebrows up. "I wouldn't want you running around with my shotgun, either. But that's the trouble with feds. They'll find anything to use against you. When they get hold, they don't let go. They squeeze and squeeze."

"I didn't tell him shit, I swear."

"I believe you. But Shay Harlowe won't give up. So you'd better have something to give him. Meantime, I expect he'll see my old man next. That's a different mess altogether, and I'll have to clean it up."

"Yeah, but what do *I* do?"

"I'm going for a drink," Luther said, standing. "My usual place, in Wilkesboro. Call him, tell him he'll find me there. It's time he and I reconnected."

"I'm supposed to sit? Just wait for the man to put me back in prison?"

"I need you to handle customers anyway. Lot of books are due back tonight and tomorrow. Collect the payments and deal with anybody who's late."

Derek sighed and got back to cleaning. "You better be right. When you rolling out, I can call the man with the phony tip?"

Luther swished coffee around in his mouth. "After another cup."

## CHAPTER NINE

"THEY HAVE KNOB CREEK?" SHAY HARLOWE'S VOICE said from somewhere behind Luther.

"I wouldn't be here if they didn't."

The marshal took the barstool next to him and ordered a glass. Luther leaned toward him to be heard over sports analysts predicting the outcomes of tomorrow's NFL games on the TV above their heads and the dull roar of conversation around them, voices coming from the other stools and the row of booths along the far wall of the narrow bar, the backlit shelves the brightest light in the room, smoke tingeing the air.

Luther saying, "Did you remember where this place was, or did Derek have to draw you a map?"

Harlowe stared into his bourbon and turned his glass in a neat circle, condensation forming a wet ring on the wooden counter. "Figured there was a fifty-fifty chance he'd tell you."

"You ought to lay off him," Luther said. "That assault charge? Some asshole stole from him, he mention that? All Derek did was reclaim his property."

"And nearly killed the man after he'd reclaimed it."

"A hardworking guy defending his living, and the police crucify *him* for what happened. There are real criminals to chase, aren't there? How about those terrorist pricks? Why go after Derek? Tell me that."

"My inclination," Harlowe said, "is to see every one of you arrested, 'real' or otherwise."

"Saint Harlowe," Luther said, and snapped his fingers for a refill from the bartender, an older man with white hair and a white mustache trimmed nice and neat, unlike Luther's.

"If only," the marshal said, and kept looking down at his drink.

"You telling me there *is* a spot on your halo that doesn't shine?"

"More than one."

Luther raised his fresh glass. "Well, congratulations, you're the same as the rest of us after all."

He finished it in one gulp and snapped again. The only cure for this marshal's self-righteous bullshit was to numb his own sensibilities with alcohol, keep himself calm and even-tempered.

Harlowe still pouring it on, saying, "What about you? There's *blood* on your halo, huh?"

"Yours too," Luther said, meeting Harlowe's gaze but keeping his expression bored and disinterested. "Or did Tucker Lee kill him*self*, while in your care?"

"I didn't send that button man."

"Neither did I, which brings us back to the central fucking point. I'm innocent of whatever charges you've imagined up. So why are you after me? That's why you're back, isn't it? The prick who shot your daddy is dead, and I'm not convinced you didn't at least let it happen. Top of that, the even bigger prick who ordered it done is on his way out of this world. Why don't you, Marshal, why don't you just go back to Charlotte and wait, and I'll call you—how about that?—I'll pick up the phone when my old man's had it, and then will you be able to sleep soundly at night?"

"I'd almost believe that," Harlowe said, "if it wasn't coming from the top poison peddler on this side of the state."

Luther pointed at Harlowe. "I dare you to prove it."

"I believe I'll take that dare."

"Been a long time, Shay."

"Thirteen years. Last I saw you, you were graduating Central. At the after-party."

"Myrtle Wilson's house. She and I spent most of it in her room, while everyone else was drinking Keystone. I told her she was taking my virginity that night, you believe it? *She* did. And she seemed to get off on it."

"I remember Myrtle."

"Most of the guys in my class and the ones above and below remember her. You ever take your chance? A sophomore. She would've eaten you up."

"I had a steady girlfriend at the time."

"Molly something, right?"

"Davis. Curly hair, short, always humming a show tune as she went down the hall with her books."

"Yeah, and you were too good a kid to step out on her, that was the real reason."

Shay tapped his fingers on the side of his glass. "I dropped by your restaurant looking for you. 'The Reformation.' Interesting name for a burger joint."

"It's fitting. I want to undo my old man's legacy. A work in progress, but I *am* doing it."

"This ought to be good."

"When you were in there, you see the bookshelf on the sidewall? I run a Leave a Book, Take a Book program in this restaurant. Help fill the county's education gap. Old Joe? He never did anything like that, never tried to make this place better. I thought you'd appreciate my little gesture. Senior year, here's this sophomore in my European history class. You were always smart."

"Remember Mrs. Kennedy?"

Luther looked down and then up again, shaking his head. "You can't forget a fifty-three-year-old Catholic woman from New Hampshire, wore white turtlenecks under black sweaters, saying she was the closest thing to a nun we'd ever have."

"You really expect me to believe you're the good guy?" Shay said. "It'll take more than handing out books to addicts."

"You want to play cops and robbers," Luther said, "I'll get my lawyer on the phone."

"If you haven't used up his minutes already."

"But of all people, Shay, you should know how hard it is for sons to move past their fathers."

The door opened with the jingle of a bell, and two guys with beards, camo gear, and hunting caps took a pair of free stools down the bar from them. Real asshole types at first glance—shouting and yelling at each other, so the whole establishment could hear them slur their words. The first one, wearing sunglasses indoors, was bragging about screwing his wife's best friend, which, in his opinion, wasn't hard to do. His buddy, hair in a ponytail, saying, Maybe he should do the same, uh? Luther glared at them, hoping they'd notice and get the hell out. But they kept on.

Harlowe seemed to ignore them. "Speaking of your daddy, I visited him today."

"I apologize."

"For what?"

"That you had to endure even a second of his crap."

"He was pleasant enough. Didn't have too many good things to say about you, though."

"His problem? He can't let go of who he was. I wish he would."

"That's right, because you can't be fully in charge so long as he's drawing breath, huh?"

"In charge of what?"

Harlowe gave him a smug squint. "Denying it doesn't stop it from being true."

"Denying *what*? You act like I wanted any of this bull-shit I was born into. So I try to put distance between myself and my old man, from his whole line of work. And what's it get me? The feds still won't believe I'm a different breed of Deegan."

"What I believe is you've taken over the whole operation."

"I run a burger joint. And I don't see as you have a reason to care anyway. Is there a warrant for my arrest?"

"Almost."

"No, there isn't. Then I ask again: Why are *you*, a marshal, after me?"

"Somebody should be."

"What if you discover you're wrong about that?"

"I'm not. No matter how many books you give away, it won't make up for everything else you do, everything your people have done."

Now the hunter with the shades was describing the screwing in graphic detail, still as loud as he could. Ponytail was nodding, yeah, yeah, laughing, cackling, adding what he'd like to do when it was his turn.

Harlowe glanced over at them, then back at Luther. "You hear that?"

"The whole place hears it."

"Let's do something about it."

"Will that prove my case to you? That I'm not such a bad guy, I have enough morality to stand up for a woman's honor?"

"No," Harlowe said, grinning. "But it'll be fun."

Luther downed the last of his bourbon, pushed the empty glass away, and stood.

"Hey, shitheads." The hunters took a second to look up. "Shut the fuck up," Luther said in a flat tone, his owl's brow furrowed.

Ponytail rose from his stool and had to stabilize himself on the counter before saying, "Who the hell are you?"

"The guy who's gonna knock every one of your teeth out for talking like you been."

"Is that right?"

"Then my federal friend is gonna lock you up. And without your chompers? You'll be the most popular fish bachelor in your cellblock."

Luther pushed his tongue against his cheek a few times to drive home the point, but they didn't seem to get it. Now Glasses came over in his sleeveless camo shirt, the man's neck in need of a good shave, body odor emanating from him after hours in the woods. Where he should've stayed, with the other animals.

"How about," he said, taking off his shades, "you shut your damn mouth and let us go back to our business?"

"No," Harlowe said, standing. "It's too late for that."

Ponytail looked the marshal up and down. "I've seen you before. But not in here. Where have I seen you?"

"When I'm through with you," Harlowe said, "you won't want to see me *again*."

"Naw, you'd be too scared to mess up that pretty suit."

"You know," Luther said, "I thought *I* was the biggest hick asshole in this county."

"Sorry to tell you," Harlowe said, "but you're only number three." Then smiled at the hunters. "Can I ask you boys just one question?" Ponytail and Glasses gave blank stares in reply. "Would y'all sign my copy of *Deliverance?*"

That got the bartender to appear behind Luther and Harlowe, showing the four of them a glimpse of the revolver tucked into his apron. "Take it outside. After that, y'all are no longer welcome here. This is no place for people like you. I'll only tell y'all once, and then I'm calling the sheriff's office."

Luther said, "The sheriff's office? My friend's a U.S. marshal."

But Harlowe, squinting at the hunters, said, "Not tonight."

* * *

SHAY GOT BACK to the house an hour later. His ma was watching TV on the couch. When she saw his black eye, swollen face, and cut right cheek, she said, "Oh my God," and rushed into the kitchen. He stood in the living room, listening to an attractive couple talk about fixing up a nineteenth-century home. His ma came back with ice wrapped in a paper towel and pressed it to his bruises.

Saying, "What did you do, kid?"

"I won a fight."

"Nobody could tell by looking at you. And don't tell me I should see the other guy."

"I won't," he said, smirking.

"Don't think it either."

"I'm fine."

"You smell like alcohol."

"Had a few victory bourbons."

"What happened?"

He hesitated, debating whether he should mention Luther. "I was at that bar in town. That one Daddy used to go to sometimes?"

"Uh-huh, and?"

"These two jackasses come in, they make a big entrance, loud, obnoxious, already drunk. Start disrespecting a lady behind her back."

"So my son the marshal had to pick a fight?"

"Imagine if it'd been you they were talking about."

"That depends," his ma said, smiling. "What were they saying?"

"They needed a good whooping, and how about let's leave it at that, huh?"

"Maybe, but they gave one, too. Come and sit, let me look at that swelling."

He took the paper towel from her, and they relaxed on the sofa.

She said, "You took on *two* guys?"

Shay nodded, deciding he'd best not speak of a Deegan to her. "They could've used a third. How it happened, we went out back of the bar, and I handled it. A drunken pissing contest, that's all."

"Well," she said, "do you need to get checked out, see a doctor?"

"No, nothing's broken."

"You could have a concussion. Kid, I just can't see you starting something. What gets into you? You never used to pull stunts like this."

"My head's all right," Shay said, "and *I* didn't start it."

"Don't say, 'But I finished it.' "

"I won't."

"Oh, but you're thinking it," she said, taking the paper towel back. "This is the second fight you've been in, that I know of."

"What was the first?"

"You punched Davie Rattner."

"Him? That wasn't a fight."

"What else do you call taking a swing at somebody?"

Shay shrugged. "He tried to wreck me coming off of four with two laps to go. Got me loose and slid by, so coming around through four again, I dumped him and took the checkered flag. On pit road, he struts up and shoves me."

"And you punched him."

"Yeah, but it's only a fight if there's fight*ing*. Davie dropped like a rock and turned tail, like the two guys tonight should've done."

They were silent for a few minutes, watching the reveal of the new and improved house. Shay looking over at his ma and wondering if she knew about his daddy's infidelity. *Alleged* infidelity, he reminded himself. He couldn't prove it either way. What it came down to, could he trust the word of a Deegan? And what if she had no idea? He couldn't spring that on her without corroborating it first.

Or was he afraid that *she'd* confirm it for *him*? Hell, Dr. Barolo would love "exploring" this.

He said, "I'll have to go back home tomorrow."

"You *are* home," she said, patting his knee.

"You get what I mean."

"Do what you have to."

"I'm gonna visit again soon."

"I hope so. Holy cow, look at that kitchen. I wish I could have them redo this old place."

"You don't like it here?"

"I do, but it would be nice to change some things. I mean, do you see that sunroom they put in…"

"I'll come back," Shay said. "Or, why don't you drive down to Charlotte?"

She turned to him and said, "Really? I'm shocked."

"What I want is for you to be happy."

He stood, stretched, and headed for the stairs to go up to bed.

"Wait, Shay." He stopped. "Is there something else you want to tell me? You have that weird look on your face. Like when you used to get in trouble at school and hide it from me, but the principal had already called and ratted you out."

Shay told himself to do it. Open up and ask her about his daddy and this other woman. Make it quick, make it honest, and be done with the whole situation.

He said, "No."

* * *

"YOU'RE IN THE CLEAR," Luther said, as he dabbed at a scrape on his arm.

Derek rummaged through a first-aid box on one of the Reformation's empty tables. "You positive?"

"Do I look like I'm in the mood for bullshitting?"

"More like a truck hit you."

"Me and the marshal, we beat the hell out of two drunks. We go out to the alley behind the bar. One with a ponytail, he tries charging Harlowe, I guess going for the slimmer of the two of us. Pushes him against a wall and starts swinging, except this guy's a brawler and can't land a hit to save his life. Harlowe elbows him in the back, guy goes down. Meanwhile, I knock the other on his ass and he stays flat. But Ponytail's not done, no. Harlowe and I drop our guard, thinking we'd already won, and this guy gets up and hits the marshal in the face. Twice, before I wrestle him away and hold him behind his back, pinning his arms. You know how I mean?"

Derek could see it like a movie playing in his mind. "Sure, pull his arms behind him like chicken wings, the dude can't do nothing about it."

"So, like that, I'm holding him. He pushes me against a dumpster, and I get banged up by the metal. But I have him. Harlowe shakes it off and goes to town. Body shots, three or four. Then one to the jaw. Like it was personal."

"They gonna press charges?"

"Against a marshal? And *me*? Shit no. They're lucky not to be in jail. Or dead."

"Sounds like Harlowe was working something out on the man."

"I got that impression, too."

Derek handed his boss a bandage and a disinfectant wipe, saying, "So y'all are buddies now?"

"Hardly, but he's going back to the city in the morn-ing. I'm not sure where he and I stand, but he's not coming after you again. Least not this trip. But he's not done with us."

" 'Preciate you sorting him out for me. But I been here thinking. Working for you? Man, it puts me in a dangerous spot. Lot of risk, no equal share of the reward."

"Just tell me how much those pills brought in tonight," Luther said, ignoring him.

"Seventeen-five."

"With how much still outstanding?"

"Another eight Gs. Expect we'll collect the rest tomorrow."

Luther wiped his mustache with the back of his hand and shut the first-aid kit. "Now that makes me feel a damn bit better."

"How would you feel," Derek said, "about making me a partner with you?"

"It's something we can discuss another time."

"I'd like to now. This marshal thing, it's got me motivated, man."

"Another time."

Derek pointed at him. "You said that when I asked about it before. And that was months ago. You expect me to just keep waiting? I won't do it, not with everything that's changing around here."

"Is that a fact?"

"The truth, man, that's the whole thing. You want me to stay on with all the shit going down around you? You ask me to take these risks for your ass? I'm gonna need compensation."

Luther gave him a patronizing smile. "I'm going to bed, Derek. Lock up and do the same."

"We ain't done."

But the man was already up the stairs.

## CHAPTER TEN

SUNDAY AFTERNOON, DEREK DROVE HIS TRUCK OUT TO Purdy Farms. Had gotten a call that morning from the man himself, with the tattoo Derek could never decide if he liked or not. Was a naked woman, which was fun. Problem was, she was inked on an ugly-ass dude's chest, and Derek could only stare for so long before it got weird.

He found Clint sitting in a van parked out front of the barn, no doubt getting ready to survey his trees. Derek hopped in the front and took a quick glance at the tat, one and done, then left it alone. Clint had a binder of spreadsheets open in his lap, and would lick his finger before turning each page.

The man looking up now and saying, "Doing my financials. You know much paperwork goes into running a farm? More'n that burger joint of y'all's."

"How's your shit doing?"

"I'm projected to make ten percent less this season. People want artificial trees. The environmentalists, they keep complaining about real ones ending up in landfills after Christmas every year. But you know how bad it is for the Earth to make an artificial, all that plastic and rubber? Not to mention, you buy a real tree, you can give it to the city when it's dried out, have them mulch it for public land, did you know that? Sometimes they'll dump 'em in lakes too, 'cause the fish, they love 'em, it's like a reef down there. Ever'body nowadays, I swear, they're uninformed but think they're geniuses, you can't tell 'em a thing."

Derek raised his eyebrow. "Man, you really do like this farming business. I mean, you *into* it."

"It's my family's legacy. Course I'm *into* it."

"Not just a convenient setup for your weed?"

"What the reefer does," Clint said, turning to him, "it supplements the money I make from the trees. And it's creative, trying to get the best blend, just the right balance to make Purdy Woman live up to its name."

"It does. I've sampled the shit. Man, you have a gift. Luther thinks so too."

Clint snapped the binder shut. "That's why I called you. How *is* your boss?"

"The man's been on edge lately. Making him check out mentally, know what I'm saying? Goes on and on about his father, what a pain in the ass the old dude is.

And he's got this U.S. marshal sniffing around, so he's had that to deal with too. All of it getting him distracted."

"You said anything to him about it?"

"He's the boss, what you gonna do?"

Clint shook his head and stared down at the binder again, then up at Derek, like he was thinking real hard, deciding something important. Saying, "He's got you in charge of his pill dealing?"

"I'm the man's number two. The man say to do something, I don't question it."

"You're real loyal?"

Derek caught himself hesitating, after his last conversation with Luther. But said, "Hundred *percent* loyal, no doubts."

"And pills are what he told you to do."

"Why you want to know so much? Ain't even your side of the business."

"I wanna know how he works it. Distributes 'em without nobody finding out."

Derek caught himself with a wide smile on his face, full of pride. "It's a slick system, man. Why don't you buy some goodies, test it out yourself?"

"I've got my own supplier. How *we* do it, we trade products and both walk away happy."

Derek flipped down the sun visor and checked his teeth in the mirror, making sure there weren't no lettuce from his burger at lunch stuck up in there. Saying, "I still can't just tell you. Not unless the man wants you to know."

"Does he put the pills in the to-go bags, with the food?"

Derek laughed. "You gonna turn this into a guessing game? Okay, man, go ahead, let's see what you got."

"Is that a no?"

"Try again."

Clint's dumbass face snorted at him, the man maybe remembering details of the Reformation and adding them up in his mind, looking for an answer. "The books," he said.

"Luther's charity. What about them?"

"They're weird. You don't expect to see 'em in a burger joint, especially one like that."

Derek had to work to suppress a grin. "They just books, man, the world's got millions and millions of them."

"No, the pill dealing, they got something to do with it."

"All right, you close. But not there yet, know what I'm saying?" Derek sighed and flipped the visor back up. "Yeah, we put the pill bottles in the food bags, our people come by and pick up their orders. But we also had sheriffs come sniffing around a time or two, and seeing our customers paying hundreds for a burger ain't gonna fly, right? We needed a discreet way to get our cash that weren't obvious." Derek tapped the top of the binder. "If they buying your weed from us, they take a book and return it with the money slipped into page 420. Why Luther likes the long works of literature. Pill people, they do the same thing, take a book and bring it back, except they put the bills into page 69. I keep a log of who got what checked out, who put what amount on which page, all that."

Clint widened his eyes into circles. "You're serious?"

This man who'd once decided to get an entire woman inked onto his fat gut couldn't believe it.

Derek said, "So how about it, man? You a big reader? Maybe I got a book *you'd* like."

* * *

Amy Barolo and her husband, Mark Hammond—she used her maiden name to keep it consistent for her patients—had finished watching act one of *The Lion King* at the performing arts center in Uptown Charlotte. They were on the first floor, in the back of the front-middle section of the theater, where the sound from the speakers converged and made these the best seats.

But she wasn't enjoying the show.

Mark, with his shaggy brown hair slicked back for their evening out, returned from an intermission bathroom run and put an arm around her. He cleared his throat, getting her attention. "Put your playbill on the floor."

"What? Why?"

"Because you've been twisting it in your hands all night, like you want to strangle it."

"Oh," she said, looking down at the booklet she'd contorted into a tight tube. "Sorry, am I distracting you?"

"More like worrying me," he said. "Work again?"

"I'm fine."

"No you're not. You're like a clenched fist in a very pretty dress. Have been all night."

"I'm okay, really. Just in a thinking mood."

"A *thinking* mood?"

"You know, contemplative."

"I thought you said this was your favorite musical."

"That was *Cats*."

"Well, these are really *big* cats."

"Mark, you stressing out about my stressing out is only going to stress us both out more. Come on, let's just enjoy ourselves."

"Usually when we come here," he said, "it's a good escape for you, right? I always thought so."

She nodded. "Okay, you want to know why tonight's different?"

"I'd love to. I want to see if I can help."

"This story is making me think about a new patient."

"Which means you can't tell me without violating your ethics."

"Sorry," she said, "but that's how it goes."

"Give me a little something."

The house lights darkened, as the curtain opened on act two.

Amy lowered her voice to a whisper. "It's starting again. We're going to disturb people."

"You wringing your program's neck is disturbing *me*. Come on, I want to fix whatever's wrong."

"It's not as simple as fixing it," she said, raising her voice just enough to get shushed from somebody two rows in front of them. She leaned toward Mark, saying, "And it's not always on you to fix my problems. I hate it when you try to do that."

"How about," he said, "we don't say anything about your patient, okay?"

"Thank you."

"No, I mean, let's talk about the lions instead."

She crossed her arms and stared at the stage, refusing to acknowledge how he was still studying her.

The chorus of colorful bird costumes and puppets concluded the act's opening number—red, green, yellow, and orange feathers leaping and diving and dancing through the air. Actors dressed as vultures replaced them, and the lighting became dim and menacing, shades of blue and purple. Set pieces that resembled gazelle skeletons appeared in the background. Then Scar took center stage, singing of madness and visions of the dead king haunting him.

Amy shifted in her seat, trying to get comfortable but unable to, Mark's eyes on her again, as the scene changed to a rushing river. Timon fell in, leaving Simba to save him. She couldn't look away from the young lion, who froze in place when a spotlight showed Mufasa's traumatic demise upstage of the main action, a childhood trauma the character couldn't overcome.

"These damn lions," she said.

\* \* \*

MARK ASKED her about it again on the car ride home, glancing at her whenever they stopped at a red light on their way out of Uptown. It was a busy night in the city. Crowds of people filled the sidewalks, musicians played jazz on the corner of Trade and Tryon, and the white-tablecloth Italian restaurant where they'd eaten dinner before the musical still looked full as they passed its glass windows.

She hesitated, weighing what she could and couldn't say, still taking it out on the playbill. "A son loses his father early in life and can't get over it."

"We're talking about Simba?"

"Yes, and absolutely not my patient."

"Okay, good, what else?"

"He grows up, he's happy—at least as far as he knows —has friends, a career, everything a healthy person is supposed to. But how would the story," she said, "be different if he hadn't been reluctant to go home?"

"I'm not following so much anymore, Ame."

"It takes him most of act two to decide he has to return and face his uncle."

"You're saying, what if he was after revenge from the beginning?"

"And what if he was so determined that nothing could stop him, even if he wasn't ready?"

"Well, it's the classic hero's journey, so the story wouldn't work then," Mark said, sounding like he was in his classroom, teaching high school English. "He *has* to grow enough to be able to topple Scar. Otherwise, the whole thing isn't satisfying for the audience ... or plausible, really. I mean, as much as lions acting like people is plausible."

She leaned on the center console, smelling the deep scent of Mark's cologne and wishing she could've relaxed and just *been* with him tonight. "But what if he doesn't care? He's so full of anger, he thinks he's a real tough guy, even has a nickname that, say, Timon and Pumbaa call him."

"What kind of nickname?"

"Something that *represents* how tough he is. And what if Simba—not my patient, remember—embraces this persona to the extent that he believes he's invincible?"

Mark shrugged. "In that case, he goes to face Scar and loses. He'd *have* to fail. Simba's the protagonist, so it's not as if he'd die. But maybe he loses a hand, like Luke Skywalker."

"Stick to the first metaphor, Mark."

"All right, but you get my point."

"Except, in real life, everybody's the protagonist in their own story, and they all think they'll get a happy ending. But that's not how life works. So if this was reality, and Simba went after his uncle too soon…"

"He'd be killed. How could he not be? It's what lions do."

"Unless," she said, "somebody intervened and helped him get over that need for vengeance. Not getting in the way of justice, but only slowing him down so he could do it the right way."

"Like a psychiatrist? Whose husband needs to ask how work is going before he buys tickets at the Blumenthal?"

"I'm glad you did," she said. "This actually helped."

"When do you see him next? This Simba guy?"

She tucked the playbill into her purse. "Tomorrow."

## CHAPTER ELEVEN

"I can explain this," Shay said, touching his bruised face and wincing.

Amy Barolo's pen stopped. "Do you feel the need to explain it?"

Shay crossed one leg over the other. In the same chair, in the same office, looking at her same degrees on the wall and wondering how many times he'd have to sit here before she'd clear him.

"Your eyes," he said, "went real wide when I came in. You seemed concerned, so I don't mind telling you what happened."

"If you want to. You get to choose what we talk about. I'm here to listen and facilitate along the way."

"Okay, then," he said.

And described the bar in Wilkesboro, trying to bring her into the memory of that night, the dim lighting, the hunters coming in and spouting their whiskey-fueled horseshit, and how he'd intervened when they'd disgraced a woman's honor. Took them out back and beat them down, hoping that would encourage them to keep their mouths shut next time.

He didn't mention Luther.

Maybe there *was* something to be gained from these sessions, something in his subconscious he could stand to learn more about. But in the end, wasn't this just an inconvenience? A speed bump on his path back to full-time service. Why give her every detail and risk slowing the process further?

She made a note or two in her file on him, but waited until he'd finished to start probing his psyche—or whatever it was she liked to do. "Last session," she said in her calm tone, "we discovered you like saving people from harm."

"From the snakes under the dumpster."

"Tell me, do you feel any difference between saving a man versus a woman?"

"I don't know. It's not something I've ever stopped to think about, especially not on the job."

"Think about it now. Is one more satisfying to you?"

"That's not the right word."

She didn't comment, waiting for him to suggest a better one.

Shay leaned forward, resting his elbows on his thighs,

one leg bouncing. "Are you asking if, as a man, I believe I'm *compelled* to save a woman?"

"Is that what you'd like me to ask?"

He shot her a look, the same he'd given her the last time she'd pulled that shrink speech on him, always answering his questions with more questions, as if to bait him. But she didn't flinch, didn't even blink. That placid demeanor never changed, no matter how much he resisted her tactics.

"You're hung up," he said, "on how I defended a *lady's* honor at that bar, huh? Would I have gotten into that fight if they'd been insulting a man? Answer's no, I wouldn't have."

"Do you take pride in the act of 'saving' a woman?"

"I didn't *save* anyone, I just knocked out a couple assholes who needed it."

"Which is contrary behavior to protecting, isn't it? Unless the hunters were threatening bodily harm?"

"Not directly."

"What went through your mind as you listened to them?"

Shay sat back again. "That somebody needed to do something, and why not me? I'm a marshal, for God's sake. It was my obligation, more than anyone else's. And I asked myself, What if that was my ma they were talking about? I'd want another person to step in."

"But had it been a man, you don't think you would have intervened?"

"I guess I like being chivalrous," he said, shrugging. "I'm a country kid at heart."

"You know, many officers who sat where you are said the exact same thing."

"So it's normal?"

"To an extent, yes," she said, "your culture and value system can shape that kind of reaction."

"Okay, so let's move on, huh? I didn't mean for this to be a whole thing, I just wanted to explain the bruises."

"Shay, in every case with those patients, there was something deeper too."

"Like what?"

"Let's explore it. Just trust me, we're getting into some potentially helpful territory. Do you and your mother get along?"

"Always have. I'm an only son. It works out that we're close."

"Did you see her during your visit?"

"Stayed with her. It was good. We did some cooking, caught up. She watches a lot of HGTV."

"How long had it been?"

"Four years and some change."

Amy said, "Hm."

"Why are you doing that? It makes me nervous when you start *hm*-ing over there."

"You say you're close, but that's a long time to go without seeing each other. Wilkes County isn't that far away from here, is it?"

"Distance hasn't been the issue. What it is, I've been busy with work. No matter how many fugitives you bring in, the list of names never gets smaller."

"Do you call, text, email?"

"Yeah, we do," he said. Then decided to be honest, saying, "Few times a year."

She played with the cap on her pen, the first sign of nervous energy he'd seen from her this afternoon. "When your father—Warren?—when Warren was killed, how did you and your mother get along in the aftermath?"

"We got *by*. What else was there to do? Had to pick up the pieces and lean on each other."

"And then you left?"

"That's right. Went to school and entered criminal justice."

"Did you worry about her, all alone, without you?"

"Of course. I still do."

"But you don't check in on her much."

"What are you getting at?"

She paused to write something in the file, then looked up, saying, "I want to switch gears. Let's discuss your nickname."

"The Intimidator," Shay said. "I'll stop you there. It's just a joke at the office. They know I raced cars, and everyone thought that was cool and different. Which it is, but I'm biased."

"You've embraced the name."

"Sure, I like it. Fits the job, too. Being intimidating is a huge advantage."

"The black suit, your tough-guy swagger," she said, wiggling her shoulders as if to imitate it, "you've taken on all those attributes."

"No, I haven't. It's who I am."

"Is that how you describe yourself?"

"You bet."

"All for the purpose of protecting others. And you felt..." She looked down at her notes. "You felt 'obligated' to be the one."

"That's right. And I know what you're thinking now. That I feel that way about women, especially. Is that what you're waiting for me to say?"

She shook her head. "Shay, you have the wrong idea of what goes on here. I'm not laying traps for you to fall into. I'm only listening and then pushing you toward progress, a better understanding of yourself. *Trust* me, okay?" When he nodded, she said, "Your father was the main force behind your racing?"

"Funded it, managed the team, taught me how to build the car from the chassis on up."

"And you were compared to Dale Earnhardt even in those days?"

"That's where the nickname started, yeah."

"So when someone calls you that, jokingly or otherwise, does it take you back?"

"Only because people have done it for a long time."

"I'm not so sure," she said, "not when you've embraced this persona so completely."

"Here's the thing: If somebody like me had been around when I was a kid, my daddy never would've..."

She perked up. "Never would've what?"

Shay rubbed the back of his neck and grinned, thinking, Hell, why not? "I learned this weekend that he cheated on my ma. And had this country crime boss, man named Joseph Deegan, help him hide it. The type of crook I'm paid to chase."

He left it there and didn't mention the connection between his daddy's murder and the Deegans. She didn't need to know that story, too.

"That must've been hard to hear," she said.

"It was hard to *believe*. See, it was Joseph Deegan who told me, so my first thought was it had to be bullshit. But my gut? It said otherwise."

"Did you ask your mother about it?"

"Almost."

"Why didn't you?"

"What if she doesn't know? Her memories of my daddy, those are all she has left of the man. How can I risk ruining those?"

"So you concealed the truth to protect her from it. To save her?"

He gave Amy a sort-of smile. "I see where you're going with this. You're good, you know it?"

"The first time you saw a snake under your dumpster," she said, pointing her pen at him, "did you want to run away from it?"

He had to think about that one to recall. "Yeah, I did. I was a boy, so of course I was a little spooked by this thing coiled up and looking all pissed off. But then they put a gun in my hand, and I was fine."

"You run from fear, except when you feel power over the source."

"Doesn't everyone?"

"There's fight or flight, yes, but in your case, everything you've been through? I think you've learned how to tame that response."

"Okay," he said, raising his hands, "I'm gonna shut up and let you tell me what that means."

"Your instinct is to run from your fear, but you also have a need to protect people, after what happened to your father. Those two actions are mutually exclusive. So you needed a way to *always* have control over your emotions, to *always* have a gun in your hand."

"You're suggesting that I became a lawman because I wanted to carry?"

"Partly. But I also mean a metaphorical gun."

"I'm shutting up again."

"You needed something threatening, something powerful and primal. Something that would consistently give you power over your fears, so you can save others from danger. You wear the black suit, you like being called The Intimidator, you've done everything you can to make the world's biggest threats—criminals, killers, terrorists—nothing more than pests you can dispose of with a quick trigger pull. Except for the one fear that not even The Intimidator can beat."

Shay drummed his fingers on the arm of the chair. "What's that?"

"Your mother. You feel an obligation to defend her, you've said it yourself. Her more than anyone. She's your *mother*, after all, the most important woman in a boy's life. And this behavioral pattern began in boyhood, Shay, and it's formed the basis for how you relate to women as a grown man. Like getting into a fight to stand up for a random lady you've never even met."

"If I'm so obsessed with protecting my ma," he said, squinting, "then why haven't I felt the need to visit her all the time? Wouldn't I be too afraid to stay away?"

"You're assuming the fight response is the one you'd choose."

"I sure as hell wouldn't flee, I'd want to be there to look after her."

"But you *have* fled."

"Every day, I pursue the worst human beings out there. I chase them, I catch them, I stare them down, and I don't feel a damned thing. You think I'm scared of my own ma?"

"Not *of* her—losing her. Or seeing her unhappy, like if you'd told her the truth and she hadn't known. It would've changed things irreversibly between you. And change is its own form of loss."

"She's the one person I should be able to talk to."

"The difference is, you're not The Intimidator to her. And you never will be. She sees you as her son, her baby. Not some tough-guy U.S. marshal. Your clothes, your attitude, your badge, they mean nothing in the face of this particular fear. So when it comes to this pest, you're just a scared little boy who ran away and never came back. Because you didn't have your gun."

Shay said, "Hm."

* * *

AMY FELT a rush of adrenaline at the end of their session. She'd thought this marshal, who worked so hard to close himself off, would be a difficult case, but she'd made serious progress already. And the more she could prove to him that her treatment wasn't a bunch of psychiatric parlor tricks, the more she hoped he'd trust her. She liked him—there was something endearing about Shay Harlowe that she couldn't ignore. Perhaps it was that balance between a little boy and a man, a line his subconscious was always riding and could never reconcile. He gave you the impression he'd protect you, while at the same time crying out to be protected himself.

He put his hand on her office doorknob and stopped,

smiling at her now, a warm expression that looked good on him. The man back again, not the boy.

Saying, "How much longer we doing this? I mean, it seems like we had the big breakthrough, so how much more do we need?"

She'd heard that argument from patients before. "That's exactly why we should keep going. Don't lose the momentum."

"My reason for asking, I wondered if you're seeing anyone, but figured it'd break some doctor-patient code."

She held up her left hand, the diamond ring catching the light. "Married."

"See," he said, "that's why I asked." And turned to leave.

"Even if I wasn't," she said, "you're correct. It wouldn't be appropriate, not even after we stop our sessions. But it *is* interesting that you were curious."

"Why?"

"Sometimes," she said, "patients will fall for their therapists. They *think* they're in love, but it's really an attachment issue. They associate the therapist with the happiness they want, and become dependent."

He shook his head. "I'm not in love with you, so let's not have a long discussion about that next time, huh? I'm just attracted to you."

"Purely sexually?"

She didn't say it in a flirty tone. No, she was still being analytical.

"Well, yeah, Amy," he said, grinning, a little bit of the boy showing through his country bravado, "I don't mean magnetically. Listen, I'm sorry for bringing it up."

"It's actually good that you did. Our next order of business should be exploring your romantic relationships."

"What about them?"

"Other women who have gotten to know the real you. Like your fiancée in college. I want to talk about how you handle love, what a healthy relationship looks like to Shay Harlowe."

"My daddy gave me one piece of advice about that," he said, "when I was sixteen, going steady with my high school sweetheart at the time."

"May I ask what?"

"Told me, 'When you're in love, don't sweat the petty stuff. Pet the sweaty stuff.' "

It caught her off guard and she snickered, something she rarely did. "Quite a quote. You can share more with me a week from today, all right?"

"Meantime, I'm glad I could make you laugh," he said, and she believed he meant it.

# CHAPTER TWELVE

VICKIE MADE THE CALL FROM A PREPAID PHONE. SHE sat on Clint's porch, enjoying the view. It was raining this afternoon, and clouds hung heavy over the hilltops. You'd see the bottom two-thirds of a mountain, and the top would disappear behind a thick haze. It was beautiful, and Vickie believed for the first time that she could be happy living in this county.

*If* she and Clint could make their plan work. *If* she could finally be the one who had it all together in life, no matter how messy the means were to that end.

Clint sat next to her on the bench. He had another smoothie, bright pink and full of fruit this time, and would look at her with anxious, shifty eyes over the rim of the glass. He still wasn't confident in what they were doing ... in *her*.

But he'd see.

Derek's voice, with that muddy southern accent, swallowed consonants, and a flavor of prison vernacular in there too, came over the line. Saying, "Reformation, what you want?"

"Hi, I'm calling for Luther."

"Man ain't in. You placing an order?"

Vickie, not buying it, said, "I have to talk to Luther about an important matter."

"He's not available, lady, you hear?"

"When do you expect him back?"

Derek's voice said, "Don't know. He's the boss, he come and go as he pleases."

She shifted the phone to her other hand. "Aren't you the guy who runs the kitchen?"

"Yeah, which is why I wanna know, do you want something? We do takeout."

"Your name is Derek?"

He didn't respond. In the pause, Clint winced at her, like he expected her to blow their chance. She held up one finger, telling him to chill out, then pointed at the smoothie. Let him drink some more, while she did the hard work.

She had to say, "You there?"

"Yeah, who is this?" Derek's voice said. "You say we know each other?"

"Listen, Derek," Vickie said, putting more confidence in her tone, "I'm calling about that U.S. marshal who's after your boss."

"Lady, I ain't seen no U.S. marshals around my burger joint."

"Slim guy, black suit, country boy like Luther, only on the opposite side of the law?"

"Don't ring a bell."

"He was there the other night."

"Can't recall nobody like that. But I'll keep my eye out, okay?"

She sensed he was about to hang up and said, "You're pushing pills out of that place."

"Say what, now?"

"I know all about it. The books, the cash tucked into the pages, like those novelty dollar-bill bookmarks you see, only these are *real*."

"You keep saying these things like I'm supposed to understand, but I don't got a clue what you talking about."

She licked her lips, sensing an opening. "Derek, I'll tell you straight up that you can't lie to me. Don't deny it, just accept what I'm saying, and let's discuss what's going to happen next."

"You not one of our customers, are you? I've met all of them, they're locals. Your voice, it's not familiar."

"No, I'm not. In fact, I'd stand to make a lot of money if that marshal took Luther out of the game. Are you following?"

"Ah," he said, starting to get it, "you one of the man's rivals."

"That's right. Is he there *now?*"

"No, lady, he still ain't in. But leave a message, I'll see he gets it."

She stood and crossed the pine planks of the porch, to the railing that overlooked the front lawn, the barn, the rows of Christmas trees that extended into the fog. "Oh, you will?"

"I'm his number two," Derek said, with what seemed like resentment in his voice. "If you can't reach the man, I'm the best person to talk to."

Her heart beating faster now, she said, "Then tell your boss I'll deliver all the information I have on his operation to the U.S. marshals—to Shay Harlowe, who I know for a fact wants to arrest him—unless he pays me the amount I'm about to specify."

"Now we coming to the point. And what would that amount be?"

"Do you have something to write with? Want to be sure you don't forget it."

"Lady, no way in hell I'm forgetting this conversation."

Vickie played with strands of her hair falling in front of her face as she leaned over the railing. "You have a pen, paper?"

"I was ready to take a food order from you ten seconds ago," Derek said, "I got the pad right here."

"Ready?"

"Yeah, I'm ready, *shit.*"

"Three million."

Derek laughed at her. She bit her lip and fumed. She hated being laughed at when she was dead serious.

"It's not a joke," she said.

"No, it's not. But you are, you think the man's gonna pay that. See, what your problem is, whoever you are? You asking for way too much. It's got to be a lot of money to be worth your trouble, yeah. But it's also got to be practical. Otherwise, the man's liable to hunt you down sooner than cut you a check. Scratch that. No checks, you'll want to ask for cash."

Vickie laughed now, too, causing Clint to mouth "What?" from the bench. "You're giving me advice on how to rob your boss?"

"You need it. Ask for one mil."

"Shut up," she said.

"Listen to me. You not holding up the mafia or a big gang or nobody. You robbing the biggest fish in a tiny pond, know what I'm saying? The man's wallet has its limits."

"Three million, Derek. What's Luther's freedom worth to him?"

"Better question. What's the difference, he in prison or free but broke as hell? See what I mean? You can't push him so far, not without taking away his incentive to give in."

"Make it two. If he doesn't have it, he'll just have to get it."

"Uh-huh, now let me ask you ... this information, it incriminate me too? Or just the man?"

"Both," she said, keeping her reply simple, giving him only enough to make him squirm.

Let him wonder.

"Reason I ask, I'm thinking *I* could call the police and let them know we being harassed. Some crazy bitch calling and making threats and accusations, into some kind of criminal activity and trying to victimize us."

"You think they'll believe that?"

"Why would they believe *you* over us?"

"It's like I said. We have proof."

"*We.* There's more than one of you."

Shit, she hadn't meant to reveal that. Clint was shaking his head now, worried he might be found out. But that wasn't going to happen. She could still salvage this.

"That's right," she said.

" 'Officer, we getting harassed by these people who called. Poor Mr. Luther, he gets blamed for everything 'cause of his pa's reputation. I ask him once if that bothers him, his bad name, he says, "Derek, all I ever do in life is try to rectify that, make up for my family's sins." And here come some real lowlifes thinking he's one of them. But all they doing, officer, they going after an innocent man. Look at how he helps the county, giving books away for free.' "

"Say what you want," Vickie said, "but they're not

going to buy what you're selling. Even if they did, we're talking *feds*. Your little county cops will be outranked. And that marshal is already after Luther."

There was silence on the line, but Vickie didn't think she'd won. No, she sensed Derek was only reevaluating.

"Okay," he said. "You know what? Give me that amount again."

Vickie pursed her lips. "Two million."

"I'll see you get what you want. No trouble."

"You tell him to have *two* million ready in twenty-four hours, or I go to Harlowe. Use this number to call me back, and I'll give you directions on where to drop it."

"Oh, I'll tell him," Derek said, and hung up on her.

Clint gulped down the last of his smoothie and said, "Are we set?"

She said, "We'll see."

DEREK STARED AT THE PHONE, thinking of the opportunity he'd just been given. A way to get something from Luther, if the man wouldn't promote him to an equal partner.

"That a telemarketer? Cable company keeps calling, offering me business internet," Luther said, coming down the stairs from his apartment and pouring himself a fresh cup of coffee.

"Nah, wasn't the cable people."

"If they call while I'm gone, tell them to screw themselves."

"Where you off to?"

"I'm going to see my old man again. Harlowe paid him a visit, told me about it at the bar Saturday night. So now I've got to interrogate my own father. What did he tell the marshal about me? That kind of thing. I could see him, after all the shit I've given him, I could see how he might decide to get me out of the way. More than that, though? I want to settle all this with him, for good. He lets go this time, or I stop holding back what I *really* want to say to him, I mean the stuff I practice in my head late at night when I can't sleep."

Derek backed away from the phone now and gave Luther his best pained expression. "That weren't a telemarketer, but they *did* want something from you."

"What do you mean?"

"Was this woman, never heard her voice before, she say she's got information on how we run the pills through here."

"She a customer?"

"No, I'd have recognized her."

"Then who is she?"

"Like I said, I don't know. But she made it clear that *she* knows all about the marshal. Why he's here, what he's looking to do to you. Seemed like she was up to date on y'all's family histories."

"Information," Luther said, swishing coffee in his

mouth, making his nasty-ass brown teeth even browner. "She threatening us with it?"

"Extorting us, yeah, that's the idea."

"Why pick a fight with *me*? And why now? It had to be right fucking now, with everything else going on."

"She say she a rival of yours."

"I have no rivals. Competitors, sure, but they're small operations. My family squeezed the others out years ago."

"Maybe she's new," Derek said, hoping it sounded plausible. "Making a move on the county."

"That's what she said?"

"I'm intuiting that, know what I'm saying? Trying to figure out where she got the stones to pull this."

Luther set his mug on the counter and wiped a hand over his slicked-back hair, the mullet in good form today.

Saying, "I can't deal with her, not today."

"I'll deal with it for you, whatever you want to do."

"My priority has to be the old man. Money can be made back if it's lost, and it sounds like we have some time to handle this newcomer, whoever she is. But my father might have already talked to Harlowe."

"How's this for an idea?" Derek said. "Get the cash together, let me do the drop, I'll see who the bitch is. Then, when we know who we fighting, we can hit them back."

"She suggested a formal drop?"

"Say I'm to call her back at that same number when

we ready to do it. She'll give us the time and place. Come on, let me take care of this for you."

"Why do you want to?" Luther said, his eyes narrowing.

"Prove I'm ready to be your partner, not just your second."

A deception the man would believe.

"We discussed this."

"I'm still hoping you might change your mind. Either way, you say yourself now's not a good time for you to handle this. So *I* will."

"Like you handled that asshole in Atlanta?"

Derek nodded. "If need be."

Luther poured another quarter-mug of coffee and drank it like a shot. "How much're we talking?"

"It's a lot," Derek said, easing him into it. "You gonna let me take care of it, though, right?"

"Sure, you want to do this for me, you can. Just tell me how much I'll be out if you screw it up."

"I mean it, it's a *lot* of money."

The man let out a short breath through his nose, not a laugh, not a snort, but something in between. "It'd *better* be a high figure, or I'll take it as a personal affront."

Derek didn't blink. "Three million."

## CHAPTER THIRTEEN

LUTHER WHEELED HIS CHEVY SS THROUGH THE driving rain, along the winding roads to Cricket, large drops from the trees impacting the roof of his car with loud *snaps*, the noise and poor visibility doing a number on his nerves, which were already shot after five cups of coffee before four o'clock. It was a five-cup kind of day.

The lot at the retirement complex was almost full, meaning the only spot he could find was under a tree, far from the doors. He was drenched after covering half that distance. Felt the gel in his hair seep down his cheeks, creating an oily slick of crap on his skin. His good black leather oxfords soaked through to his socks. Not to mention, it was cold, and his coat weighed him down as it took on water.

What he wanted to do was go home and sleep, take a nap as the rain hit his window—nothing was more relaxing. Brew decaf, something warm to drink that wouldn't keep him up, and shut down for a few hours. But he had to be here. Had to settle this shit with his old man, make it final, no more holding back, not with Shay Harlowe only a short stretch of interstate away.

He checked in at the reception desk. The nice girl behind the computer knew him well enough to give a sideways glance, and that was all. He proceeded to a bay of golf carts with the keys in them. Drove one over to the villa, the storm coming at him through the sides of the cart, Luther doing his best to miss the sections of ponding on the paths.

A minute later he was dripping on his old man's porch and ringing the bell. Hoping beyond fucking hope this would be the last visit.

Joseph answered the door, saying, "Son, take your coat and shoes off before you come in."

Luther pushed past him without a word. His shoes squeaked on the hardwood floors as a puddle formed around him from his clothes.

"What did I just say?"

"*I'm* paying for the place. I'll enter it how I want."

Joseph turned and went into the sitting room. "You're in one of your tantrum moods. Sound like a little child. Seeing me, it's that bad, is it?" Luther let silence fill the space between them. "After all I did for you?"

"Don't start on that again."

"I gave you a life, son. One that let you be a free man."

"Free?" Luther said with a harsh laugh. "I've been a slave to the bullshit you created. Been that way every day since I took my first breath. You passed it on like a disease, and you're *proud* of it?"

"You never had to sell your soul to nobody. Give up your time, energy, your talent for a wage that doesn't come close to covering what you need. Never got worked to death and still had to struggle to make ends meet. Son, I *am* proud of that. I've seen how the county's changed, what people are dealing with now, and you're lucky I done these things for you."

"Maybe I *wanted* to work."

"They came into this county promising money and stability, they used us for our labor, and then abandoned us when they could get cheaper overseas. We whored ourselves out and got beat. You didn't want that."

"Your problem? You never asked me *what* I wanted. It was assumed I'd fall in line."

"This place, my legacy, it's who you are."

"No, it's really not."

"Our name goes back generations," the old man said, his voice weaker today, catching in his throat, but still stern. "You have a responsibility to it."

"Screw your responsibility," Luther said, running a hand through his hair, "and our name. You have any idea what it stands for?"

"Freedom, son. We're a dying breed of folk not dependent on anybody for anything. We made our own way. We got to *be*, son, we got to *be*, and most people, they only dream of that."

"We're the shadow that follows every addict and junkie in these towns. They can't escape us, and every time it seems the sun is about to shine on them, they know the shadow will be there again, so why bother having hope?"

"You read that in one of your fancy books?"

Luther put his hands in the pockets of his coat. He liked the extra weight now. It made him feel solid, strong.

He said, "It's what *I've* seen. And I can't change it, not while I'm a Deegan."

"Destroy my name if it'll make you happy, son," Joseph said, taking on pitiful eyes and a soft tone. "I just hope the Lord takes me first."

"There have been moments," Luther said, "when I've thought about helping the Lord along." His old man's melodramatic expression changed, fear spreading over his reddish-pale features now. "Moments when I've said to myself: Fucking do it. End him and all of this. *That* would be freedom, and for more than just me. But I haven't, and you know the reason? You're my flesh and blood. Killing you because of our differences would be the Deegan thing to do, so I never followed through on those thoughts. And here I am. The best I've got is to lock you up in a luxury retirement home and visit whenever shit goes wrong."

"Wrong?"

"The marshal was here."

"He was."

"What'd you tell him?"

"He came asking after you."

"Same fucking question."

"I begged him not to punish you for my sins."

"I'm to believe that?"

"It's the truth. Told him I'd failed you, which I suppose I have. I'd ask your forgiveness, but—"

"You know I won't give it."

"What I know is only the Lord can set me right."

"What else did he say?"

"He's on us because of that business with his daddy. Sons and fathers, it's not easy for anyone, it seems."

The muscle under Luther's right eye twitched. "Not when you're involved."

"He wants to take you in if he can. Looking for an excuse to do it."

"Did you give him one? Sell me out so you can take the reins back from your disappointment of a boy?"

Now Joseph stood and came over to him, putting a hand on his shoulder. "Never. You can think of me as an old fool, son, but I'll be killed before I see you lose your freedom. It's all I ever wanted for you. It's all that's ever worth anything. Other people, they trade theirs, day in, day out. We don't have to. You can hate me for it, that's fine. I only care that you have the *choice*."

Luther backed away. "You don't get it. You made me what I am. Turned me into a younger version of yourself, so you could pass on the business, keep all that money in the family, where you could get your hands on it if you wanted. For all your grandstanding about greed, look what you've done. And then look at *me*, what I do for a living. It's a terrible thing, profiting off misery. But what else can I do? This is what I know, what you raised me for." Keeping his expression disinterested, he said, "Maybe I ought to stop fighting it."

He walked to the door and opened it. The storm raged on.

"Son," Joseph said. "Luther…"

But he went outside and stood on the brick walkway, his face turned up to the clouds. Let the rain soak him to the bone before he left for the last time.

* * *

SHAY WENT OUT THAT NIGHT.

Maybe if he forgot about Luther, if he rode out the remainder of his suspension and shrink appointments like he was supposed to, it would be the progress Amy wanted him to make.

At the very least it would take his mind off her, the

married woman he couldn't stop thinking about. Why was it that everything he wanted was forbidden?

Except for good bourbon, and he intended to satisfy that desire.

The Uptown bar he went to was four blocks from his building. An old hotel that had been converted into a two-floor cantina with apartments above, where the rooms used to be. It attracted a local crowd, younger people who liked the vintage charm. Not a rowdy clientele. They handled their drink with maturity, one of the reasons Shay enjoyed coming here.

He sat at the counter and perused the list of bourbons. Had to pick just the right one to go with his mood and the Lumineers song playing in the background.

There wasn't another badge in the place, the *other* reason he came to the old hotel. It wasn't a cop watering hole, which meant he was safe here. No shop talk, no temptation to slip back into his persona and go tearing after Luther Deegan. This was a hangout for DYPOGs, as his ma called them. Dynamic Young Professionals On the Go, mingling shoulder-to-shoulder on the main floor in front of the bar, some dancing and swaying to the music, others in groups, talking.

Shay had a third reason for being here. The bartender, a young woman named Mandy, was about his age, blonde, had a good figure and knew it. Wore slim blue jeans, cowboy boots, and a black T-shirt that hugged her body in a comfortable way, not too showy, but confident. She wore a light blue Panthers cap and was a major fan of the team. She'd once told him she had a serious crush on Cam Newton. He had the best teeth, she said, and that wasn't even the best-*best* part of him. Shay had stopped in one Sunday to watch the game and had ended up watching *her*. She put on a show, hollering at the TV and getting competitive as could be. Every time the other team got an interception or a sack, she'd yell, "Cam, baby, what are you doing to me? Oh, but that's okay."

He'd asked if she thought the Panthers would go to the Super Bowl this year. She said, How should she know? She didn't pay any attention to the stats or which teams were good or bad. He raised his eyebrows, asking, Then why was she so intense?

She'd leaned across the counter. "Because I love Cam."

Shay had laughed. "You ever meet him?"

"No, and I probably never will."

"That's the saddest love story I have ever heard."

"I know," she'd said, returning his trademark grin. "I'll just have to hope that one night, some tall, dark stranger comes into this bar and gives me a new dream."

He hoped that would be tonight.

Now she brought over two glasses of bourbon.

"Don't you dare look at that drink menu," she said, with a pronounced Carolina accent that was both cute and strong. "All this time, you think I don't remember what you like?"

He raised his hands. "I swear, I didn't even glance at it."

"Good, because I ordered these two whiskeys especially for you."

"What are they?"

"Oh, just taste them. Don't you trust me?"

"No," he said, and downed the first glass.

She crumpled up a cocktail napkin and threw it at him. "You jerk, you can't just gulp this stuff down. This bourbon is meant to be savored."

He tipped the second glass into his mouth, taking his time emptying it. "That better?"

"Oh, it's too late now. You already ruined the moment."

"They're both good," he said. "But let's do this second one again."

She filled the glass, then shifted her weight and said, "I've been meaning to ask you something."

"Only meaning to, huh?"

"What do you do?"

"Take a guess."

"You look like a musician. The only guys I see dressed like that are in bands, and they think being all moody is cool."

"They're right, aren't they?"

She shrugged. "But I don't think that's what you are.

Oh, please tell me you're not a banker. I see them in here all the time. Junior execs in navy suits and brown shoes. Pant legs always just a little bit too short, because that's apparently the style."

"You know who probably wears his slacks like that?"

"Who?"

"Cam Newton. He's into all kinds of modern fashion, ain't he?"

"Yeah, but he can wear *any*thing. Or nothing, I wouldn't mind that."

"But bankers ain't your type, huh?"

"Too pretty. Perfect hair, everything all ... coiffed. *So* forced. It's like hitting on a Ken doll. And they think they're *so* slick. They tip me well, though."

"You've got them figured out," Shay said, grinning. "Now, I'm not asking because *I* want to know, you understand. But what *is* your type?"

She poured another bourbon for him and said, "You should be careful with that little country-boy smirk of yours."

"Why's that?"

"A girl could find herself in love."

## CHAPTER FOURTEEN

DEREK ASKED ONE OF THE TREE FARMERS, A HAPPY-looking dude who spoke good Spanish and not much English, where he could find Clint. The dude grinned and said to look for a shed about a half-mile down the hill, among the rows of firs. He used his hands to indicate the direction and distance.

There was a rusting blue tractor parked out front of it. Next to that was Clint Purdy's white van with the logo on the side. The building itself was bigger than any utility shed Derek had ever seen. Was the size of a small house, but made of pine boards that still carried a trace of their smell. Night had fallen, and two exterior spotlights burned orange in the darkness, from the front corners of the roof.

He pushed through the double doors that clattered against the side walls and was now standing in the center of a single room with a high ceiling. Wooden beams crossed above his head but weren't for structural support. Clint's marijuana plants, the more mature ones, hung from them. To his left and right, Derek was surrounded by racks and tables that held additional pots. A watering system of thin pipes that reminded him of the produce section at the market circled the space, misting the plants with a hiss.

Clint turned around when the door opened and looked scared, not expecting Derek to be there.

Good, keep this man on his toes after the shit he was trying to pull.

Except Derek knew Clint to be a man who was cool, and it weren't wise to underestimate him. His eyes carried surprise in them for only a moment, and then it was like Mr. Purdy had caught up to what was happening. The man's iPhone rested on the table in front of him, and a bluesy Joe Bonamassa song played from it. Sounded tinny coming through those small speakers, but still not bad.

Clint said, "Who told you I was in here?"

"One of your workers. They all legal?"

Clint held up his hands, motioning toward the thousands of dollars in reefer growing around them. "Does it matter?"

Derek shook his head, laughing. He wanted to say something that would match Clint's coolness.

Had an idea and said, "Did you know that pigeons and doves, they're really the same bird?"

Setting it up. Clint didn't respond, like he was confused.

"Yeah, man, scientifically speaking? They're the *exact* same, I'm not kidding you. But people don't know that. They see a common gray pigeon, they don't recognize that it's more than that, know what I'm saying?"

"You lost me," Clint said. "And I still can't figure what you're doing here."

"I'm coming to that," Derek said, wishing the man would just let him talk. "People look at you, what do they see? Man with a naked woman on his chest. She looking good tonight, man. Maybe they think, Wow, this dude is a walking hick stereotype, man, hillbilly through and through. *Common.* Hey, they think that about me too."

"Do I look like a fella who cares what other people think?"

The man still being cool.

Derek said, "I'll tell you my opinion, right? You a dove, but you look like a pigeon. There's more to you than meets the eye, only it's hard to understand until you get closer."

"We could've had this weird conversation over the phone."

"For sure would've been less interesting than the last call I got from you."

Clint's face didn't change, not even a twitch. "What?"

"I answer the phone, this cute voice say to me, Pay two million dollars or *we* go to the feds. *We*, not I."

"Nobody's ever called my voice *cute*."

"Don't treat me like an idiot, man, I'm not suggesting it was you on the phone. Only that you had the idea to extort Luther. Inviting me out to the farm the other day, asking about how we distribute pills. Then, whoever this girl is you put up to doing it, she threatens to spill that exact information to the marshal been around."

Clint turned down the volume on his phone, a new song playing now. Derek could feel his body moving to the groove, his foot tapping. It was natural. He didn't mind it, neither. Show he was comfortable, not afraid of this man or his little scheme.

"Why," Clint said, "would I work against Luther? He's my main buyer."

Derek rubbed his thumb and first two fingers together. "Why do most people do stupid shit?"

"I got everything I need right here."

"Everything ain't enough, not when you find a way to make a slick something-something on the side. I get it, man, I don't hold it against you. Your setup, you got the weed business with Luther, but now you start to thinking about how to get more of his cash. He has it, trust me. He and his daddy, both of them loaded as fuck. You should see the villa the old dude's living in. You understand what I'm saying?"

"Suppose you're right," Clint said, stepping closer to

him, "and I'm running a grand conspiracy against the Deegans. What're you gonna do? Come to put me out of action? You do anything to me, the weed supply dries up, there go your profits."

Derek sighed, disappointed that the man had lost his cool so easy. Put a tiny bit of pressure on him, he folds.

"Naw, I ain't here to pop you. How long we known each other?"

"Since you joined up with Luther," Clint said.

"About a year and a half. Been a while now."

"It ain't *that* long. Something you learn, time moves a good bit slower in the country than it does in the city."

"Shit, you think I don't know that? But in that year and a half, haven't we gotten familiar enough to understand each other, even a little?"

Clint squinted, a dumb expression on his face, the man a master of hiding how crafty he really was. "Depends on what you're here to do."

"Be straight with me. Was it you set up the phone call?"

Bonamassa wailed a smooth lick on his Les Paul, and Derek felt a pleasant chill.

"The marshal created an opportunity," Clint said. "Might be the first time anyone's had a legitimate shot at making a move in this county. When the law gets involved, well, it changes the status quo. You got to jump on that or miss out big."

Derek smiled. "See? I *knew* it. And who does that cute voice belong to? I'd like to meet her."

"You already have, I'd guess."

"I'd like to meet her *again*."

Clint stared at him a moment. "You're not pissed?"

"How I'm feeling right now," Derek said, "I'm excited. You just raised your middle finger to the man with the biggest dick in the crime business. You shaking his ass *down*, and I expect you believe you'll get away with it 'cause you're part of his operation, right? Hit him from the inside, the man won't know where the sucker punch came from. But now you got a new problem. I know about it."

"Just tell me, what is it you want?"

The pipes hissed.

"In."

* * *

"I DON'T DO the whole casual sex thing," Mandy said to him.

"There's nothing casual about what we did tonight."

They were in her bed. It was three in the morning, two hours after she'd gotten off work.

He'd hung around the bar until they were able to have a private drink together. She did most of the talking, which he liked. Telling him that she lived in an old condo complex near Queens University, where she was studying for her MBA. Hoping, she said, to own a place like the one where she worked. She'd always wanted to be an entrepreneur and had waited tables and tended bar in enough restaurants to know that business well. He asked her what she'd call her own joint. She'd said, Mandy's. Keep it simple for the male crowd of regulars who'd come to watch games on Sundays. A sports bar, of course, because she liked the energy in places like that.

But mostly she wanted an enterprise that was all her own. Created, maintained, and grown from her hustle, her drive, her ambition. She was competitive, too. Liked the idea of beating the other restaurants in the area and being *the* neighborhood place to go.

She had a sister and a brother, both of whom stayed in South Carolina, where she'd grown up. When he asked why she'd left, she said they were from a small town where the only opportunity was to do what your parents did. That was true for the boys, at least, but for a woman? There were even fewer options. She wanted to live in a city, where you could take from the place what you put in. And she planned to put in a tremendous amount of work, to "show her teeth," while she did it. Shay said he could relate to leaving a hometown behind for a brighter future. But he did not reveal his own past.

For some reason, he didn't want to bare his soul to Mandy.

She went on to explain that her dad owned a diner, where she'd served sodas and burgers from the age of sixteen until she went to college at nineteen, after taking a year off after high school to bank additional funds for her move. Went to Queens University for undergrad and fell in love with Charlotte. They had an MBA program, so she'd figured, Why not stick with what she knew? Except she still had to work for somebody else until she was ready to be the boss. She didn't mind it, saying the bartending job had allowed her to meet some nice people.

One in particular.

At that, Shay had taken the opportunity to say he hadn't been to the area around Queens in a long time. Could she give him a tour? That tour had ended in her bedroom.

Now they kissed. She laid on her stomach, with her face turned toward him.

"I don't fool around with guys. There has to be something real."

Shay ran his hand over her naked back. "You're not even sure what I do for a living."

She flipped over and sat up, letting the sheet fall. Looked at his black suit, which was scattered on the floor, between her bed and dresser.

When she dropped back onto the pillow, she said, "A few American Airlines pilots come in about the same amount you do, when they're not traveling."

"You think I fly planes?"

"Well, you're not an every-night customer. So either

you have other pretty bartenders you're seeing ... or you have a job that keeps you busy, maybe even away."

There weren't any other bartenders, but he did think about Amy. Not that he wanted to. Here he was with a woman he'd imagined being with since they'd met. He wasn't about to ruin that.

He refocused on her, touching her chest, her belly, and then moving further down. She drew close to him, and it didn't take long to find a spot that made her body tense. Her hand reached up and gripped the side of the pillowcase, twisting it.

"I'm not a pilot," he said.

"Thank God. I like having you here."

"Where?"

"Right *there*."

"How about I give you a hint?"

She kissed him again and whispered as she pulled away, "Okay, but just one. I'm going to get this."

"I work at the federal courthouse."

"You're not an attorney, are you?"

"No, but I have to try to get along with them, from time to time."

"How does that go?"

He recalled sitting in a bright conference room, trying to explain to a surly assistant United States attorney why he and Earl Tucker Lee had switched clothing that night on the overpass. "Lately? Not so well."

It was odd, being so intimate with this woman who didn't know the first thing about him—except what his favorite bourbons were. All the while, he couldn't have this same experience with Amy, the woman who had the deepest parts of his mind catalogued in a file folder. The woman who encouraged him to discuss whatever he felt like. He could tell her anything, despite his reservations about doing so.

Still, his night with Mandy had been fun, and maybe he didn't need to make it more complicated than that. Maybe this could be a part of his life that didn't require analysis.

"You're a judge."

"No, but I work with them a lot, too. Protect them, actually."

Her eyes widened. "Are you a Secret Service agent?"

"You're close," he said. "That's what most people guess when I mention judicial security."

"A cop?"

"Of a kind," he said, smirking.

She reached down and stopped his hand, pushing it away. "Now, what did I tell you about that grin?"

"C'mon, what's the worst that could happen?"

She didn't say anything. Just raised a teasing eyebrow and then gave a brief gasp as she fitted him between her legs.

Before they got too far, he said, "I can just go ahead and tell you."

"Shay, stop talking."

* * *

VICKIE CAME in from the dark front porch that didn't have any working lights. She crossed the living room and glanced once at the sleeper sofa, like she considered plopping onto it, but then stood and played with her hair as she looked Derek up and down. Vickie in an orange knit sweater, jeans, and blue Vans.

Clint had to smile. After all the times she had conceived some wild plan without ever consulting him? It was good to be the one who knew what was happening.

"I remember you," Derek said. "Woman from the Reformation the other night. Got a burger and sat in the corner, didn't say nothing. Looking at your phone like it could tell you the meaning of life. Or trying to make everybody think you weren't listening to Luther and the marshal."

Vickie didn't miss a beat. "Would you like to know the meaning of life?"

Neither did Derek. "Shit, I wouldn't ask *you*."

"That's too bad. Because I have the answer."

"Yeah? Me too. Comes down to one thing—getting yours. Ain't no more or less meaning to be had, and you heard it here first."

Vickie gave a slight smirk through pursed lips. "I was going to say something similar."

Feeling that now was the time, Clint made formal introductions.

The smirk disappeared, Vickie saying, "Why's he here?"

Derek spoke first, and Clint shot him a look that didn't stop him. "Wanted to meet the woman behind the voice on the phone. I'm not disappointed, neither."

"Do you have the money?"

"It look like I'm carrying two mil about my person?"

Clint said, "Now, look. Derek wants in on our deal. Told me he can help make it work, you know, being as close to Luther as he is."

"That's what I have you for," Vickie said. "At least, that's what you promised me when we started."

"But I ain't close with him like Derek is. I'm Luther's herb farmer, not his right hand."

"We don't need him. A third player in this game? It's asking for trouble." She shook her head. "One more potential talker, if this goes bad."

Clint didn't disagree with that, but also wasn't inclined to let her win this. It was his turn to decide their next move.

"Who was it, not long ago, got real worried over how much experience we *don't* have in this kind of thing, huh? Well, I found us somebody who's got a bunch."

"Say that again," Vickie said, "and really listen to yourself, and then tell me why you think that's a good idea."

Derek cleared his throat. "Would y'all prefer I go outside so you can chat about me?"

"No," Vickie said, "I want you to stay where you are so I can keep an eye on you until I figure this out, how to fix the mess Clint's made."

"Don't got to watch me."

"Oh no?"

"Keep your eye on the money, girl. What else is there to worry about?"

Clint stepped between them, looking back and forth from Vickie's icy glare to Derek's wide grin. "What Vickie and I don't have," he said, "is Luther's ear. If we want to be sure he cooperates, we need somebody to convince him it's in his best interest to pay us and be done with it. That's what *I* figured out," he said to Vickie. "Took your plan that had a great big hole in it, and now I'm filling it."

"My plan was fine," she said. "I'd thought it all through."

"The man ain't gonna play dead," Derek said. "You want to rip off the baddest mug in the county? You need help from inside his circle. Otherwise, what's to stop him from ending your shit before it gets going? He's tough. Not tough like his old man Joe, but that's still saying something, right? Something significant you can't ignore, 'less you *want* to get killed."

Vickie sighed, maybe coming around now. "You can convince him to deliver the cash?"

"Better. I already talked him into letting me handle the whole affair, so he can focus on other matters more important to him. You see? He thinks I'm looking after his interests. I'll get the money, do the drop." He scratched his chin stubble, thinking. "How about at the abandoned racetrack?"

"Why didn't you bring the money tonight?" Vickie said, crossing her arms in the sweater.

"You think I'm a damn fool? Nobody has even a glimpse of that cash until I know I'm gonna get mine."

"That's all that matters to you?"

"Like I said before ... no more, no less."

Vickie turned to Clint. "How much does he want?"

"Hadn't asked him," Clint said. "But if you'll wait a second, I'm sure we'll find out."

He could tell she was pissed at him for taking charge, which pissed him off in return.

Derek raised his hand, fingers spread wide. "Five hundred. Call it a handler's fee."

"Way too much," Vickie said. "*Way* too fucking much, are you kidding?"

"Or you can take your chances with the man. And me working *against* you, 'stead of helping you pull it off."

"Four hundred," Clint said, maintaining control. "Vickie and I each take eight. Only right, seeing as we did all the work so far. And we'll do the payoff at the track, like you suggested."

"Deal," Derek said, before Vickie could argue. "Only problem I see, though?"

Clint didn't want to hear about any more problems. Part of him wished he could get in the van, start driving, and keep going until he was far away from the both of them.

But he said, "What's that?"

"The marshal. You won't wanna be around him and Luther when *that* pot of shit boils over, know what I'm saying?"

Clint sat down on the edge of the sleeper sofa, the mattress pulled out into the living room and covered with an old sheet and beige blanket. Clint always slept here. Didn't much care for his master bedroom, which he still felt belonged to his parents, rest their souls. That was what happened, he supposed, when you lived in the same house, on the same land, that your kin had owned for so long. What he preferred to do every night, turn on the gaming console he'd bought so he could watch Netflix and YouTube on his TV. Crank up the web browser and find an old college football game or a NASCAR race from the 1990s. Then drift off to the sounds of the motors and the crowds and the announcers with their practiced way of speaking, a distinct rhythm that was as good as a lullaby if you were tired enough. And after hours in his fields and grow houses? Or dealing with Miss Vickie?

He was *bone* tired.

"We're counting on it," he said.

"That's right," Vickie said. "We *want* Harlowe and the marshals to arrest Luther."

It only took Derek a second. "And then you—*we*—fill the power vacuum the man leaves behind," Derek said, his expression opening up. "We run this place."

Clint pointed at them in turn, starting with himself. "Reefer, pills, and whatever you'd see fit to do, I guess."

"Do whatever *I* see fit?" Derek said, like he was marveling at the prospect of it.

Vickie said, "That's what I call the meaning of life."

## CHAPTER FIFTEEN

The next morning, Luther watched Derek prepping food. Pulling wads of ground beef wrapped in plastic out of the refrigerator and forming the pink blobs into patties. Processing batches of fries and dumping them into a metal tray, so he could microwave and then scoop them into grease-stained paper bags later. Washing lettuce and tomatoes. Mixing mayonnaise, barbecue sauce, and pickle relish to make a dressing he liked to put on the bottom buns. Then taking more wads of beef from the freezer and setting them in the fridge to thaw over the next twenty-four hours. Derek in a white cotton T-shirt and red sweats, comfortable.

He was silent as he worked, which was strange. It was more than just deep concentration. He'd done this same routine every day for months. How much focus could it take?

Luther had on a brown long-sleeve shirt and slacks, with his black sport coat over the top. Held his customary morning mug of coffee in one hand as he pulled a chair from the house to the kitchen with the other. He sat by the grill and crossed his legs, waiting for Derek to ask, What's up?

Finally, Derek's head turned. "Can I help you?"

Agitation in his voice. No, it was defensiveness. Over what?

"You tell me," Luther said.

Derek scrunched up his mouth like he had just tasted something awful, but didn't say anything.

Luther pressed him. "I recall, last we spoke you were taking care of a three-million-dollar problem for me."

"That's right, and I'm still seeing to it."

"Fix me some eggs," Luther said.

"What? Ain't got time. It's already nine-thirty."

"Scrambled."

No reply, but Derek went to the fridge and pulled out three brown eggs, the kind Luther liked for his breakfast. He had the sense that his number two was forgetting the hierarchy here. First getting ideas about that equal partnership, even though he wasn't in the Deegan family. Then requesting to manage this con job being run against them.

And now?

Look at him taking out two kinds of fury on the eggs as he cracked them on the side of the grill, tiny pieces of shell getting in there because of his aggressive sloppiness, Derek fishing the bits out with a spoon.

"I have the cash together," Luther said, and waited to see how Derek would answer.

Still nothing, except the metallic clatter of spatulas on the surface of the grill.

"Three million in a roller suitcase. It sounds like a lot, but when you see it lying there? It's not all that much."

"Maybe not to you."

"That's right, because I'm sitting on a fortune built up over generations," Luther said without pride. "Does that piss you off? You think I'm a privileged man?"

"Doesn't do nothing for *me*."

"Except pay your salary."

"Yeah, my *wage*."

"And I give you a cut of all the business we do here."

"Man, a small damn cut."

Luther sipped his coffee. "How much of my three million were you promised?"

"Look, I told you—didn't I already tell you? There's nothing like that going on. I ask to handle this for you to show I *can*."

"If it were me and I got that phone call? I'd have gone to my boss and said they wanted more. Say they demand two million, I report they want three. That way, I can keep the differ—"

"Man, that ain't how it is. How many times I got to repeat myself?"

Luther waited a moment, blinked, and said, "Oh, I'm sorry, did the middle of *my* fucking sentence interrupt the beginning of yours?"

Then bared his teeth under his mustache and kept quiet long enough for Derek to squirm, Derek scratching the side of his neck before plating and serving the eggs.

They were overcooked.

Luther made a ceremony of looking down at them, standing up, and then dumping them into the sink along with the plate, which shattered. Derek gave a slight jump at the clatter, but the same look of indifferent arrogance remained planted on his face.

"The hell you ask me to make those, you didn't want them?"

"Just keep prepping your burgers."

Derek went back to his work, shaking his head.

"Did you arrange for the drop to take place?" Luther said, setting his mug down on the counter, next to the register.

"Tonight. Eleven o'clock."

"Where?"

"The abandoned speedway."

"What about their security?"

"Gonna just leave the money on the finish line. We be in and out real quick, they won't know."

Luther reached down to the shelf below the register. "Or maybe you can slip the guard a couple grand out of your take."

"Not gonna discuss that with you no more, you got it?"

"Hey, Derek? Look at me."

Luther raised the shotgun as Derek half-turned toward him. Didn't even leave the prick time to change his expression from smug to surprised.

Shot him once in the close range of the kitchen, Derek flying back onto the grill and letting out a howl as his skin and sweats made contact with the hot metal. His reflexes allowed him to jump away from the scalding surface, before his body seemed to realize it was missing its middle, Derek sliding down the stainless steel now, leaving behind a red stain on his short path to the floor.

Luther poured himself a second cup.

CLINT AND VICKIE were both on the sleeper sofa. She'd stayed over, but they hadn't done anything—she'd taken the master bedroom and had come downstairs this morning wearing her little athletic shorts and a bad mood. Had her legs stretched out on top of the blanket. Fiddling with her hair as she stared at the TV and seemed to be somewhere else. That was fine with him. She hadn't been her usual self since they'd brought in Derek, like she was pissed Clint had made that call without consulting her.

Her problem, the woman was all talk. She was real

*good* at talking, that was for sure. Could get you on her side and make you believe anything that came out of her mouth.

But where were the results?

Vickie said, "You're lazy, you know that?"

"I run a farm."

"So?"

"I run a *farm*," he said again. "You do realize what that entails?"

"I mean about *our* work."

"Hey, I'm the one who found us some specialized talent."

"Oh, is that what that shit with Derek Mooney was?"

"You're mad you didn't think of it." He poked her head, causing her to swat his hand away. "Can't take it if you ain't the smartest cookie in the room."

"What has me upset," she said, "is that you gave away part of our haul, and why? Because you wanted somebody else to do the heavy lifting."

"I delegated," he said, proud of that term he'd learned from watching *The Apprentice* years ago.

"We had it covered. Just us."

"Derek's a smart man. We're lucky to have him. You just can't see it through all your pride."

"We didn't need him."

"See, now, you ain't the genius you think you are, and *that's* what's got you riled up." When she shot him a look that about killed him, he said, "Hold on. You have the will but not the experience. Same with me. We *had* to hire Derek, a guy close to Luther, to get this done. Otherwise, where would we be? Still talking, always talking out our asses, about some plan that's never gonna pan out, 'cause we ain't the people to pull off something like this, least not by ourselves."

"You know what, Clint?"

He didn't say anything. No good ever came from a question like that. Because he never did *seem* to know what, not with Vickie Beaumont.

"I think," she said, "you only want to sit here and grow your trees and be left alone."

"Amen, sister."

"But you also want the money, no?"

"Sure, and so do you."

"But I'm willing to work for it. To keep trying. You'd rather pass the job on to somebody else."

He turned down the TV. She wasn't letting up, and he couldn't hear the rest of the seven-day forecast anyway.

"We had a need. I filled it."

"*Had*," she said.

"Yeah, no way around it."

"*Had.*"

"You can't just speak in one-word sentences and expect people to understand you."

"We don't need him anymore, Clint."

"What do you mean?"

"After Luther gives us the cash tonight, Derek's part

in this will be over. Why should we keep the guy around?"

Clint sat up, agitated by her attitude. "We made a deal with him. You want to go back on our word? I'm a lot of things, but I ain't a man who goes back on his word."

"This is serious crime we're talking about. It's time we started acting like serious criminals."

"I don't like making false promises. It's like breaking something sacred."

"How much is it worth to you?"

He shrugged. "Even if we did cut him back out, he ain't gonna just say, Oh, I understand, go on ahead. Goodbye and good luck."

She flung her legs over the side of the mattress and stood. "Do you have a gun?"

"A Springfield rifle in the foyer closet, next to the broom."

She left the living room. Saying from the old house's entryway in a loud voice that carried, "You think all I do is talk and talk, huh? Too much discussion, not enough action?"

"You said it, not me."

"But you've been thinking it."

"I didn't know you could read minds now too. Hang on, I had other ideas about what we could do to kill time before this evening. Right here on this comfy couch, too.

Come on back, how about it? What I'm thinking of, it won't involve no talking at all, not 'less you're into that."

"No, Clint," she said, coming back into the room and standing with the butt of his Standard M1A against her cocked hip, holding the rifle to the side like a model in a firearms magazine. "But don't worry yourself. Tonight, when we see Derek and Luther, I won't say a word."

\* \* \*

SHAY'S PHONE woke them up.

The first time it rang, he ignored it and shoved his face farther into the pillow.

The second time, he heard Mandy groan that he should just answer it so it would stop.

He picked up when whoever it was dialed him a third time in five minutes.

"Shay." It was the voice of his friend at Highway Patrol, Trooper Martellus Long. "Man, you don't sound awake."

"They should make you a detective, Marty."

"Get your ass out of bed and into the car."

Shay could picture Martellus smiling into the phone at his grogginess. Martellus a twenty-eight-year-old road warrior, black, with wraparound shades that he wore because he thought they made an impact when paired with the gray shirt and black pants of the NC state police uniforms. Shay agreed. He and Martellus enjoyed the same intimidating style.

Trooper Long was also the *second* best wheelman to ever come through the agency, in Shay's opinion.

Mandy's brown eyes were looking at him from her side of the bed now, a curious gleam in them.

Shay said, "What if I said I was busy? And it would take something really important to pull me away?"

"County sheriff up in Wilkes got a call, about an hour ago, loud shot reported at the Reformation."

Shay was awake. "What happened?"

"Couple of deputies got called out to investigate, do a routine business check, thinking they'd take a look around, fill out a form saying they did."

"And?"

"That man you had me look up, Derek Mooney?"

"Yeah, you ran his plate for me."

"Dude's killed. Shotgun to the midsection, burns all up his forearms, legs, seared through his sweatpants and T-shirt, like the blast knocked him onto his own grill."

"Shit."

"I 'magine that's what Mr. Mooney was thinking when it happened," Martellus said, with the dark humor cops so often developed on the job. "You were looking into the guy three days before he was killed. Figure you should be here."

"I'm suspended, Marty, what help could I be?"

Mandy frowned at him, sensing trouble. She slid out

of bed and slipped on her robe. He nodded at her, before she went into the bathroom. He heard the shower come on.

Martellus's voice saying, "Hell, how about you come be my witness? I'm hooked into a task force interested in this."

"I know whose gun it was. At least, I have a hunch I'd stake my life on."

"Let me guess, same dude who owns this shithole but has mysteriously vanished today, nobody seen or heard from him?"

Shay threw the sheet off himself and stood, stretching. "I'll be there by this afternoon."

"Eat on the way. You sure don't want anything from *this* kitchen."

They hung up, and Shay looked at the bathroom door. It was open a crack, maybe an invitation.

He said, "Mandy, I have to go."

She poked her head through the door, and he could just see her bare shoulders and chest through the gap. "Right now?"

"It's a long drive for an urgent call."

"You have to protect a judge somewhere?"

"Not exactly."

She gave him a coy grin. "But you can't do your job— whatever it is—with your hair looking like that."

He feigned offense. "Like what?"

She shrugged and let the door open a tiny bit more. "All oily and matted."

"Guess I should wash it first, huh?"

"Yes, we should."

* * *

WHEN THE MARSHAL ARRIVED, the county homicide investigators had already processed the scene and loaded Derek Mooney's body into their morgue wagon. Police tape blocked off the entrances to the restaurant. A reporter from the *Journal-Patriot* reviewed the scribbles in his notebook as he watched the last of the uniformed deputies strolling to their radio cars, white Chevy Caprices and Ford Tauruses with thick forest-green stripes stretching from the front wheel wells to the back quarter panels.

Martellus got out of his silver-and-black Highway Patrol Charger when he saw Shay Harlowe approaching, the dark suit a dead giveaway.

They'd been troopers in and around Statesville, North Carolina, where Shay had learned about the U.S. marshals at the federal courthouse there, a colonial-style redbrick box that fit the small-town charm of the area—at least until you got inside and were greeted by a couple of those marshals, packing and dressed in Kevlar. They were friendly, but you got the impression right away that the building and the people inside meant business.

Martellus had never wanted to be a federal agent of any kind. He liked the open roads too much to give up his current job.

He'd grown up in a nice home in Raleigh, the state capital. Went to a charter school with other kids from nice homes, many of them wealthy. His parents did fine, his father pulling down a comfortable hundred grand every year, his mother making forty selling decorating and interior-design products from a blog she'd grown since 2009. Years of racing video games nurtured his love of cars and driving. He'd run full-length grands prix on Formula 1 games, do all 500 laps at Bristol in NASCAR Thunder, and test his hand-eye coordination with rallies on virtual versions of skinny dirt roads in Europe.

It was an ideal childhood, he'd tell people. Never wanted for anything, got a good education, went to Duke University on a scholarship, and planned to go into law.

Then his uncle had passed away from an overdose. He'd been hooked on H, and nobody in the family had told Martellus.

Sheltering him.

It was then he realized just how sheltered he *was* and always had been.

Didn't care for that kind of insulation from real life. So he finished pre-law at Duke and went into the enforcement branch of the criminal justice system, choosing to catch drug traffickers on the North Carolina highways, rather than convict them in the courtroom.

He and Shay got along, Martellus believed, because they'd both lost somebody to crime.

Harlowe stopped a few feet from the Charger, taking it in. Then walked around the side, the back, and around to where Martellus waited at the front.

"You miss these?"

Harlowe nodded, tapping the metallic silver hood with his knuckle. "They're fun to drive."

"Not fun to maintain."

"I remember. Reliability was always the problem. But they look good."

"Marshals have you in an SUV?"

"Tahoe. Great for transporting prisoners. Not bad off-road, though I don't find many occasions to do that, working out of Charlotte."

"Take-home vehicle?"

"Mine is, but they're phasing them out."

"Budget constraints?"

"Money's tight. Can't have every deputy driving around in a high-performance ride."

Martellus led him over to the edge of the scene, the front door to the Reformation closed and locked, the activity concluded.

"County won't want us getting closer."

"Don't blame them," Shay said. "A marshal has no business here. Let their homicide people do their jobs."

"At least until they put out a warrant for Luther and can't find him." He knew that was the outcome

Harlowe was hoping for. "Then you'll be all over it, I expect."

"I'm not here for work, Marty."

"You said you're suspended?"

"Marshals don't investigate local crimes. The only reason I'm back in Wilkes is *because* I'm suspended."

Martellus said, "Uh-huh, but you're here for *some*thing more than a friendly visit. You don't have to tell me, you don't want to. But I have to know, why were you looking into Derek Mooney?"

"I'm interested in his boss. Needed leverage to get Derek talking to me."

"You're after Luther Deegan?"

"Who I'm pretty sure killed Derek."

"But you're not here on official business? Now you've got me curious, Harlowe, you really do. Matter of fact, I wish you'd let me in on the secret, maybe I could help you."

Shay looked at his shoes, like he wanted to say more but couldn't. Or simply wouldn't. Martellus hoped that would change.

But the marshal only said, "Did County find the murder weapon?"

"I'm not in the loop. Highway doesn't have a dog in this case yet, either. Although I'll tell you this—I mentioned a task force before, on the phone? Well, I'm working closely with DEA on one now, and they've had their eyes on Luther for some time. County brought some dogs in, sniffed and searched every inch of this place. If they found a hint of drugs, top of anything pointing to Luther as the perp? My phone and theirs start ringing, you can believe that."

"They like him for pushing opioids, huh?"

"Plus herb. DEA also been on this man named Clint Purdy, owns a Christmas tree farm on the line between Ashe and Wilkes. Rumor has it he's cultivating for Luther."

That got Shay to grin in a way that reminded Martellus of the Cheshire cat. "Here's what I'm thinking, Marty. You keep me updated on the Mooney murder. I want to hear what County's doing, as much as you can find out."

Martellus gave a quick nod, then grinned back. "And what do I get in return?"

"While I'm suspended, I can run down some leads for you, like this pot farmer. Off the books. When your people are ready, you will be too. Give them everything I give you."

"I feel you on that. It'll be good to work with The Intimidator again. Assuming you haven't lost your mojo."

"One more thing," Shay said, thinking faster than it seemed he could speak, "listen closely to the scanner. Specifically traffic about this Clint Purdy, next day or so."

"Like what?"

"If Luther Deegan did shoot his number two, he'll

already be on the run. I'm willing to bet he'll go to his next closest associate. Either for help ... or to cut ties."

"Expecting Luther to start some shit?"

Shay put his hands on his hips and stared at the empty restaurant again, wind catching his black jacket. "He'll be dangerous, because he'll be desperate."

"We still have to see if he's even our guy, though. The investigation is only just getting started."

"So am I."

## CHAPTER SIXTEEN

It was Shay's ma who called him at eight o'clock that night.

He said, "Did you think about my offer?"

"No. I mean, which offer?"

She sounded different, unsettled. Not scared, but something close to it.

"To visit Charlotte."

"Oh, that's right. Sure, kid, we'll do that soon."

"What is it?" he said, and looked around his motel room from his spot on the queen-sized bed.

It was a modest space in a two-story building outside Wilkesboro, not far from 421. A blue roof, exterior hallways with blue railings, and a front office with no working air-conditioning. The kind of place Shay could afford during his suspension. The room had a small flatscreen atop a worn dresser, a narrow bathroom with a single sink, and one chair with a table by a window. It wasn't much, but it was clean.

"You're *in* Charlotte. You didn't come back up here?"

"I would've told you," he said.

"I hope so."

He didn't like her pointed tone. "Don't believe me, huh?"

"It's just ... there was a story on the news tonight."

"The local report?"

"Yes, and it made me wonder where you were."

"I'm sitting on my couch," he said, "watching the Weather Channel. I heard this is what people do when they retire or take a day off or get suspended."

"They're saying Luther Deegan shot a man. Earlier this afternoon. I couldn't take my eyes off the screen."

"Hadn't heard."

"You're not lying to me?"

"No, Ma."

"You wouldn't."

"Not about this."

She sighed. "Remember Luther? A little older than you, two years, I think? Graduated from Central."

Shay squinted at a cheap painting of a field and a barn across the motel room. "I recall the name."

"They're looking for him." There was another pause on the line before she said, "Kid, I never told you it was Joseph Deegan who had Warren killed."

"No, you didn't. But I knew."

She drew in a deep breath and let it out. "How'd you find out?"

Shay rubbed the back of his head. "Every marshal has sources. An associate of the Deegans told me. Matter of fact, it was one of the last things the fella ever said. Before you ask ... no, *I* didn't kill him."

"That's why you're suspended. Isn't it? You don't have to tell me what happened, but that's it."

"Yes."

"So you stayed with me last weekend to, what? Investigate without anyone at work knowing?"

"And to see you."

"Liar," she said, and he thought he could hear a smile in her voice. "Another thing," she said, serious again. "If Luther's gone, if he's on the wind..."

"*In* the wind."

"If he's in the wind, I know there's a chance the marshals will chase him down."

"It's what we do best."

"And you'll volunteer."

"I would, you're right about that. But I still don't have my badge."

"Something tells me," she said, "that won't stop you." When he didn't say anything, she continued. "But Shay? Don't."

He tried to appeal to her emotions. "After what they've done to us?"

"You stay suspended. I thank God you're suspended.

You watch from the sidelines, hear me, kid? Let some-body else take Luther."

"Daddy would want me to settle this score."

"Warren was an idiot, and it's time you realized that," she said with venom. "Taking that money, trusting a man like Joe Deegan. Sleeping with another woman and having those hicks cover it up for him? Tell me, kid, did your sources fill you in on that bit of history, too?"

"I wondered if *you* knew."

"I do. I did, even back then. Warren and I made it work and didn't let our problems show, for your sake. But trust me, there were *problems*. So don't go crusading after Luther because it's what Warren would've wanted. Your daddy's dead, and there's a reason for it, you listening? There's a reason, and I can't let you follow in his footsteps."

"I'm in a position to do something about it," he said, and felt a strange sense of self-righteousness.

"Don't you dare, Shay. Don't you *dare*. Go to therapy and watch the Weather Channel, keep watching until you're qualified to be a meteorologist. Switch careers while you're at it. That would add years onto my life. But do not put yourself at risk chasing that Deegan boy. He shot somebody? Good, an excuse to get him off the streets. But it's not your burden. I want your word."

"I promise."

"Warren broke *his* vows to me. I know you loved him,

and he loved you. But I could've killed him myself when he finally confessed to everything he was doing."

Now Shay got up and paced back and forth in front of the bed. "Did he ever say why?"

"The money was for the race team. I assume you've figured that much out."

"Yeah," he said with guilt. "Yeah, that was clear."

"Don't go blaming yourself. And don't think you're obligated to catch Luther Deegan because Warren's death is somehow on you. It's not."

"What I meant, I wondered why he ever stepped out on you."

"Like I said, Warren was an idiot. I'm sure he had a reason at the time, maybe no more complicated than he wanted this woman. Probably seemed like a good idea to him. But the truth is? I don't care why. Only that he did what he did, and look how it affected his family."

"That's what I have Dr. Barolo for. My concern is how you're holding up."

"I'm fine. Here's the secret, kid, what I've learned. I have to love and hate your daddy all at once."

"You might be interested to hear," he said, "the doc thinks I'm terrified of losing you. According to her, that's why I became a marshal. I'm afraid to even see you upset."

"Good," she said, still serious as he'd ever heard her. "You stay that way until Luther's behind bars."

\* \* \*

YOU COULD STILL SEE the faded speedway sign sticking through the pines on the edge of 421, westbound. It was about two miles ahead of a billboard that read "HEAVEN OR HELL?" and gave you a number to call, if you were curious about where you'd be going and why.

Luther had attended several races here as a boy and saw big names win the 400-mile events. Terry Labonte in October of '87 and April of '88. Rusty Wallace that same autumn, followed by the infamous Dale Earnhardt in the spring of '89.

Legends. Names that meant something and represented legacies. Luther could still hear the roaring crowds, especially when Earnhardt's black 3 led the pack of forty-two other cars, all of them a blur of many colors as they went by each lap. Could still smell the fried food, beer, and gasoline. It was an atmosphere that told you how alive you could be, if only for three hours on a Sunday afternoon.

The races were also where his old man had introduced him to the family business. Did it by explaining the past—moonshiners, like his grandfather, in the Wilkes County hills. Their antics running from lawmen gave birth to stock car racing, Joe had told him. The days of making a living from 'shine were over, but drugs? They were the new cash cow. Reefer, then pills. It was about achieving freedom from corporations, from the government, even from the forward march of time. Their culture had to be preserved, because it was pure and worthy of preservation. Only through *their* way of life could you have the freedom that everyone wanted but few folk ever experienced.

And, like the thunder of forty-three V8 engines, the desire to be free was raw and primal.

Now Luther heard the eerie silence of the derelict track. Crickets, highway noise on 421, and the faint but shrill scream of rusting metal catching the breeze inside the crumbling infield buildings. Young trees pushed through the gaps in the grandstand bleachers, like they were fans watching an invisible race between the ruins of the speedway and time itself, always moving to overtake what remained here.

Luther had paid the lone security guard to leave the gate off Fishing Creek Road wide open. Now the younger Deegan set an *empty* suitcase down at the start-finish line —these pricks wouldn't be getting their three million tonight. He took a position atop the flag stand. He crouched behind the rim of the solid railing with his shotgun in hand.

Like the rest of this place, he waited for a new legacy to begin.

"SEE ANYBODY?"

"It's dark," Clint said. "I can't tell shit from Shinola."

Vickie couldn't either, and now had to ask herself how she really felt about this. Derek Mooney had made a lot of promises in this deal. It was on him to convince Luther to pay up. It was on *him* to make sure Luther didn't show tonight but let his man handle the drop alone. Could she trust him to do all that? It didn't matter now. Thanks to Clint, her future depended on a slimy hick who sounded fresh from the cellblock. A guy you could tell would do anything to get his.

So, no, she couldn't trust him. But he stood to gain from their success, too. Maybe the money was enough to keep them aligned. Still, her gut told her to stay on guard.

"Starter stand's on the other side of the infield," Clint said.

They were in her Jeep. She'd wanted to take his van, keep her own vehicle out of this, but no. Clint had made his usual fuss, insisting that they couldn't use a car that could be easily identified. Referring, of course, to the Purdy Farms decal on the side of the van. He had a point, but her Jeep could be recognized without much trouble too. He hadn't given in, and she was getting tired of fighting with him.

"Do we just drive in?"

He craned his neck to look out the windshield at the dark drive leading to the tunnel under the back grand-stand. "Gate's open. *Some*one's here. Park on pit road, we'll hop the wall. You collect the money, I'll man the rifle."

"Oh, *I'm* the one running out into the open? You're cracked. I don't even know where pit road is."

"Go right on through the tunnel, round turns three and four, and then down the left side of a wall you'll see on the front straightaway."

Vickie didn't move. Just kept her foot on the brake and glared at him, hoping he'd realize how it was going to be.

"Look," he said, "you even know how to shoot a rifle?"

"It's a gun. I've handled guns before."

"Shit," Clint said.

They didn't say more and didn't need to. Vickie was getting her way this time, whether or not Clint understood that yet.

She drove them down the middle of the track, through the sweeping corner, Clint explaining now that if they were in a stock car at speed, she'd want to hug the inside line tight and wrestle the wheel. Vickie said they weren't in a stock car, so would he just shut up and get ready to grab the cash? They might need to *be* at speed on the way out of here. The Jeep bounced over the broken pavement and the veins of grass spreading through the cracks. Clint rolled down the window and let in the quiet. Having some weird spiritual experience looking at the speedway.

Vickie wasn't a race fan and didn't get the hype. But it was interesting to see Clint like this, so dazed and solemn, shaking his head now, saying it was a damn shame what had happened to this place. Saying the speedway was rotting, just like everything else, it seemed like.

She didn't ask for specifics.

He told her anyway. "This is what's wrong with the world, right here. People forgetting where they come from, letting tradition decay. Everybody focused on the almighty dollar, 'stead of what's important."

"Like me," Vickie said, and snapped her fingers in his face. "Which is why I need you to pay attention."

"I'm just saying, you know why they ain't racing here no more? The sport got corporate. Moved the event to a bigger track, more people to nickel-and-dime. What's our county left with? This mess."

Another Clint Purdy nugget of wisdom.

She turned left onto pit road and rolled the Jeep along, until he pointed out the flag stand to her, on their right.

"Pull up to the wall, even with the line," he said. "What we're gonna do, we'll use the wall for cover. Get the rifle, stabilize on the car's hood, and cover me."

"Where's Derek?"

"I don't see him."

"Dammit." She opened her door but hesitated to step outside. "How do we know the money's even here?"

"I see a bag under the stand, right where he said it'd be."

"But what about him?"

Clint grabbed the rifle from the back seat and passed it to her. "If he *is* here, don't you miss."

\* \* \*

TELLING her not to miss didn't give Clint any more confidence. Even if she'd been a great shot, she never listened to *any*thing he told her.

But here he was, getting out of the car. Opening the rear door on the passenger side, in case they needed to make a quick escape. Pushing his bulk over the pit wall and wishing he'd started drinking those nasty green smoothies months ago, gotten fit for this. Walking real careful now, placing his feet on the faded outline of the checkers painted across the width of the front straight.

He took a glimpse at Vickie, who had the Springfield pointed at the stands ahead of him but held it all awkward, the rifle swaying and bobbing as she tried to stabilize it against the Jeep's hood.

One thing bothered him a whole lot.

No sign of Derek.

Clint thought of calling out for him. Then decided, no, that would be stupid. If the guy didn't want to be seen, he wouldn't be. Could be this was a trap, a setup.

But all Clint could do was fall into it and find out if he'd make it out.

There, under the flag stand, was a rolling suitcase, its handle raised and ready for him to collect it. Wasn't that just peachy and all too convenient?

He advanced, less and less comfortable out here in the dark and the silence, with no idea who was waiting for him. This place, all abandoned like it was? There weren't no shortage of spots to hide.

Clint grabbed the bag's handle, and that's when the shooting began.

VICKIE SAW a man rise in the starter stand but couldn't tell who it was. He was looking down at Clint, and she took in a short breath, readying herself for a fight.

She fired a shot from the Springfield and missed high with the kickback. Dammit, come on, reposition the sights, hold the gun steady. Squeeze the trigger, squeeze, squeeze ... there.

The second shot forced the figure to duck behind the railing again. Clint was moving toward her now, dragging the case behind him. She let another couple of rounds go, missing again but keeping whoever it was suppressed.

When Clint was almost to the Jeep, she took the wheel again and set the rifle against the passenger seat. As she shifted into drive, Clint chucked the suitcase through the open back door and launched himself in after it, on his stomach and twisting around to reach for the door handle.

A muzzle flash erupted from the top of the stand. The metallic clang of buckshot contacting the side of the Jeep rang in her ears, followed by a howl of pain from Clint. He pulled the door closed and pounded on the headrest in front of him, clamoring for her to go, go, get the fuck out before the sumbitch started shooting again.

She sped down the old pit road and pulled onto the low banking of the turn, staying right on the inside line like Clint had told her.

"Are you hit?"

"Yeah, I'm hit. Shit, feels like my skin's on fire where it went in."

"How bad?"

"It sure as shit ain't good, I got to tell you that?"

They were on the backstretch now, out of range of the attacker's shotgun. The Jeep bounced over the rough asphalt without trouble, and they built up speed as the engine came to life.

She braked hard when they came to the entrance to the tunnel that fed under the back grandstand and out to the main road, where they'd come in. Clint's breathing was heavy but not labored. He moaned and hissed air between clenched teeth every time the wheels hit a deep rut in the pavement or a thick mound of earth growing in a crack.

"Clint, how *bad*? Tell me so I know what to do."

"I ain't sure and I don't give a fuck. I'm bleeding all over your back seat, I need a hospital."

"No, we can't. What would we say? And there'd be a record of it."

"Hunting accident. Took a blast by mistake, gone shooting with somebody ain't never done it before." She could feel him glaring at her and shot him a look in the rearview. "Feed them your usual bullshit," he said. "You're real good at it. They're not the police, they won't care." When she didn't agree right away, he said, *"Now."*

"We'll get some supplies at my store. *I* can fix you up."

"Hell no. I ain't putting my life in your hands."

"Gee, thanks."

"Thanks nothing. I want a real doctor at a real hospital."

"Where did he get you?"

Clint hesitated. "Hang on, you think that was Derek? He's gonna be pissed, 'cause we got the money. I wasn't leaving there without it."

"We'll find out what happened, but first I have to know where you've been shot."

"Would you believe it?" he said. "Bastard got me square in the ass."

## CHAPTER SEVENTEEN

SHAY RECEIVED A CALL FROM MARTELLUS THE NEXT morning, nine o'clock.

"Got a lead for you to run down," Marty's voice said on speaker. "If our deal's still on."

"Something on Luther? Course it's still on."

Shay capped his shaving cream and got to work on his face.

"Clint Purdy was in the Wilkes Medical Center last night. Late, at the ER."

"You know what for?"

"Can't breach patient-doctor confidentiality without some legal firepower we just don't got. But see, I'm thinking about what you said before."

"Remind me," Shay said, being careful not to move his mouth too much as he passed the razor under his nose.

"Twenty-four hours after Luther may or may not have shot Mooney, that's when something happens to Clint Purdy gets him to run for the emergency room. You called it, telling me to keep an eye out for anything related to the guy. Well, here we go."

"They admit him?"

"Nah, he was discharged. Check for him at his residence. I'll text you the address."

Shay cut off the hot water and wiped himself off with a rough motel towel. "You got it. Has county homicide been in touch?"

"They gonna be looking for Luther Deegan's shotgun, see if they can run ballistics and get a match to the shot they pulled out the vic's torso. Far as I know, they're inclined to suspect our boy. Drug search didn't find anything in the Reformation. We think he took the product with him, knew we were coming. DEA's still hungry for more."

"What are the odds we see an arrest warrant soon?"

"You could take these odds to Vegas."

"I'd best get myself reinstated then, huh?" Shay said.

"Speaking of your ... let's call it vacation time. See, this Clint guy, he's got a reputation for being a pain in the ass. Been that way for county and DEA, thinking he will be for you, too. Wait till you see the tat on his belly. It's how he was recognized at the hospital. My point, much as you might want to shoot him," Marty said, pausing to set it up, "it'd help if you didn't."

Shay grinned at his reflection in the mirror. "Man goes to the ER in the middle of the night, with Luther on the run and cutting ties to his people?"

"Seems that way, yeah."

"Sounds like somebody *already* shot him."

HIS FIRST IMPRESSION of the Christmas tree farm, it was a legitimate business that happened to make an ideal front for growing marijuana. Fir trees sprouted for acres, providing plenty of cover for the drying sheds and grow houses that blended into the hillsides. Not to mention, Purdy's staff could tend to both crops without drawing suspicion, or at least without giving law enforcement the proof they'd need to search the land.

Shay drove his black Tahoe, with black rims and aluminum caps, up the dirt road that went all the way to Mr. Purdy's green-and-white house, traditional southern architecture in desperate need of some love and maintenance. Not unlike a lot of places throughout the county, once you left the quaint town limits of North Wilkesboro. He put on his smoke aviators, the style of shades he'd worn since his tenure as a state trooper. It was a sunny morning, no trace of rain clouds left in the sky, and a slight breeze tugged at his clothes as he glanced at the barn, the branded van parked inside it, and the festive cabin on its trailer. All of it innocent enough on the surface.

He strode through the wooden gate in the fence that could've used a fresh coat of paint. Climbed the steps to the porch, the boards complaining under his weight.

Shay knocked on the door, and was surprised when a woman he recognized answered it.

He said, "I guess that burger didn't kill you, huh?"

She looked at him funny in her red plaid shirt and neon yellow exercise shorts. Then her expression opened up in a corny way, overdone, like she'd only pretended to forget him.

"You're Luther Deegan's friend, right?" she said in a sweet voice, playing with a strand of her auburn hair as she put on an act.

"Oh, I wouldn't call myself that," Shay said, hands on his hips now. "But I am curious who *you* are."

"Call me Vickie."

"Vickie what?"

"Beaumont. You're a ... sheriff? Isn't that what you told Luther?"

"Federal marshal. Come to see Clint, check up on him."

"He's not here."

"Then I sure hope he knows somebody's in his house. You live here?"

"No, I'm just visiting."

"After he went to the hospital last night? Very kind of you."

She clenched her jaw a couple of times, giving herself away and maybe not realizing it. "Are you *Clint's* friend, too?"

"I'd like to be. Here to see if I can help him. Heard it on good authority he's in danger. How about you? Hanging around Clint and eating at Luther's restaurant? You can't feel safe right now either." He gave her a slick smile. "I can help you, as well."

"Look, Marshal," she said, and Shay could tell from her tone she wasn't taking the bait. "I'll tell him you stopped in."

She moved to close the door, but he said, "Wait, you didn't ask my name."

"What?"

"How're you gonna tell him I stopped in if you don't know my name?"

"I'm listening."

"Shay Harlowe, deputy U.S. marshal, as I said." He took a business card, the same kind he'd given Derek Mooney, from his wallet and passed it to her. "You get in a tight spot, you can call me. You or Clint. What I'm really here for, I'm looking to bring in Luther Deegan. I don't particularly care what Clint's got going on."

That was true. But he omitted the fact that Marty and the DEA did care.

Vickie Beaumont played with her hair again, twirling

it around one finger and looking at the card. Then looked up with wide eyes.

"Give me a minute to change," she said. "And then I'll answer your questions."

He hadn't expected that. "You will, huh?"

"Yes, let me just slip something on."

"Mind if I wait inside?" Hoping to take a look around. She'd already shut the door.

*  *  *

VICKIE RAN upstairs to fetch a pair of jeans from the closet in the master bedroom, where she was now keeping a small supply of clothing.

Clint shouted from the living room, "Who was that?"

She pounded back down to the ground floor, still buttoning her pants. "Quiet, I told him you weren't here. It's Harlowe."

"Shit, what good is being quiet gonna do? He wants to see me, he's gonna. That's how these cop types do things. They always get their way."

"Shut up, I'm thinking. He's expecting me to come out and explain what happened last night."

"How's he know *anything* happened?"

"I told you in the car, your hospital visit was going to create a record. He can't have gotten the details of why you were there, but he knows you were."

Clint was lying on his stomach, with his head turned

sideways on a pillow. Splayed out on his sleeper sofa like usual, only he wasn't wearing anything on his bottom half except for a thick bandage that looked like an adult diaper. She'd put a blanket over his ass so she wouldn't have to look at it every time she came through the living room.

"So," he said, "what're you gonna do?"

"Stay there and don't make a sound. I'll handle it. 'Kay?"

Clint snorted. "He's looking for Luther. Ain't he?"

"Oh yeah, he hasn't given that up."

"You know, I'm damn near certain it was Luther who shot me. Left that empty suitcase and set a trap for us. Derek must've pulled a double-cross, and now look at me, the mess I'm in."

Vickie thought about that, saying, "Well, how about we tell Harlowe the truth?"

* * *

"I HEARD what you did to Derek."

"No," Luther said, "you don't know a damn thing about that. And if anyone asks, you'll say as much."

"What do you want? I've never heard you sound as ... anxious as you did on the phone."

Luther stood over his best customer, a junkie who bought hillbilly H from him, a regular face in line at the

Reformation whenever a new shipment arrived from Florida.

She was sitting on the couch, her legs crisscrossed and bouncing with nervous energy. Would've been a pretty woman, except her hair was long and stringy, disheveled. There were deep bags under her eyes, and her split-level in Cricket was as much of a mess as its owner. Laundry scattered on the chairs, the kitchen table, and piled up on her floor. She had a treadmill in front of the television. A bottle of water was in one cupholder, a bottle of pills in the other. Running gave her something to do when she was high, he supposed. She was too skinny, and he didn't usually find that attractive. But he'd always liked *her*.

"I need a car," he said.

"I don't have two."

"That's why I brought something to trade."

He pulled a Reformation to-go bag from behind his back and dropped it onto her coffee table, between a pizza box and a heap of T-shirts, all the same cut but in different colors, like they'd come in a cheap bulk package. Oxy capsules rattled against each other when the bag hit the table.

"What's in there?" she said, perking up.

"All the stuff I have left. I'm leaving the county. No clue when I'll be back. So you get the rest of my supply."

Her mouth fell open. "I can just have it?"

"In exchange for your Nissan."

"It's got, like, 200,000 miles on it. Not worth all *this*."

"Right now? It is to me."

"I need it to get to work, the midday shift," she said, but was already reaching for the bag and peeking inside.

"You'll figure something else out."

She nodded and looked up at him with a sickening admiration. She was *grateful* to him for dumping those pills off on her and stealing her car. That much product to an addict could be a death sentence. He was taking everything from her, and she was thanking him for it.

Looking at him in a different way now. "Is that *all* you wanted?"

He was a Deegan. His family lived off taking from others. Take their money, their sanity, anything to get yours. Maybe it was time he stopped fighting that and enjoyed the freedom his old man had preached about.

After all, how long did he have left?

"Get up," he said.

She stood and adjusted her shirt, which fit small after too many runs through the wash. He was gentle as he pushed her toward the wall between her living room and bedroom, undoing his slacks and raising her loose cotton skirt.

"We can use my bed."

In a bored tone, he said, "No."

Took her against the wall.

\* \* \*

"A RE you aware what kind of man Luther Deegan is?"

Shay thought that was a good opener, pit the two of them against Luther, maybe get her to talk by working on her conscience. They sat on one of the benches on Clint Purdy's porch, glancing back and forth between each other and the morning horizon over the hills. She knew her rights and still wouldn't allow him into the house.

"I hear rumors," she said, taking on a distant expression. "Like he's into some serious things."

She wasn't as good at this as she thought she was.

"They're not rumors," Shay said. "Take it you don't watch the local news."

Vickie shook her head. "Neither does Clint. What he does? Plays old NASCAR races on YouTube. Not every evening, but a lot. He doesn't have time for TV during the day."

"The marijuana plants need a lot of care, huh?"

It didn't faze her. "Don't know what you mean."

"If you *did* keep up with things, you'd know Luther's believed to have shot a man who worked for him."

The phony distant look disappeared.

Shay gave her a sad smile, doing some acting of his own. "Yeah, took a shotgun and splattered his cook, the guy who made your burger the other night, you remember him? Splattered the poor soul's guts all over the kitchen. You thought it was nasty in that place before? You should've seen it after."

She was rigid. Didn't fiddle with her hair this time, which confirmed she'd been playing dumb earlier. This was the real Vickie Beaumont.

Saying, "When was this?"

"Yesterday morning."

"Are you sure?"

He hiked an eyebrow.

"It's just," she said, recovering, "it's hard to believe he'd do that."

"County Sheriff's Office is looking into the why of it. Meantime, Luther's still out there somewhere. So, after the fella blows away his number two, I find out his pot supplier is in the ER. Health concerns happen, they do. But I'm more inclined to think *Luther* may have put him in the hospital."

She shifted back into her bullshit mode, one hand going to her hair again. "You keep accusing Clint of, what? Growing drugs?"

The phrasing made Shay want to laugh, but he kept his cool. "It's known what he does for the Deegans. And I'm betting you know it too, otherwise why would you be lying out the ass for him? If he *did* take a bullet last night, he's got to be in the house. So let's say Luther's doing what I think he is. His friends are all potential snitches now, and he's trying to fix that. He'll come for Clint, finish the job. You understand? Where does that leave you?"

"I have nothing to do with any of it."

"Luther wouldn't buy that, and I don't either. You were at the Reformation just before all this shit went down. And here you are, tending to Clint? No, you're connected somehow."

She pursed her lips. "You can't prove it."

"I don't care to," he said. "I want Luther. Not you. Not even Clint."

"Clint asked me," she said, speaking real slow, easing her way into it, "not to tell anybody what happened to him. It's embarrassing."

"The more truth you give me, the more I can help you."

"Luther came here around midnight. Clint and I are ... together, why I'm staying here and have my clothes with me. I was upstairs in the bedroom, and Clint was in the cabin, cleaning it out for the holiday season. All the sudden, I hear two people shouting. And I look out the window and see Luther holding a gun on Clint."

Shay pointed to the dirt drive, the cabin, the barn. "Right out here?"

"Mhm."

"What happened next?"

"Clint keeps a rifle? So I got it and opened window and yelled for Luther to drop the gun or I'd kill him. Clint turned and ran for the cabin, but Luther got him once. I shot back, but I'm no good. Luther drove off before I could try again."

"Where'd he hit Clint?"

She screwed up her face, wrinkling her nose. "That's the part he doesn't want getting around. The butt."

Shay said, "Uh-huh. And he went to the ER to get a bullet plucked out of there."

"That's right."

Shay squinted at her. "What kind of gun? Could you tell?"

"I think it was a shotgun. Maybe the same from when he ... killed his employee?"

"How far away from Clint was he when he fired?"

She looked over at the cabin, pretending to recall the distance, when really it seemed like she was judging it now, trying to think of something plausible.

"Fifteen yards?"

"I'd sure like to see Clint, check on him."

Shay thinking, A body pumped full of buckshot at fifteen yards couldn't be put back together. Her story was bullshit. Question being, how much?

"Not without a warrant," she said, her tone still innocent.

He rose from the bench and straightened his black suit. "Fair enough. You think of anything else you want me to hear..."

"I have your number."

As he walked away, he said, "And I have yours."

# CHAPTER EIGHTEEN

GWEN HARLOWE FIRST NOTICED SOMEBODY following her at nine o'clock, when she went for a jog up and down D Street. She could feel it and slowed to a fast walk, surveying her surroundings. The quaint bungalow houses framing the road, the hills of orange and red leaves, and blue sky in soft light as the sun haloed the church steeple.

A green Ford F-250 passed her twice, going one direction, making a U-turn just before reaching the town, and approaching her again. She saw a man in a red hat behind the wheel. He never looked right at her as he drove by, but she sensed he was watching. She doubled back and returned home, increasing her pace to a light sprint.

A couple of hours later, she spotted him again at the Food Lion. She wheeled her basket to the cart return. There, at the back of her aisle of cars, sat the same truck, the driver's red hat visible through the windshield. Gwen thinking, A red hat was an odd choice if you wanted to follow somebody and be discreet.

But that's what worried her most. Maybe whoever this was intended for her to know he was there. A real and present threat she was meant to fear.

She pushed her basket into the corral and, before it even made contact with the other baskets, she had her back to the stranger and didn't give him another glance.

The third instance, the one that made her call the police, happened in her kitchen. She was emptying the dishwasher and had the cabinets on either side of the farmhouse sink open. The routine she'd developed was to do the plates and bowls first, then the silverware, and the glasses last. She placed the last tumbler into its spot and closed the cabinet door, which had blocked her view of the window above the sink.

Now a flash of red in the lower right pane made her jump. She didn't gasp or scream, and was proud of that. No, what she did, she grabbed the vintage shotgun she'd had for so many years and ran out to the backyard, ready to use every sentence of North Carolina's home-defense laws to her advantage.

But the man in the red hat was gone. She couldn't even be sure he'd been there, not really. Maybe she'd imagined him in the window, gotten paranoid after seeing him twice earlier. That could've just been a coincidence, right?

No, she was positive.

A pair of sheriff's deputies responded to the house and secured the property. Which meant they walked the perimeter of her small yard, checked in the bushes and landscaping, and looked for footprints or signs of an intruder near the exterior wall of the kitchen. Telling her now that they found the tracks of what looked like tennis shoes in the mud that hadn't yet dried after the rains, but their guess? Probably a Peeping Tom or a teenager. Was she sure she didn't have anyone coming to the home today? A lawn care company or an exterminator treating for termites? Sometimes people didn't remember what they'd scheduled and got spooked.

Yes, of course she was sure. Look at the house. Did it seem like she had constant work done to the place?

Well, they said, it was still probably nothing. Call them if there was any more trouble.

She knew better.

Her son picked up on the second ring, and she told him what had happened, that she believed the man in the red hat wanted her to be afraid.

She was.

He said to stay put and lock the doors, he'd be there in a few minutes.

"Kid, what do you mean, a few *minutes*?"

\* \* \*

"IT *WAS* LUTHER," Vickie said.

Clint felt a strange satisfaction in that. He'd taken a bullet from the baddest son of a bitch on this side of the state. And he'd lived.

"Where the hell was Derek with our money? All that trouble, losing my ass over an empty suitcase. He must've told Luther what was really going down. Must've been it. Luther shows up instead, starts shooting. You think?"

Vickie paced next to the sofa, what she always did when it was thinking time and her body had to be moving as quick as her brain. Clint hoisted himself up and twisted around to face her. The pain meds he had in him—legally this time—had been working just fine, but her grave expression killed any euphoric vibes from the pills.

"Derek's dead."

"What do you mean?"

"Not alive, that's what that word means."

Clint snorted. "Don't have to get snippy."

"He didn't meet us with the money because Luther shot him earlier. He must've caught on and set a trap for us. Which we fell right into, like the couple of amateurs we are. This is what I was worried about."

Clint felt nauseous now, like there were critters squirming around in his stomach, and he remembered Vickie's eyebrow caterpillars from that evening she'd asked him what kind of crimes he'd committed. He should've known then that they were out of their depth, challenging a Deegan.

He flipped onto his side to take pressure off his gut, let his belly woman breathe.

"Luther shot him too?"

Vickie nodded. "That's what Harlowe told me. Luther's gone, they don't know where he is. And that's a big fucking problem, Clint. If he knows who we are, that it was us?"

"What did the marshal say about me? He ain't coming after my reefer, is he?"

"I don't think so. It's like we guessed, he's really after Luther. Here's what I told him. I said that Luther was here last night and shot you."

"Shit, Vickie, c'mon. You're getting me mixed up in something real serious."

"It's one more charge they can put on him, one more reason to lock him up and get him out of our way."

"This means I'll have to talk to the sheriff's office. For real this time. And Harlowe. You realize the position I'm in now?"

"Yes," she said, crossing her arms. "*We* are in the best position. They'll catch Luther, and we'll be able to operate in the county without fear of him coming down on us."

Clint rolled back over on his stomach, groaning. Not from the pain, but anticipating the lies he'd have to sell to the police to pull this off.

He said, "And what if Luther saw me at the track? IDed me. Could be he comes to finish what he started."

"All the more reason to have the law on our side, don't you agree?"

He let out a long breath. "I hope you're right." After a moment he said, "Hey, Vickie?"

She sat on the edge of his mattress and patted his back, an odd tenderness to her touch. That was new, and he liked it.

"I'm telling you," she said, "it's going to be fine."

"Hey, Vickie," he said, enjoying screwing with her after she'd dragged him into this mess.

"*What?*"

He tossed the blanket off himself. "I need a fresh bandage."

"Wait, you want *me* to do that?"

"You're the healthcare professional. Ain't that right?"

"You want *me* to..."

"Relax," he said. "I ain't asking you to *kiss* it and make it better."

\* \* \*

SHAY FOUND his ma in the kitchen. She didn't look up from her sauté pan when he came in.

"Are you hungry?"

"I had a late lunch," he said. "Stopped at the smokehouse, got Daddy's favorite pulled-pork plate."

"Hm."

He took a seat at the table in the dining L and tried not to focus on the silence between them, the sizzle of frying hamburger the only sound in the room. He wasn't sure if he should speak first, apologize for hiding his visit from her.

For breaking his promise.

Would it be better if she brought it up?

She fished two patties out of the oil with a spatula and dropped them each onto a plate. Scraped potatoes from a pot and added ground pepper and grated cheddar to the top of heaping portions next to the meat. Then set one of the chop steaks in front of him.

"I can't eat any more," he said. "You remember how many sides you get at the smokehouse. And hush puppies."

"You're too thin," she said, and sat down with him.

Stabbed her fork into the browned hamburger and brought the pieces to her mouth in a cold, mechanical motion, chewing without looking up from her supper and then going back for more without a word.

Shay pushed his food around. Made a well in his potatoes, which was pointless given there wasn't any gravy. But it was something to do. He felt like a kid again, at this same table.

In trouble.

Except his ma no longer used a time-out chair to express her disappointment in him. No, this was new territory. All he wanted was to repair the damage he'd done. He couldn't think about anything else until he'd set this right.

"Tell me about the fella who followed you," Shay said.

She shrugged. "He was short, wore a red hat. I didn't get a good look at him."

"Doesn't give me much to go on."

"You're suspended. What could you do anyway?"

"That'll be over soon enough."

"After they decide whether you lied about whatever happened. That's what they're waiting for."

"Ma, I know you're pissed, and you should be. But I need to make sure you're safe."

"I'm fine, aren't I? You can go back to Charlotte knowing you checked up on me, been a good son."

"I haven't yet. But I will."

She took a sip of ice water from one of the tumblers he remembered from childhood, glasses with the letter H printed on them. His daddy had gotten them as a gift from the bank when he'd opened an account there. The same bank that had refused to loan them more money for the race team, causing Warren Harlowe to turn to Joseph Deegan for funds.

His ma saying, "Your daddy, he loved my chop steak."

At least she was talking now, but he sensed this was only the next phase of his punishment.

"I like it too," he said, trying to be nice but sounding lame as hell.

"You're his son. I can't change that. Just like I couldn't change him."

Here it was.

"He made mistakes," Shay said, "big ones. But he tried to be a good man, didn't he?"

"Trying doesn't count for much," she said. "Oh, he *was* a good man where you were concerned. Always told you about making positive choices and owning the consequences. But with me? I saw a different Warren."

"I know I chose badly this time, Ma."

"I know you know," she said with a smile.

That was the thing about Gwen—even when she was furious with him, she couldn't keep from finding humor in everything. Shay had always loved that side of her.

"I shouldn't have misled you," he said.

"You didn't."

"Course I did."

"You didn't mis*lead* me, kid. You went back on your word. What's worse, you made me a promise with zero intention of keeping it."

"You're right," he said, still playing the fork around his plate, dabbing it into the potatoes, the beef juices.

"We always talked about how you were Warren's son, like that was never a bad thing. But there are times, well, I wonder what I wouldn't give to make sure you ended up different."

Now Shay pushed his supper aside. "You haven't forgiven him, huh?"

She took another bite, still with that mechanical motion. "I have. Does that surprise you?"

"I bet it was tough, is all."

"I just wish I'd seen the signs. Back then, you know? He was so impulsive and stubborn and put so much energy into being a man's man. When your team ran out of money? He wanted the best for you, but it was really an issue of his pride. He was never going to give up, no matter what it took, and I should've understood that. And then the other woman..."

"Ma, none of this is on you. You had to remind *me* of that, now I'm gonna do the same."

"He needed somebody to chase. He loved me, but a man's man can't sit still, can he? Needs women, more than one, to validate his manliness."

"How am I supposed to respond to that?"

"By not making those same choices, kid."

"I'm not taking dirty money or stepping out on anyone."

She gave a quick nod. "No, but you're working even though you're suspended. And you're lying to me."

"It's not that simple," he said, and reached for his food again.

His ma had finished hers and stood now. "Truth is, I'd give a lot to keep you from repeating history. Doesn't matter how simple or complicated it is."

"And I'd give that same amount," he said, "to protect

you. So, tell me what happened with the man you saw, huh?"

She walked to the sink and rinsed her plate with the sprayer.

Dropped it into the empty dishwasher and said, "Like I told the sheriffs, a guy in a red hat and a green truck was spying on me all day."

"You've never seen him before?"

"Not that I remember."

It only took Shay a second to decide on the best course of action. "Come with me, to Charlotte. I'm going back tomorrow, try to sort out the suspension. You can stay with me until the local cops figure this out."

"Kid, they told me I was a crazy old woman seeing ghosts. Besides, I *will* not be scared off my property. We didn't run when Joseph Deegan's goons came to shake us down, and I'm not about to now."

"What if he comes back? Breaks in or attacks you? I can't just sit by and do nothing."

"You won't," she said, but it wasn't a compliment. "Warren wouldn't, and neither will you. You're going to Charlotte to talk your people into giving you the Deegans. You've probably already connected them to the guy in the hat. *I* have—it only makes sense, what with Luther on the run and you back in town. Then you'll be here again, risking your life, and I'll still be in this house dealing with the fallout if you get hurt. Or worse."

"I'll find out who this is. And see he's put away, whether or not I get to take him to jail myself."

"Do what you want, kid."

She started to walk out of the kitchen, making an impactful exit, as he sat in silence with his still full portion of chop steak. But she turned around, and it seemed she couldn't stop being his ma.

"You're leaving tomorrow?"

"In the morning. Want to be in the city before lunch."

"And just where have you been staying?"

"Motel," he said, "off the highway."

"Well, you're staying here tonight. I won't argue about *that*."

"You won't have to."

# CHAPTER NINETEEN

W HEN M ARTY CALLED HIM IN THE MORNING WITH A Cricket address to find, Shay said, "You say jump..."

"Why you complaining, man? I'm keeping your suspended ass close to the action."

Shay was already in his car, driving down Main and thinking about where to stop for breakfast. "Only screwing with you. Although, didn't you just send me on an errand, asking me to check on Mr. Purdy?"

"He give you anything?"

"Didn't see a sign of Clint. But I spoke to a Vickie Beaumont, white female, who's with him at the house. She gave me a good bit, and without knowing so."

"Fill me in when you arrive."

"Do I have time to grab a pumpkin muffin at the Artisan? Haven't had the chance, not once since I've been back. It's funny, half of the café's building used to be a post office. So was the federal courthouse I work out of in Charlotte."

"Oh, am I interrupting your wake-up routine? City boy needs his pampering?" Good-humored sarcasm in Marty's voice.

"What's so important at this new address?"

"Luther's killed again," Marty said, the humor gone.

"Shot somebody else?"

"If only."

THE SCENE WASN'T dissimilar from the homicide at the Reformation. County radio cars, a morgue wagon, crime techs. Marty's silver Charger parked at the curb outside the run-down split-level. An ambulance crew with long faces.

Shay strode up the driveway in his black suit and looked down at the oil stain covering the center, toward the top. A car had been parked there every day for years, he'd guess, but wasn't there at this time.

Marty was on his cell, standing with one hand on his hip and stopping sheriff's deputies and techs as they brought out evidence bags and photographs of whatever had happened inside. When Shay walked over, Marty held up a finger and signed off his call.

"Busy day," he said, dropping the cell into his pocket. "Tomorrow's gonna be busier, I promise you that."

"Good news?"

"This shit right here? It gave our task force's AUSA what he needed to bring Luther's case before a grand jury. I expect they'll move to indict. Your boy's about to be a federal fugitive, top of the warrant on him already. Come on in, you see why that is."

Shay followed him into the dim lighting and musty air of the house, shades drawn over the windows, clutter and dust on every surface. A camera flashed from the bedroom and illuminated the dirty carpet over the threshold.

In there, on the queen-sized bed with its sheets pulled down, was a dead woman, her face pale, her lips and fingernails purple.

"When she didn't show for her early-morning shift," Marty said, "her supervisor called the police. Knew she had a habit, after she'd disappeared once before. That time, they'd made it soon enough to get EMS, save her."

"*That* time."

"Today, she was already gone."

Shay spotted a paper to-go bag in the space between the bed and nightstand. It had the Reformation's branding on the side.

"What did he sell her?"

"Oxy, Percocet, everything. We know why County

didn't find nothing at the restaurant when they tossed it. Luther took the last of his product and gave it to this poor woman. Here's the real heavy shit, you ready? Boss says she had surgery to fix a bowel obstruction. This was a year ago. Got hooked on the meds and been using ever since. See her lips and nails?"

"Signs of respiratory depression," Shay said.

"Drug suppresses her brain activity, including the part that controls breathing, carbon dioxide levels, she chokes to death with no oxygen. Fucking awful way to go."

"I know it," Shay said.

"Anyway, this amount of product in a Reformation bag, we got all parts of his operation mapped out. The runs to Florida to get the stuff, using the restaurant as a front, clean the money. And now we see the impact."

"It's a bad sight."

Shay didn't feel much sympathy in that moment, and it troubled him. He was glad this had happened. Not that a woman had died, of course. But that Luther had given them the opening they needed to make him a federal fugitive.

He said, "Her car's gone."

Marty nodded. "An '09 Altima, gold. We got a BOLO out on it."

"Luther took it," Shay said. "Probably dumped the SS. Hell, maybe traded his pills for the Nissan."

"He gets to unload his merch *and* scores a clean ride.

Well, not clean anymore. But who knows how far he's gotten already?"

"I bet he didn't expect her to die so quick," Shay said.

He got closer to the body. She had nice features that were frozen in a sad, peaceful expression. Had been wearing a cotton skirt and a bra. She fell asleep and likely never realized that her breathing had stopped. The drugs sedated all of the natural reflexes that would have saved her from asphyxiation.

Marty joined him in his somber observation. "I know you and I, we're feeling the same thing right now."

"A personal obligation to catch him."

"This is how my uncle looked. *This* is how the man went out."

"I'm sorry, Martellus."

"Just tell me one thing, before you leave for Charlotte. You think I ought to haul in Clint Purdy? He'd make a hell of a grand jury witness, assuming I'm right about him."

"No," Shay said, and watched Marty's eyebrows raise in surprise. "Wait until I get back, hopefully with my badge."

"He ain't gonna run, is he?"

"What I'm guessing? He'll come to *me*." Another funny look from Marty. "This Vickie Beaumont told me that Luther shot Clint. They didn't go to the police, for obvious reasons if they're involved with the drugs. I made it clear that Luther would be back to tie up loose ends. What I'm thinking, we offer protection in exchange for grand jury testimony."

"You believe they're reliable sources? This works, it'll go a long way toward convicting."

"I believe that Luther shot Clint. But Vickie lied about how it went down."

"What she tell you?"

"A shotgun at fifteen yards."

Marty laughed. "That close? Bits of Mr. Purdy would be fertilizing his trees."

"She's hiding something. But that doesn't mean she won't need us. Give me some time, if you can."

"But, man, how you gonna pull getting your badge back?"

"I have an idea. Still a stretch, but what have I got to lose?"

"Meantime, I'll keep you posted on what DEA wants to do, see if the marshals get involved. You'd best hit the road."

"I will," Shay said. "After one more stop."

\* \* \*

SHAY LEARNED at the front desk that Joseph Deegan had booked the retirement home's putting green for the entire morning, nine to noon.

It was just past ten when Shay walked through the

flower garden, with its quiet stream, beds of colorful petals, and benches occupied by other residents. A few of them looked at him, this young stranger in black, as he went by. A series of stone steps led down a hill, from the garden to a brick path going all the way to the edge of the property, where he saw the elder Deegan casting his shadow over a small bucket of yellow golf balls positioned at varying distances from a red flag. The green was in the open, out of the shade from the pine and oaks that stood beyond a worn wooden fence blocking off the lawn from the slope and valley below.

Shay let his own shadow fall over Joseph Deegan's line to the hole, but the old fella did not look up.

Only said, "Should've called. I could've gotten you a bucket."

"Never was much for golfing."

"Charlotte must have some nice courses. Was a time I lusted after such things." He tapped the ball and missed the putt long. "Too much Wheaties for breakfast."

"Why I never liked it? The game's too slow for me," Shay said. "Always had fun driving the carts, though."

Deegan snickered and held out the putter to him. "Have a try. It's good for you." When Shay took the club, the fella went on, saying, "Teaches a man patience. Something I surely need, now more'n ever. To win, you have to control your mind as much as your arms, legs, torso."

Shay studied the break of the green and let Deegan keep talking.

"I was the same as you, boy. Loved going fast in everything. Couldn't never slow down, I expect because then I'd have had to think about myself in the still moments."

"I understand that," Shay said, setting his feet.

"But now? The stillness is all I've got. So here I am, learning how to live in it."

Shay stroked the ball, and it came up short.

"Not enough Wheaties," he said, rising. "As it happens, I didn't have *any* breakfast. Had to drive out here to Cricket. Not to see you. There was a crime scene, a mess Luther left behind." Deegan didn't respond. "An OD. Part of the legacy I believe you told me about last time."

Shay handed back the putter and watched Deegan take up his stance over another ball.

"You haven't let up on my son."

A statement, not a question. The son of a bitch knew damn well how it was.

"It's been his decision more than mine. He shot one man, caused another death now, likely shot somebody else for good measure."

Deegan paused, mid-pull of the club. He backed away from the ball and crouched behind it, holding the putter in front of his eyes as a vertical reference against the break.

"Patience," he said.

Deegan lined up the putt again and let it roll. The

ball dropped into the hole with a satisfying, if unceremonious, click on the plastic cup, the only sound apart from the birds and rustling orange leaves on the lonely hilltop.

"Patience leads to results," he said, and then nodded at Shay. "Why I've tried like hell to have it where you're concerned."

Shay's hands went to his hips. "That so?"

"A *suspended* lawman, something you tried to hide from me. A suspended marshal comes and threatens my kin. You'd be dead as your daddy, if not for my fucking patience."

Shay squinted at him and stepped forward. "All these years, that's still the best you got? Huh?"

"I mean what I say. You, of all people, have no reason to doubt me."

They stared at each other, neither blinking, Shay grinning.

Deegan said, "Tell Gwen I send my best to her."

"She does too. It's why I'm here."

"Except you still didn't bring your gun."

"Next time, I will. Unless you stand down, let Luther face the consequences of his choices."

"You back off my kin, I'll do the same."

Shay shook his head. "Threatening the family of a federal officer. I could bring you in for it right now."

"You could," Deegan said, "if you still had a star on your belt. No, boy, you can't do jack shit to me."

"I don't need a badge to put you down."

"You do if you want to kill me right. Ain't that true? Keep it legal, by the book. Be a hero. Ain't that what all y'all lawmen want?"

The last thing Shay said before walking away, he said, "Not this one."

## CHAPTER TWENTY

AMY BAROLO SAID GOODBYE TO HER FINAL PATIENT OF the morning, a mother of two who was a serial adulterer with abandonment issues, after *her* mother had left when she was eight years old. It had been a productive session, one that had cost Amy a full tissue box, and it made her feel good to see how much progress the woman had achieved.

Amy admitted to herself that in a way, she lived through her patients. Their accomplishments were hers as well, and she sometimes believed she'd become addicted to the pleasure of helping others. It wasn't just professional ambition that drove her. Rather, she knew she wasn't so different from Shay Harlowe—she had her own proverbial gun and carried it as often as she could. Perhaps that was why she understood him at such a deep level. She'd discovered that a psychiatrist could learn much about herself from her conversations with patients. Each one presented a new angle on the human mind, and there was often a connection to draw between their struggles and her own psyche. Sometimes it was slim; other times, she felt much more in tune with them.

But when Amy stepped into the waiting area of the office and saw Shay standing there in his black suit, her mood changed. He wasn't scheduled to come in today, and his presence worried her. His eyes fell on her with the same intensity they had during their very first session, before they'd had their breakthroughs. The marshal's demeanor was much the same as his clothing— dark, brooding. A handsome face hiding an ugly heart. No, that wasn't quite right. Not ugly so much as damaged and fighting to repair itself.

It was like he'd regressed since their last meeting.

"I'd like to take you to lunch," he said, giving her what felt like a restrained smile.

"We already discussed that it would be inappropriate for us to—"

"Not that kind of lunch. Strictly business."

"If there's something you want to talk about, make a note for Monday."

"It's pressing. I wouldn't be here otherwise. You know that."

She did. He'd been resistant to treatment from the beginning. But what about everything they had worked on? Hadn't she shown him how useful their sessions could be?

She slung her purse over her shoulder. "Just lunch?"

Part of her—a shameful part—found the idea exciting. God, what was she thinking? It broke all her professional and moral standards to even let her thoughts drift in that direction. But she wanted to find out what had happened in the last few days to undo all the progress she'd made with him. She *had* to know.

And had to fix it.

He grinned like the Cheshire cat. Mischievous, charming. She didn't like it, except for the part of her that did.

"You got to eat, don't you?" he said, with a bit more Carolina mountains in his voice than before.

She said, "Just lunch."

And followed him out.

THEY WENT TO THE EPICENTRE, an Uptown shopping and dining complex on East Trade Street, across from the Omni on one side and the Ritz on the other.

Shay frequented a '50s-style diner on the lower level. Red-vinyl seat cushions, chrome chairs and booths, classic rock and rockabilly on the radio. Burgers, shakes, and thin-cut fries, not to mention breakfast served all day, his favorite part of the menu.

Today he ordered a burger, keeping it simple, and she asked for the same. When their waitress, a twenty-five-year-old in a carhop outfit, had left them, Shay didn't waste time.

"I have to ask a favor."

She didn't say anything, but narrowed her eyes, like she knew his request wasn't going to be easy or right.

He said, "Clear me to get back to work."

She'd started shaking her head before he'd even finished, her long hair swaying and wafting the scent of her minty shampoo at him. "I can't. Not unless I feel that we've accomplished everything we need to."

"What I need, it's something that can't be talked out, you understand?"

"Then what is it? What do you think will help?"

Once again asking him what he *thought*.

"I've mentioned the Deegans but didn't tell you everything, what went down between our families," he said. "Joseph Deegan's the one who had my daddy killed. It's a long story that starts with him taking their money and ends with a funeral. Now the son, Luther, is a fugitive. Shot at least two people, killing one. Directly caused a woman to die also."

"I had my suspicions there was more between you and them. But that's a lot to process. Are the marshals looking for him?"

"If not, we will be soon. We're the best at tracking down guys on the run."

"And you want the case."

"What I want, I'd like to put this whole sorry business to rest. Only way that happens is if—"

"I see, you're tired of 'talking' it out, so you're going to try shooting it out instead."

"I'm looking to arrest the man, not kill him."

Their food came, always quick in places like this. The waitress scrutinized Shay, like she'd overhead the tail end of what he'd said. Then brushed her white apron with one hand and left the table in a hurry.

As Shay started in on his fries, Amy said, "I can't clear you to chase the person you're projecting all your anger and hate onto. You're not ready. Even if you were, it would be totally irresponsible for you to work that case."

"I'd get justice. What's so bad about that?"

"You'd get revenge, and they're not the same thing."

"This is one situation that doesn't call for psychoanalyzing," he said, as she took a bite of her burger. "This is real simple. They shot my daddy. I intend to bring them in. Don't make it something else. I'm fully conscious of what's at stake."

"It's anything *but* simple."

"I just want this to be over," he said, and heard a weariness in his voice that surprised him.

"Shay, if I clear you? If I let you go storming after this fugitive, it will be putting *both* your lives at risk. For nothing." He opened his mouth to argue that point, but she raised a finger, stopping him. "Because you don't really hate this man—Luther? You don't hate Luther Deegan. He isn't the one who pulled the trigger, right? He's just the latest object of your anger."

"You don't know him," Shay said, stabbing his ketchup cup with two fries, Chuck Berry riffing on the radio now. "He's his father's son. I hate his daddy, that's for sure, but trust me. Luther's no different."

She sighed and wiped her mouth, being careful to preserve her lipstick. He liked her lips. And hoped her husband appreciated what a lucky man he was, even if this doctor drove Shay nuts and was the only thing standing in his way.

"It's not *his* father you really hate."

Her eyes studied him now, in a way they never had before.

"You're not telling me I hate my *own* daddy," he said, giving her his best look of disbelief.

"For doing what he did, yes. It would be unnatural for you not to be hurt by that."

"I don't *feel* that way."

"You haven't recognized it or admitted it to yourself yet. But this is what I've been trying to get you to see. Once I heard you talk about him and your mother, your job, the Deegans ... I knew this was central to what's troubling you. You have to come to terms with what your father did. Right now? I think that anger is what drives you to be a good marshal. But I want to help you be a whole person, at peace."

Shay realized he was wringing his napkin in his hands, under the table. "How can I hate him? When I was a kid, he was my hero. Hell, he still is, even though he's been gone, what? Twelve years. Twelve damn years, and the man means the world to me. I guess that's what I wanted *you* to see."

"And as heroes always do, he let you down. Heroes are human. It's inevitable for them to fall short. But as children, we tend to see things in black and white, good and evil. It's a shock when that gets disrupted. Our entire worldview changes in a way we can't understand. And if we never resolve it? Well, it affects us as adults."

"I wasn't a kid when he died."

"There's no age limit on these patterns of behavior."

"So his death, it broke my pattern?"

She pushed her empty plate aside and leaned forward. "It turned your world upside down. And of course it did, such a traumatic experience for anybody, let alone a boy of seventeen who had everything—a racing championship, good family, promising future. At our very first appointment, you told me you liked picturing yourself as the *villain* to criminals. Remember that?"

He nodded, wondering where she was going with this.

"In my opinion, your hero failed you. He ruined your life—or at least the plan for your life. So now you see the fugitives you chase as the heroes in some grand story, and you're the villain. It's like you switched who's good and who's not, because as a kid, your whole view of morality became confused."

"I also told you that the people I chase are the worst human beings on the planet. How can *any*one be confused about that?"

"You aren't, at least on a conscious level. But what I'm referring to is deeper than just what you intellectually know. We need to address what you feel."

"My subconscious again," he said, frustrated they were back to this.

"You're trying to make sense of the world after everything that's happened to you. Tell me something, what changed after he died?"

Shay tossed the crumpled napkin onto his plate and ran a hand through his hair. "I gave up on racing, for one."

"The dream you and your father shared."

"Then I left for Charlotte, went to school."

"And left behind your family, your home, anything that could be associated with him or your past."

"I went into law enforcement."

"You became a new person with a new dream. One that seemed to make sense, one that reconciled how you *had* to see the world now. But it's a flawed way of thinking, Shay, because it's not really you. It's your response to tremendous pain, like a reflex action."

He tapped his fingers on the Formica tabletop. "How

do I get past it, then? If I'm that screwed up, what can I do?"

"It's not that you're screwed up. You have to forgive."

"I can't," he said. "My daddy's dead. So is the guy who put him in the ground. Not like I can go converse with them."

She shook her head again, like a teacher whose student had almost grasped an important concept but wasn't there yet. "Forgiveness has nothing to do with the other person. It's internal. It's for *us*, not them. I can guide you through it. In our next sessions, I'll try to get you to make peace with what your father did and what his memory represents now. But don't give up."

"I can catch Luther," Shay said, his tone even. "I can do it before the marshals even get involved."

Stating a simple fact.

"He's not the person you need to confront, and your persona won't be able to help you this time."

"Because I'm really confronting myself?" he said, and received a thoughtful nod from her.

When the waitress came back with their ticket, Shay offered to pay the tab, since it had been his invitation. He told himself it was as innocent as that. But every time he saw Amy Barolo, he couldn't keep from feeling an attraction to her that wasn't proper, given their situations.

She declined his offer to pay and pulled her wallet

from her purse. Saying, "If you'd like, we can move your next appointment up. Friday?"

"Sure. I must be making progress."

"You are."

"Still want to discuss my romantic life?"

She laid a twenty on the table.

Smiled again, a little teasing this time. "Especially why you asked a married woman to lunch."

He wanted to flirt in return, keep it silly and foolish and fun. Instead, he felt a surprising urge to be honest with her.

"Amy," he said, "they've threatened my ma."

"Who have?"

"Old man Deegan and however many people he still keeps around to do his dirty work. I back off or she's dead."

"How do you know?"

Shay told her about his ma being followed, about his conversation with Joseph Deegan at the retirement villa, and Gwen's refusal to leave the county. She listened in silence, no commentary, no questions. Giving him her immovable psychiatrist's expression.

"He's protecting his son," Shay said. "So I need my star and gun to protect my family, too."

Amy rubbed her eyes and took in a deep breath. Finally, a reaction from her that wasn't restrained.

"Can the police there protect her?"

"They told her it was teenagers snooping around," Shay said. "They're useless."

"Maybe if *you* talk to them..."

"You're right, I am the one who can stop this," he said, "but not by calling in somebody else. This is *my* ma. It was *my* daddy. In the end, I want it to be me and the Deegans."

"I can't clear you," she said in a sorrowful tone.

He believed it was genuine.

Saying, "You have to let me do this."

She shook her head. "We'll have our next appointment. I'll get you in as quickly and as often as I can, okay? But that's all."

"I won't let anything happen to her," he said, leaning over the table. "Suspended or not, you understand?"

Her expression changed to one of grave concern, eyes falling, lips pursing. "I know you won't. You'll make your decision what to do. But I have to stand by my principles as a doctor. I'm sorry."

A moment's pause settled between them.

Then Shay said, "I'm afraid of losing her. You told me that yourself."

"Do you remember what else I told you? That your persona, the version of you that exists in Charlotte, where you ran to escape that fear? It can't help you fight these battles from your childhood."

Shay did smile now, a warm, earnest smile meant for her. "Amy, my persona started *there*. It's as much a part of my past as it is my present. Who I am today? It all began on a slick asphalt track on a Saturday night, up in the Wilkes County hills. You're right, I did try to leave everything behind. But the one constant? My persona. Which tells me it's not a persona at all. It *is* who I am, who my ma and daddy raised me to be."

She gave him a thoughtful tilt of her head. "What do you think that means?"

More of her shrink-speak, except now he didn't mind it. Because he finally had an answer for her.

"I don't need to forgive my daddy. I have to come to peace with myself, for ever leaving in the first place."

"Stopping the Deegans will make you feel better?"

"It'll set things right, restore order. In more ways than one."

"Do you really think that will make you happy?"

He sensed that was a personal question, not part of his treatment.

"Yes." When that didn't seem to ease her concern any, he said, "It's time for The Intimidator to go home."

# CHAPTER TWENTY-ONE

WHEN AMY GOT HOME AT SEVEN, SHE FOUND MARK grading papers at the kitchen table, Mark in a navy sweater vest and white button-down, his reading glasses pushed to the tip of his nose, his leg bouncing under the table. He was all wound up and in full educator mode, the same way he'd get in stressful situations, like when their car had been towed a block from the Smithsonian on their fifth-anniversary trip to D.C. Or in arguments when he thought of a point that would win it for him and couldn't wait to get it out.

He could be such an intense man. Not in the same sense that Shay was, with his easy disposition, the way he played it cool even under pressure. No, Mark wore his intensity like the sweater vests he put on every morning, his self-prescribed teacher's uniform. He had a closet full of them, in every variety of colors and knits. The season dictated which he'd wear, but he was never without one. Sometimes it was an attractive look.

He waved at her, looking up for only a moment before going back to his work. She poured a glass of water from their filter pitcher in the fridge and sat next to him at the table, watching him fiddle with his papers, licking his finger every time he turned a page, a habit that irked her. When he wasn't making a comment in red ink, he clicked his pen.

*Click, click, click.*

She wanted to reach over and take it from him.

Instead, Amy waited a full minute. When he didn't say anything, she spoke first.

"I saw Simba again today."

*Click.*

"He came by," she said, "without an appointment. Wanted to ask me for a favor."

"How's that going?"

"The favor or my patient?"

"Both."

She got the sense he was only answering to answer. "He's making real progress. But what he wanted was to ask me to clear him early."

"That's not good, right?"

"No," she said, "it isn't."

She wanted to vent about everything Shay had said. Especially the part about going home, what she was most afraid of with him, that he'd rush into a violent and final confrontation with his demons and lose, all because he wasn't ready.

All because she'd failed to make him ready.

*Click, click.*

Where was the Mark from the other night, the one who was jumping to fix her problems? It was one extreme or the other with this man, and neither was what she needed. When he tried to help her, it was about him. He solved her issue, and look how wonderful he was for doing so. Why couldn't he ever just listen? She had made a career out of listening, and it was hard to understand his inability to really hear her.

"This student," he said, "is trying to draw a parallel between modern political discourse in America and the man-versus-monster themes in *Beowulf*."

"Is there one?"

"Don't know yet, they can't write a thesis statement to save their life. Something I'll have to go over again when half the class gets Cs on this essay. Honestly, Ame, I'm reading a parent's words here. Not that they wrote the paper, but the kid got it all from them."

"You'd be surprised how much of an impact parents have on us," she said. "Like with the lions."

He nodded again.

*Click, click, click.*

She pressed on, hoping he'd engage with her. "I think I'm getting through to him. You want to know the truth? I've helped him a lot, and I think he's going to be my new favorite success story. But I'm worried about him. I don't know if he'll stick it out or do something reckless."

"Are we still talking about your patient or the play?" he said, as he crossed out an entire paragraph with a red *X*.

"It was a musical, not a play." She hesitated. "Hey, have you ever considered *not* wearing a sweater vest to work?"

Now he looked up. All you had to do was change the subject to something about him, and you'd have Mark's attention. It was probably why he'd become a teacher in the first place. Sure, he loved English and literature. But her suspicion was that he loved being the focus of five classes of high schoolers every day. The one who knew more. The one with wisdom to impart. The one who held the power of grades, their futures.

"You don't like my vests?"

"They're fine, but don't they feel a bit ... outdated?"

"I think they make me look scholarly."

"I suppose," she said, and waited to see if he'd try to continue the conversation.

"What do you suggest?" he said, setting his pen down and really concentrating, his vanity giving him focus.

She felt herself smile. "Well, you could try a suit. A trim one, a little more youthful in its cut. And maybe a different color shirt? Something not so bland and starched."

"Suits are for corporate men," he said. "I'm in academia. It calls for a certain style."

"Maybe I'll take you shopping, so you can put one on and see what I mean."

He shrugged. "All right, if you want."

And that was it. He returned to the stack of papers.

*Click.*

She said, "A black suit."

SHAY KEPT three guns that weren't issued to him by the marshals. The first, his favorite, was a .40-caliber Glock 27, a firearm he sometimes used as a backup on the job because it was compact and hit hard. The second was a SIG Sauer P226, the same weapon he'd carried as a state trooper. He liked Glocks best, but the SIGs were reliable and high-end.

The last was a true beast, a Taurus model 513 Raging Judge, chambered in the .45 Long Colt, with a black-and-red rubber grip, and a cushioned insert to assist with controlling the piece. Shay had always wanted a big revolver. A year into his tenure as a deputy marshal, he'd bought one, and it had taken him since then to master it at the range. He'd never packed it in the field, as it wasn't a sanctioned option for official business.

But if Amy wouldn't recommend that the chief

deputy return him to active duty, why not carry it for his pursuit of Luther Deegan?

Shay placed all of them on his dresser and stacked boxes of ammo next to each one. He looked for a bag to stow them in for the ride up to the county. It couldn't hurt to bring his entire personal armory. Who knew what kinds of firepower Luther could get his hands on? As the son of a former crime boss, he no doubt had connections who'd equip him.

A few minutes after he zipped his gym bag closed, Mandy texted him, asking if she could come and stay at his place.

* * *

"THERE WAS AN ELECTRICAL FIRE," Mandy said, as he poured her a glass of sweet tea from a pitcher in the fridge. "Some wiring sparked or something? Apparently melted a pipe on the second floor, and *that* flooded the hall and the whole lobby."

"Was your floor affected?"

"No, only one and two. But now the fire department's kicked everybody out. The place needs an inspection and there's liability, and I don't have a home for at least tonight."

Shay handed her the glass, and they relaxed on the couch together. His condo was in a tower next to the federal courthouse on West Trade Street. He kept the décor simple and sparse. A living room sofa and two chairs, a pine coffee table, and a flat-screen. A quartz countertop separated the sitting area from the kitchen. There was a small dining space by a window, but he didn't have a table there. Instead, he kept an exercise mat and free weights. Most evenings, he ate dinner in front of the television. Other times, he'd be at work, either in the office or in the field. Why did he need a formal dining set? There were four paintings in the unit, all landscapes depicting mountain scenes. He hadn't chosen them to remind himself of the Blue Ridge. They just looked good on his off-white walls.

Mandy saying, "I have a huge paper to write, and I really don't want to dish out the money to stay in a hotel. Is it okay if I, you know, get a handle on my life here for now, maybe a couple days?"

"Fine with me. But I'm planning a trip, starting tomorrow morning, early."

She crossed her legs and sipped her tea. "Again? Wow, a lot of judges must need protecting. How long will you be away?"

"Not sure. Could be awhile, depending on how events transpire."

"Is it something serious?"

Shay tried to keep his expression upbeat but could tell he was failing. "My ma, she's in some trouble."

"Oh, I'm sorry. Is she all right?"

"For now. Why I have to hurry and help her."

"Yeah, no, I get it. Is there anything *I* can do?"

There wasn't, but Shay didn't say that. Mandy didn't know him, likely wouldn't understand what he was dealing with if he explained it to her. There was too much to say and not enough time to walk her through it. The one person who *did* understand had refused to do anything. So here he was, about to push forward alone.

Still, he appreciated Mandy's offer. She was kind, and he believed they could be happy together, if he could only fix himself. Then again, he'd had that problem in his love life before.

"You can answer a question for me."

She pushed some hair behind her ear, and he sensed she wasn't comfortable, like she could feel that something was off between them. "Shoot."

"Do you ever think about moving back to South Carolina? Go back to your roots?"

Mandy shook her head. "No..."

"You don't feel any obligation to where you come from, your people?"

"The only person I'm *obligated* to is myself," she said. "And I belong here, not there."

"But do you ever doubt what you're doing? What I mean, the choice you made to leave?"

Her eyes lit up and took on a dreamy sparkle. "Have you seen this city? There's so much opportunity. So much going on, always. I sometimes wonder if I should visit my family, but I never want to leave Charlotte."

"Be careful of visiting," Shay said. "You might find yourself going back a lot more'n you expected."

"Is that how it is for you?"

"Lately? You have no idea."

Mandy rubbed her arm, her discomfort becoming more obvious the longer they talked. Her delicate features were sad now. Beautiful, but with traces of fear and sorrow directed at him. She was everything he should want.

Why didn't he?

"Shay, this isn't the 'I'm moving away and we're done' talk, is it?"

He didn't know. When he confronted the Deegans, it was almost guaranteed they'd come to violence. And if he, a suspended lawman, pulled the trigger, even in self-defense or to protect another, he'd lose his star for good. Then what would he be? Would there be anything to keep him in Charlotte? He could go back to Wilkes, maybe try to restart his former life there. Try his hand at racing again, although he was too old to climb the ladder now. The teams wanted young guns, the next generation of champions—what he would've been had he not given it up. He'd find something, though, he was sure of that.

But would a relationship with Mandy be enough to make him stay in the Queen City?

"No, it's not that talk," Shay said, "so don't worry. But I *will* need to see how my ma's doing before I know how long I'll be gone."

Mandy stood and glanced at a suitcase of her things by the door. "So ... can I stay?"

"Watch the place for me," he said, smiling. "I'll get you the spare key."

"Thanks." She looked down, then back up. "Are we together? I have to know if you're in or out. If it's a bad time," she said, "I get that, but don't make me hopeful if there's no reason to be."

He nodded. "Far as I'm concerned, just because it's a bad time, that doesn't mean we shouldn't give this a shot. We've wanted to."

"Yes, we have," she said, and pulled him up into a kiss.

They made breakfast for dinner, since Shay had skipped it that morning. Eggs, frozen tater tots, and homemade waffles in a two-bay waffle iron that Shay's ma had given him for Christmas the year he'd gone to college. It wasn't the same as warm heirloom pumpkin muffins at the Artisan in North Wilkesboro. But it was good and it was hearty.

Without a table and chairs, they ate at the kitchen counter and washed down the eggs with two beers. Shay told her about his past relationships, one thing he'd never discussed in detail with Amy. His high school steady, his fiancée, the fact that he'd only dated around in Charlotte, never anything serious. She listened and drank her beer. Didn't seem to be the type of person who minded her partner's romantic history, even the part with the diamond ring. She did ask him why it had ended.

"My job," he said, and took a long pull on his own bottle. "She and I wanted different futures. We got 'em."

Mandy set down her fork. "I think our little game has gone on long enough. What *are* you?"

Shay said, "For now? A deputy United States marshal."

\* \* \*

AFTER THAT, Mandy brought her belongings into the bedroom, and Shay went outside to make a phone call. Took the elevator down to the street and stepped into the city.

Leaving his condo tower, he could turn left and see the Panthers' stadium rising over the tree line. For a major urban center, Uptown Charlotte was green and full of trees, something he admired about the atmosphere here.

He took a right, as he did every morning, going toward the Charles R. Jonas Federal Building, the largest United States courthouse in the Western District of North Carolina. As he dialed, he stared at the historic structure that had once been a post office. It was two stories, constructed of limestone, with Greek columns in a full-length colonnade and a temple pavilion over the central doorway at the front, facing West Trade. The building would have looked natural in Washington D.C., except the people who worked *here* actually got something done.

Inside, it still had the L-shaped lobby that had once accommodated the post office sales floor. There was an ornamental plaster ceiling, plus the original marble floors and woodwork from 1915. That continued in the upstairs offices. Now, the government was working on an annex tower behind the main building.

It was a place of great history, which Shay respected. You didn't join the U.S. Marshals, the nation's oldest law enforcement agency and the legends of the American West, without an appreciation for where you came from.

Would he still be able to walk through those courthouse doors when this was over? Hell, he hoped so. What was stopping the Deegans really worth?

His ma answered on the first ring.

"Are you okay, kid?"

It was a good question, one he had planned to ask her.

"Yeah, Ma, I'm fine. It's you I'm worried about."

"You're in Charlotte?"

"I'll be coming back home tomorrow."

"You just left. All this back and forth, I hope you get to write off gas as a business expense."

"Ma, I know who's threatening you."

"So do I—Joseph Deegan. I'd like to think I'm smarter than your average country girl, but even a dummy could put this together." She hesitated, then said, "Did they reinstate you?"

"No," he said, still looking at the courthouse, "but that doesn't mean I can't protect you."

There was silence on the line again. He expected her to argue with him, tell him to stay away and be safe. Try like hell to convince him she could take care of herself.

But her voice said, "Sure, kid. See you soon."

## CHAPTER TWENTY-TWO

GWEN MADE HERSELF A CUP OF HOT GREEN TEA AND settled into her spot on the couch to watch HGTV. The show was about a retired couple who had to decide between renovations to their current house or buying a new one that met all their needs.

What a choice that would be. Have a professional team come in and redo the entire home, something Gwen still hoped to do herself, or have the network find the perfect place to move. It would be a tough call, she had to admit. This house had so many memories. Little Shay, the good years with Warren. Even the time since his death, when she'd been alone, had been rewarding. She had figured out who she was. Endured as an individual, gotten back in touch with her personality, separate from her husband, son, and the expectations of her family.

So, what would she do, given the option to stay or list?

She could stick with her current plan and improve the bungalow. The change wouldn't be quick. She'd be looking at a long project. But it would be worth it, especially if Shay was going to continue visiting so much. She hoped so, and supposed that was the main reason she'd never left for a new address. Wishing Shay would come home. And now he had.

Would it last?

Gwen turned up the volume. She wanted to think about the show, not what could happen to Shay if he tried to avenge Warren. The kid was tough like his father, but full of hate and anger. And, as with Warren, there was nothing she could do to stop Shay. That terrified her.

What if she lost him, too? Then there'd be no reason at all to live here.

The window shattered. Four gunshots rang out. Bullets hit the front door and the external walls of the old home. Gwen dove for the floor, spilling her tea and placing her hands over her head. A car's tires screeched, and she heard somebody yell "Whoo!" as they sped away.

She stayed down for another minute, just to be sure the silence wasn't a trick. Then stood and looked across the room at the broken window, cool fall air creeping in through the jagged gap.

A brick rested on the carpet beneath the sill. She picked it up and felt its weight in her hand. Rubber banded to it was a folded sheet of paper. She opened it and read:

DEAD HARLOWES

The *s* was in red.

She knew who it was from and why they'd done it. Another scare tactic, so she'd beg Shay to let Luther go, for her sake.

But this time? She wasn't afraid.

Gwen walked out the front door and inspected the four deep holes in the wood and siding. Those would have to be repaired in the renovations. Then she went to the side yard and crumpled the note on the way.

Tossed it right into the dumpster.

\* \* \*

NINE O'CLOCK, Vickie came downstairs in her gym shorts and one of Clint's black-and-red flannel shirts. *He* never wore it, so why not take it for herself? It was soft and warm, perfect for fall in the hills, where the air had taken on a chill.

Clint was an odd one, even more than she had understood when she'd met him. She found him on the sleeper sofa again, his territory, and she couldn't figure out why he seemed to ignore most of the other rooms. He had his arms crossed.

Pouting.

In one of his moods, upset that his contribution to their plan, bringing in Derek, had caused trouble.

Vickie sometimes worried that *she* came across as petulant. The girl from the family with means, who'd screwed up at every step. In trouble since she was little and first learned the word *no*. It was simple. When Vickie Beaumont failed at something, she put the blame on society and its rules. People designed so many hoops for themselves to jump through, and for what? Why not take the easier ways? Who in their right mind wouldn't, given the choice?

The only solution Vickie could ever find was to defy those rules when she didn't get what she wanted, when it wasn't easy. It *should* be, and how was it her fault that it wasn't? She'd tell herself she was a dreamer, a visionary. If they'd just put her in charge of the world for a month...

She wasn't a cog like the rest of the population. Who wanted to be a cog, anyway?

That was a disappointment to her father, who'd given up on her and now spent his days on the coast, forgetting her existence with a fishing rod, a motorboat, and a bottle of tanning lotion. That was fine. She'd found her path. Got a bachelor's in biology from a tiny in-state school with a low ranking and a lot of television commercials. Found work in a local drug shop, because where else could she get hired with those pathetic credentials?

Nowhere.

She worried that this whole career change, entering

the crime profession, was just one more in a long line of hissy fits. It was all she knew, wasn't it? When you don't get your way, raise hell until you get *some*thing.

Clint acted all wise, made you think there was more to this shirtless redneck than his appearance suggested. But *he* was the petulant one. Look at his face, brow furrowed, biting his upper lip with his bottom teeth, all tense. And...

Pouting.

"Any sign of Luther?" she said.

"No," Clint said. "I'm starting to think he ain't gonna come for us after all. He's on the run, gonna leave us be."

"Then we're ready."

"Are we?"

"We've done everything we set out to."

"Except get that money."

"That was always a bonus. But it's peanuts compared to the business we're about to do with Luther gone."

He gave her a look and rubbed his chin and the unshaved stubble on his jawline. "You sure, and I mean absolutely positive, you wanna do this? 'Cause I'll call a meeting with the Deegans' dealers, guys I've supplied again and again. They see it's me, they'll pick up, and they'll hear me out when I update 'em on all that's changing. But, Vickie, these fellers ain't the type who'll cut us slack if we can't manage this shit. They want their money, and that's all it comes down to."

"I'm with them on that."

"You don't understand. We fail at this? It's *us* gonna be dodging bullets next. They'll take it that far, if it means keeping the cash flowing."

"Clint," she said, "call them."

He glanced at his phone, on the end table beside the sofa, and frowned. "I ever tell you about the first time I brought a crew of hands onto the farm?"

She rolled her eyes, growing impatient with him. When he was in a mood, that was when you *really* had to endure his little speeches, his lectures about life. Always with some interpretation of what you were doing and why it was wrong. Telling stories and speaking like some kind of authority on human nature, this man with a naked woman on his chest and thousands of reefer plants hidden among Christmas trees. He was either the absolute worst person to dispense that kind of wisdom, or the best.

It annoyed the hell out of her.

"You're about to," she said.

If he was going to be in a mood, then so was she.

"I'm serious," he said. "This was back when I'd just taken over the place, after my daddy left it to me. It was different being the owner, not like working the trees as the owner's *son*."

"All right," she said, giving the man with that gaudy tattoo what he really wanted—attention. "What's the story?"

"I was twenty-one. And there was this spot in town, a

street corner by an auto-repair shop, where you could hire crews of laborers, most of them immigrants, legal status questionable for a good quarter of 'em."

"How is that different from the guys you have in the fields *now?*"

"I'll tell you, if you'll slow down for a freaking second and stop talking."

Pouty, pouty, pouty.

"So I hire a crew, seven bucks and a quarter an hour, and there were maybe eight of 'em. Then I had to lead 'em, you know, instruct 'em in the jobs I needed doing."

"Did you wear a shirt back then?"

That got her another look.

"Know what my problem was? No, you don't, 'cause you ain't realized you got two ears and one mouth for a reason. I *thought* I had what it took to lead, no sweat. Since I was young and smart, I knew just enough to think I knew everything, when I really didn't know shit."

"Same question, how is this any different?"

"See, I didn't handle the crew well. First couple days, all was fine, but then what happened, they figured out I was naïve and stupid and weak. So they started slacking, but still expecting to get paid. One feller in particular, he'd run his mouth and have excuse after excuse for why he couldn't prune the trees. Couldn't cut 'em, couldn't bag 'em, nothing. His arm was broken, when it weren't even in a cast. His ankle was sprained, but the feller weren't limping. Know what I did?"

"You haven't told me, so how can I?"

"Screamed and hollered at 'em. That was all I had. Couldn't command respect, and they saw that. I even tried to fire that one feller, but he said no. You believe that? This migrant who ain't even in the country legally says to me, *No*. And goes on not working but wanting his seven twenty-five."

"You're trying to teach me something. But you forget who got us this far."

He shook his head, not giving in. "All I know is, you like talking and mouthing off. Pull that shit on these dealers, don't back up none of your words with dollar signs? We're gonna command exactly zero respect, and it'll cost us. If all you got is noise, they'll shut you up real quick."

He stood and stretched, but still didn't make the phone calls.

"You like talking as much as I do, you know that?" she said, moving closer to him. "Love hearing your own voice impart your unique brand of wisdom, even when nobody cares to hear it."

"Somehow I've survived this long, and I've learned a thing or two."

"I'm not a silly girl you need to instruct. Got it? I'm a survivor, like you. Always made my own way, never bowed to anybody. You don't think that's made me strong?"

He was silent.

"Well?"

"We'll find out," he said, and started dialing.

She reached over and put her hands over his, stopping him. And smiled, gave him a real sweet one to charm him back to himself.

"What're you doing?"

"Before you talk to them, I want to be sure you see me as an equal. As a woman."

"You want to show me you're a woman," he said, his face screwed up in the grin of a horny teenage boy, "there's a way you can."

"No, Clint," she said, and found herself grinning too, unable to help it.

"Here I thought we were getting closer."

"We have been. I do like you, okay? When you're not in a funky mood."

"*Me* in a funky mood?"

"Yeah, when you're not popping my pills, you're incorrigible sometimes."

"Know what'd make me a happy man?"

She snickered. "Yes, but I think you're going to be sad a while longer."

"You're not saying never, though."

"You don't, like, have anything, do you?"

He tilted his head, taken aback. "Like a disease? Shit, Vickie, is that what you been worried about?"

"Well," she said, hesitating, "I don't know who you've been with. I *am* in the healthcare industry."

"Healthcare? You sell people their hemorrhoid cream and dollar candy bars. Hey, I swear I'm clean," he said, moving closer to her, putting his hands on her waist now and pulling her in. "You want, I'll rubber up."

Now she pushed him back down onto the sleeper sofa. "Easy, tiger. You have any in the house?"

"No," he said, and looked embarrassed, like he was ashamed he never needed them. "I'll go get some. How about it? Will that put your mind at rest?"

She laughed and patted his cheek. "We'll both go for a drive. I need to clear my head."

"You want to do that, we'll smoke some Purdy Woman first. Nothing like it."

"Sure, but, Clint? I am *so* not doing anything on this couch."

\* \* \*

JOSEPH DEEGAN'S doorbell sounded at midnight. Years ago, he would've assumed it was a rival for the county crime business come to kill him.

It had happened twice. On both occasions, his personal bodyguard—Earl Tucker Lee, before his promotion to pill runner—had dealt with the attacker.

But now? He was an old man, out of the game and almost out of days in this life. There weren't no rivals anymore. He'd seen to that prior to handing over control of his empire to Luther, now his biggest regret.

The only people who knocked on your door at this hour were the law. Had to be his boy was in custody or dead, and this was the call to inform him of that. It would make sense, seeing as he hadn't heard from Luther since the afternoon of the storm.

Joseph got out of his bed, which was positioned by floor-to-ceiling windows that looked out over the hills, the dark mountaintops only visible as black mounds blocking the starry sky, no lights to pollute the air out here.

This view of Heaven might just be the closest he'd get, after everything he'd done. And everything he *would* do, if there was still a chance to save his boy.

He put on his robe and slippers, drank half of the bottle of water he kept on his bedside table, and pushed his stiff body through the gloom, to the light switch. The bell rang again. Kept ringing, as he went to answer it, his slippers dragging on the hardwood. He turned on the foyer chandelier and opened the door, expecting to see a couple of sheriff's deputies with somber faces.

"You fucking snake," Gwen Harlowe said.

He had time to glimpse the vintage shotgun in her hands, before she shot him in the chest.

# CHAPTER TWENTY-THREE

CLINT COULDN'T HARDLY WAIT ANY LONGER AND TOLD Vickie so as they climbed into his van, Clint being gentle with himself as he lowered his wounded rump onto the upholstery. He'd been waiting for this, had a baggie of Purdy Woman reserved in the bread box for them. All's she had to do was stay in the mood until he was well equipped for the evening.

She didn't look up from her phone. Just said "Uh-huh" from the passenger seat.

Hell, they were fixing to spend the night together, and that was all the response she'd offer? It irked him, it really did, same as every other time she'd ignored or waved him off. But not enough to keep him from driving the thirty-three minutes to the local drugstore. He'd buy a box of rubbers and head back in a hurry, before she had a chance to irk him some more. Or change her mind.

Maybe even indulge in another dose of the pain meds before they got hot and heavy. Let the euphoria take it to a whole new level. Then thought, Nah, what he needed was his own stuff, nothing else. It was good enough on its own, and he took pride in that.

When they got there, he told her he'd be there in a jiffy, just sit tight. She nodded, said "Aisle three," and kept browsing Reddit on her phone.

Well, whatever made her happy.

He ran into the pharmacy, going so fast he almost didn't close his door all the way. The place was empty, only one feller behind the checkout desk. Quiet, too, except for the fluorescent lights humming overhead.

Clint found what he was looking for in the far right aisle, not where Vickie had told him they'd be. Made him wonder what she actually *did* here all day. The woman wasn't content with her station, that much was obvious. Why she was hanging around with him, plotting to get into crime, instead of doing something better.

He grabbed a box, hesitated, then took another, practicing some positive thinking. Made sure to stop by the rack of bandages on the other side of the store and restocked on those too.

He shoved thirty bucks in the cashier's face.

Saying, "Keep the change."

\* \* \*

CLINT DIDN'T PAY much attention to the headlights getting brighter in his mirror. He had a box of the condoms in his lap. Opened it with one hand and peered inside to look at the wrappers.

Vickie said, "What kind did you get?"

"The real thin ones, you can't even tell you got one on. So they claim. They're lying, I'll send 'em a letter calling 'em out."

"Why don't you ever sleep in the bedroom?"

Clint felt his face get all screwed up at the question. "It's my house, I can't sleep where I want?"

"Sure, but I'm curious. Seems odd not to use that nice master suite."

"It ain't mine."

"How's that?"

"The master was my folks'. Don't feel right for me to move in there. I know most people would. But, I don't know, I always saw it different."

She flipped down the sun visor and checked her hair in the mirror. He thought she looked good tonight. When *didn't* she look good?

Vickie saying, "You were close with them?"

"You run a family farm, you're bound to be tight. Everybody has to do their part or the operation goes under. You rely on each other in a way most families don't understand, I'll tell you that right now. Sometimes, and this is gonna sound weird, but sometimes I swear I sense them in that house with me. In the fields too, when

I'm riding around alone. Not like ghosts, I don't believe in those. But like there's another *some*thing beyond death, a way you can see people and go places, check up on your loved ones. That sound as crazy as I think it does?"

"I've heard stranger ideas. Guess things would've been better for me," she said, her voice sad and reflective, "if we'd been farmers."

"You mean your pap forgetting you?"

"Traded me in for a forty-foot fishing boat. After I disgraced the Beaumont name by wanting a different path than the one my parents took. Once my mom died? The only thing left for me and him was to part ways."

"Different path ... that what you call what we been doing?"

"Yes," she said, "and so far it's working."

"Well, you were never a disgrace in my eyes. Fact, I think you're scrappy."

"Most people would leave off the *s*."

"You *are* a survivor. You don't just fall in line with nothing, you make your own decisions and work hard to get there. Even if it means clocking in at that store every day until you hit it big."

"With you," she said, and he sensed genuine feeling there.

Would you believe it? After all this time, she was coming around to his charms and manly wiles. Or maybe she just wasn't used to being appreciated. He could relate.

The car hit their back bumper going at least twenty miles per hour faster than they were. The van wobbled on its skinny wheels, shifting from one side of the lane to the other, but Clint held on.

Vickie said, "Shit, what is this idiot doing? Didn't he see us?"

Clint about pulled over, assuming it to be a traffic accident. When the second collision happened a moment later, he floored it instead.

"Yeah," he said, "I expect he sees us real clear."

The van's back end slid out going around a tight corner. It scraped the guardrail, snapping the wheel in his hands and almost breaking his wrists. He could just make out the snout of a Nissan sedan in the red glow of his taillights, its grille looking snarly and evil in the dancing shadows.

And, hell, coming for them again.

This time both vehicles hit the railing, side panels and sheet metal grinding on the barrier that separated them from the drop-off down the side of the hill, into the scrub oak and pine. The Nissan kept pushing, and Clint's eyes went wide when he saw yellow-and-black arrows dead ahead, signaling another hairpin. Except there was no guardrail here, just a few trees and rocks separating the road from the sky.

The sedan's engine revved.

Clint tried to pull the steering wheel to the right, away from the ledge, but the vehicles were locked together at the bumpers now, the van's size advantage not enough to compensate for its thin tires or the engine power of the Nissan. They plowed through the brush and bounced off a young tree trunk, pine branches scratching the roof and windshield with shrill screams. Then Clint and Vickie were flying, the vehicle pitching down, its rear wheels spinning and spinning as Clint kept his foot planted, the condoms levitating from the open box and appearing suspended in midair.

A boulder stopped the van from falling the rest of the way into the valley below.

VICKIE PUT a hand to her head, checking for blood on her fingertips when she brought them down to her eyes. Nothing, at least that she could see in the darkness of the still van. Her waist and abdomen hurt where the seat belt had cut into her. She twisted herself around, testing her range of motion. There was no pain when she took a couple of deep breaths.

Good, no signs of internal damage. But her body ached. The airbag had saved her life, but her face felt bruised and swollen from the impact with it.

She managed to reach to her left and unbuckle. Then wrestled to get out from under the airbag and open her door. She slid from the crippled vehicle and stepped onto the slope, her shoes hitting a soft floor of fallen leaves, pine needles, and scrub. Standing now, she continued her self-evaluation, the pharmacy cashier playing doctor in the middle of the woods at night, unable to see a foot in front of her.

Her limbs and joints had sustained trauma but moved well. There were no indications of fractures or major injuries. She gulped in the cool air and was proud of how clear and focused her mind was.

See? She *was* tough. Look what she had just endured. An attempt on her life by Luther Deegan. Who else wanted them dead? He was the only person it could've been.

That led to a question that frightened her—was he still here? Stalking them in the dark, making sure he'd finished them. Or had he driven away after running them off the road?

Regardless, they had to get out of here.

She wanted to call out for Clint, thinking he'd probably already left the van and was hiding somewhere nearby. He would have reached the same conclusion about Luther. But if Deegan was close and he heard her...

No, stay quiet and listen. Footsteps, breaking branches, swishing leaves. Was there any sign of another person's presence?

But she heard only the chirps of bugs in the brush and the soft swaying of what leaves remained on the tree branches this late in the year. A cold wind gave her goose bumps, and she shivered.

Farther off was the soft hooting of an owl on the hunt.

Satisfied that she was alone, Vickie stepped up the slope, judging the grade as she placed her feet with care. Her left ankle throbbed, and pain radiated up her leg. Shit, she *had* been injured, but she pressed on, ignored it for now.

Limping, she curved around the back of the van, keeping a hand on its side paneling, passing her fingertips over the Purdy Farms holly-leaf graphic on her way to the driver's door.

When she reached it, she said, "Clint?" Keeping her voice low but fierce in the silence.

No answer.

The window had broken open in the crash, and she thought she could make out Clint's form slumped in the seat. But, God, it was pitch-black, and she could barely see the length of her own outstretched arm.

She had to tug on the door handle to get it open, and then the van's interior lights flickered on and off and on again.

Vickie said, "No ... Clint? No, no, fuck. Clint?"

Dried blood from his crushed forehead caked his cheeks and the skin around his eyes like war paint, his mouth open, his jaw askew. More of his blood tinged the gray vinyl of the steering wheel crimson.

Clint's airbag hadn't deployed, and the momentum of the fall had sent him forward with greater force than the seat belt could stop. She touched his neck for a pulse, knowing there wouldn't be one.

Look at her, the *healthcare professional* in action.

He was dead, his body already going rigid and surrounded by colorful condom wrappers. The orange bottle of pills she'd given him had flown from his pocket and now rested on the floor by his feet, which had been crushed when the front of the van crumpled against the boulder. His side of the vehicle had taken a harder hit than hers, but she suspected that had been the source of her own ankle injury.

Now what? Call the police? Absolutely not. So far, there was nothing to implicate her in anything that had happened. Right? And there was no hope for Clint, no rush to call 911.

So, what if she just left? Let the authorities find the wreck on their own. Don't give them any reason to connect her to Clint, to Luther, or the crash. This was her chance to make a clean break.

But could she leave Clint, just abandon him in the woods?

Yes, because she was a survivor. He wouldn't care. In his strange wisdom, he would've given her the same advice.

She closed the door and stared at the shape of him. The thing was, she had always run away from her problems. But Luther Deegan was still out there. When it hit the news that Clint had been killed, without any mention of her? He'd know she was alive, and he'd come for her again.

She needed help, and not from the police. It had to be somebody who understood the pure hatred she now felt, who wouldn't care about her role in everything that had happened, not when there was the common goal of catching Luther.

Somebody who had also lost a loved one to the Deegans.

# CHAPTER TWENTY-FOUR

AMY BAROLO CANCELLED ALL HER MORNING appointments and pulled Shay's file. She entered his address into her car's navigation system. It turned out to be a condo building next to the federal courthouse on West Trade, which shouldn't have surprised her.

She parked in a lot around the corner and enjoyed her walk in the glow of the morning, passing under the shade of trees lining the sidewalks, taking in the sounds of traffic flowing through the city, Charlotte awake and beginning a new day. The sides of the skyscrapers to her left glistened in the sunshine, set against a crisp Carolina blue sky.

At the door, she buzzed his unit. There was no response, so she tried again, wondering if he'd already gone out.

A woman's voice finally said, "Hello?"

"Sorry, I must have the wrong one," Amy said, hiding her surprise. "Can you tell me which condo is Shay Harlowe's?"

The voice hesitated. "This is it. Who's asking for him?"

"His psychiatrist. We didn't have an appointment today, but I wanted a word."

"Was he expecting you?"

"No, but it's pressing."

"Oh, okay. Well, he isn't here..."

Amy tapped her foot on the cement and had an idea. A crafty, adventurous idea that wasn't at all something she'd entertain under normal circumstances. But right now, it intrigued her. She needed information on where to find him. Asking herself, What would Deputy Marshal Shay Harlowe do in this situation, if he had to chase somebody down in a hurry?

She said, "In that case, can I come up and talk to you?"

\* \* \*

THEY SAT in Shay's living room, with a perfect view of Uptown. The Hearst Tower, the Duke Energy Center, the Carillon Tower. And, rising highest of the many skyscrapers, the Bank of America Corporate Center. It was sights like this that made her proud to live and work here. Perhaps Shay felt the same way. Maybe that was a reason he'd bought this unit, with a view to remind him of why he chose the Queen City to start over.

But the condo itself didn't feel like a home. He had some paintings on the walls, but minimal furniture, nothing too comfortable about the space. It served a purpose, a roof over his head so that he could recharge and walk the short distance to the office.

This was the apartment of a man who considered himself the only person standing between dangerous criminals and their innocent victims. Any time spent here could be devoted to his duty, and the condo's design reflected his fear of failure in that mission.

They made introductions. Mandy—who called herself Shay's girlfriend—was beautiful, spunky, and had the same cool confidence about her as Shay. She studied Amy with her eyes, making the doctor feel like the patient.

Amy didn't like it.

She said, "Shay didn't mention being with anyone."

Mandy shifted in her seat, the desired effect. "We haven't been together for long. Finally decided to take the plunge."

"When will he be back?"

"I don't really know." Amy gave her a quizzical look. "He said he might be awhile, helping his mom back in his hometown."

Amy's heart beat faster. She'd known that he would go to Wilkes again. He'd made that clear over lunch. But if Shay hadn't even told his girlfriend about his plans, then Amy's fears were valid. She had to find him before he got himself killed.

"Is he doing all right?"

Mandy gave a curt nod, like she didn't believe her own answer. "Other than fretting over this trouble his mom's in? Yeah, he seems to be his old self. You know, happy. He didn't tell me he was seeing you." She paused, then said in a pointed tone, "A shrink, I mean."

They both understood each other. Two attractive women vying for the same man. Mandy must have sensed that there was the possibility of more between Shay and his doctor. But Amy was a married woman. How could she allow herself to contemplate that for even a second?

Still, she couldn't help feeling jealous. This would be interesting to analyze later, when she was alone. Maybe she needed to review the ethical standards of her job, as well.

"Really? Well, it's required for his work," Amy said. "He was involved in a shooting a couple of weeks ago. It's standard procedure before he can be reinstated."

"Reinstated?"

"That's right. He's dealing with a suspension until I clear him. We're nearly finished, but I get the sense he won't be at his next appointment because he's ... gone somewhere."

Mandy shook her head. "He didn't tell me any of this. But, like I said, we haven't been together that long."

Justifying his actions to herself. The poor girl didn't know a thing about Shay, did she?

"How did you two meet?"

"I was his bartender," Mandy said. "We started talking. He's always been nice. Likes his bourbon." Her eyes wandered to the floor. "Should I be worried about him?"

Amy couldn't keep herself from lying. "Not at all."

"I've shared everything about myself with him. Why hasn't he done the same? I mean, at first we were playing this game, kind of? He wouldn't tell me what he did for a living, I had to guess. But I thought it was fun, not that he didn't *want* to tell me."

Amy's mind went to Shay's former fiancée. Seemed he had a habit of ruining relationships, all for the sake of his work. Everything, down to his spartan décor, was for the sake of his work. Clearly, he was making similar mistakes with Mandy.

Well, she wouldn't let him backslide and undo the progress they'd made together. That was *her* duty as his doctor.

Now who was justifying?

Amy said, "Did he leave contact info for you?"

"Like what?"

"I'm thinking his mother's address."

\* \* \*

SHAY WAS twenty minutes out from North Wilkesboro

when Marty called to tell him Gwen had shot Joseph Deegan.

Marty saying it had gone down at the retirement villa in Cricket. She knocked on the man's door, middle of the night. He opened it, she pulled the trigger quick.

Somebody dialed up the police to report the gunshot. County responded to the scene and found her in his kitchen, with a glass of his best whiskey, the murder weapon right on the counter, not hiding anything. She wanted everyone to know she'd done it.

"Made her initial appearance this morning," Marty said. "Good news, what she's got working for her, record's clean, no history, plus she's a fixture of the community. Not to mention, you ask anybody who they think killed your daddy, they tell you Joe Deegan. There's sympathy for her, you know what I'm saying? That counts for a lot with the judge."

Shay could picture the scene, his ma tired of being threatened, probably also hoping he'd back off if Deegan was dead. In truth, he wasn't surprised she'd shot the man. What he couldn't figure, why the hell would she wait around for the police?

"Is she looking at murder first?"

"Was clear she'd planned it. Now, County does have that complaint she reported about the dude following her, threatening her. She says he even broke her window. Tossed a brick through it and fired some shots, left a note. It's entered into evidence. I expect—and I'd *advise* her—she better use it to back up a self-defense claim."

"You think that'll work?"

"Like I told you, ain't no one up here who didn't want Joe Deegan gone. She frames it as getting the man who was gonna kill her, after he'd already killed her husband? She got a chance at beating this."

"We'll need a good attorney. She have one yet?"

"Not sure, man, but I'm only going by what my sheriff's office contacts been giving me. I ain't in on her case." Marty got quiet, then said, "How's your finances looking?"

Shay glanced in the mirror and winced, anticipating what was coming. "Just tell me how much I'd need to post."

"Fifty grand."

"Well, shit."

"People in town, they already taking up a collection to help her pay for her freedom, cover her legal bills too. She's a hero, what she did."

"Always was. Where are they keeping her, the county jail?"

"Off Courthouse Drive, down from the sheriff's."

Shay passed the speedway, the faded Winston Cup sign sticking up from the trees on the side of the road, brush and foliage overtaking the grandstands that were visible from 421. He got ready to exit and drive to the Wilkes lockup. Hell, to see his ma there. He never would have imagined this happening to them. But, in this moment, he still wasn't surprised she'd made this move. Wasn't one to rely on others for protection, especially after the authorities had already shrugged off her concerns. She was never going to let him put his life on the line for her, not after losing Warren.

And not after getting Shay back.

"I hate to ask," Marty said, "with everything else. You heard from Victoria Beaumont and Clint Purdy yet?"

"You'll be my first call when I do."

"I better be. We close to ending this, you see that?"

"You bet," Shay said, thinking he'd use the revolver, bring the Glock 27 as backup. "One last question for you."

"Hope I got one last answer."

"When my ma shot him, did she use a vintage shotgun? A Fox Sterlingworth."

"Shit, how'd you know?"

* * *

WHAT HIS MA SAID, after they sat her in front of the glass partition, the two of them speaking into black phones, she said, "Before you ask, I'm fine, kid. Brown isn't my color, but otherwise..."

Shay looked at her in the DOC jumper that reminded him of the evening he'd transported Tucker Lee and seen him die. This was his fault, he knew, for making that decision. His actions that night had sparked the chain of events that had brought them to this point. *He* was to blame, and so were the Deegans. Yet the person suffering the most, once again, was his ma, who was the only innocent one among them.

He wouldn't let the last of his family be destroyed.

"Why didn't you call me?"

"What could I say that would explain it?"

Shay said, "Try."

"You were so determined to protect me."

"Still am. I'm gonna use every bit of my influence as a marshal to get you clear of these charges."

"Kid, I was never the one who needed saving. You were. And you wouldn't realize it."

"If this is about my leaving or my going after Luther—"

"Listen to me. I'm okay, really. Being in here's not exactly a vacation. But they're treating me all right. You'd be amazed the respect an aging widow gets when she's accused of shooting Joseph Deegan. From the guards, too. But you, kid, you have everything ahead of you. Let the past go. Lock it away. Move on and make sure the things we've gone through and the things we've done are worth it."

He twisted the phone in his hand. "How could you put this on me? *I'm* the reason you were threatened. This is my doing, you look at it straight."

"I'd rather you put *this* on yourself than your daddy's

death. But neither one is your fault. Okay, kid? Never was, never will be."

"I was gonna fix things. I still can."

His ma tilted her head and gave him a sad smile. "There's nothing more to do."

"I *will* get you out of this."

"You have fifty thousand dollars?"

"What I'm told, the town is working on gathering the money. We'll get you the best lawyer, and we'll tell the truth. Self-defense."

"I don't doubt it. Until then, keep an eye on the house. You'll see some bullet holes in the front door. And a broken window."

"You should've called me the second it happened."

"So you could come up here, challenge Joseph Deegan, and get killed for me? Kid, you have to understand why I didn't."

He nodded. "Amy Barolo, my doctor? She thinks I understand a little too well. That what I do as a marshal comes from your influence. Growing up, everyone thought I was my daddy's son, but I was always yours. It's showing now, I suppose."

"Seems she has you figured out. I like her. So, has she fallen for you yet?"

"She's married."

His ma looked down. "See? You *are* more like me than Warren."

## CHAPTER TWENTY-FIVE

"So this is where you come after you leave my office."

Shay couldn't believe she was here. Amy Barolo on his ma's front porch, leaning against the wooden railing with her heels off and set aside. The wind tossed her curly hair, and the afternoon sun made it shine.

He strode up the front walk in his black suit of clothes, wondering how the hell this would go, Amy seeing his childhood home. She knew something about it from their sessions, but he'd still managed to keep his two worlds separate. Not anymore. He felt uncomfortable, exposed.

Worst of all, he expected she'd try to intervene in his business.

Amy smiled at him, as he took the wooden steps and

joined her on the porch. Despite his reservations, he was glad to see her.

"I wasn't aware you *made* house calls."

"I don't."

He drew up beside her and leaned over the railing. "Then am I to understand you ain't here officially?"

She hiked her eyebrows, challenging him. "Kind of like you."

"I recall, I told you my intentions at lunch. It's yours that are in question."

"Would you believe I'm here to help?"

"As a doctor?"

"And a friend, if you'll let me."

Shay stood tall again and put a hand on his hip, making a deduction. "You spoke to Mandy."

"She was worried about you."

He didn't say anything else, just went to the door and examined the bullet holes his ma had mentioned. Felt Amy watching him as he traced the small craters with his finger.

"I noticed those when I knocked. Nobody answered. Where's your mother?" He still didn't care to respond, so she said, "You won't tell your girlfriend, but will you clue *me* in on what's happening?"

He smirked. "You don't have my file folder. What would be the point of us talking, if you can't fidget with your pen and scribble all them notes about my subconscious?"

She crossed her arms. "You're an asshole, Harlowe."

"It took you this long to realize that, you may want to consider a different profession."

"What if we talk like two people, no more doctor and patient?"

He turned toward her, curious where she was taking this. "What'd you have in mind?"

"It's almost dinnertime."

"You're screwing with me. I ask you to lunch, then you show up here, want to have *dinner*."

She shrugged. "You have to eat. Don't you?"

HE TOOK her to the smokehouse, figured he might as well show her the rest of his childhood hangouts. They ordered two fryers with veggies, one of which was mac and cheese. In the South, it counted as a vegetable, and you were never too old for a big helping. They ate their chicken and washed it down with cold beer, sitting in the small dining room. Red-and-white-checkered tablecloths, ceiling fans, and a brown tile floor, the same design the restaurant had sported for the last six decades, in the same spot on Main.

"Your husband know you're here?"

She finished with a thigh and said, "He's used to me having to assist patients in distress. It doesn't happen often, but he'll always ask if he can help out, then I say no, and he doesn't put up a fight. Mark wants it on record that he offered."

"We'll come back to the false notion I'm in distress. But it didn't strike him as odd you were driving all this way?"

"He knows my work is confidential. I can't share too much."

"Uh-huh," he said, and grinned.

She shifted in her seat, her body language telling him she didn't want to discuss it further. That was fine. He didn't want to play psychiatrist to *her*, twist this whole dynamic around on its head. If she and her husband were having problems, that was no concern of his.

It was interesting, though.

He took a sip from his bottle of Coors and said, "What makes you think I need help? I thought we'd resolved this, last we spoke."

"Hardly. You grandstanded about your plan to finish off the Deegans, have your revenge. I *had* to try and stop you, before you make a terrible mistake. You could ruin your career, your life. As if that wasn't enough, when I arrive, I see somebody took shots at your mother's house. And you haven't said a word about it. What's going on, Shay?"

"You put it together fine. An associate of Joseph Deegan fired on her."

"Okay, let's break this down. First, is she all right?"

"She's in jail," he said, and glanced over at the front

counter, a glass case full of desserts, pecan pie, red velvet cake, peach cobbler, "for murdering the man himself." He looked at her again. "Hey, how about a slice of pecan?"

"My God, when Mandy said your mom was in trouble, I had no idea..."

"Mandy doesn't know the extent of it. And I'm already working on Ma's defense. What it comes down to, there was a snake under our dumpster all these years. Bit and killed my daddy, tried to strike at her. She knew it was gonna try for me next, or that I'd go after it, and she didn't want me to get hurt."

"So she took care of him. And you think she was right to do it."

"Yes or no on the pie? It was always my favorite part of having supper here. Came with my daddy, never left without something sweet."

Amy gave him an incredulous look and pushed away her basket of chicken bones. "This bothers you, doesn't it? She sacrificed her freedom to protect you. Knowing you were about to do the same for her."

"Not just for her. That family's been a disease in an otherwise beautiful county. Spreading their poison and misery. Profiting off death. She did this place a favor, and I'd have done the same, she hadn't beat me to it."

"A villain to villains," Amy said, and pursed her lips.

"You're finally getting the idea, huh?"

"I'm not sure I want to live in a world without heroes. Where, to defeat the bad guys, the good guys have to be just as awful. And I don't believe you're really as tough as you want people to think."

"Stick around," he said, "and you'll see otherwise."

He picked up his last drumstick and got to work, Amy saying now, "After all this, you're still going to chase after Luther. You won't learn."

"We're down to the last Deegan. That's one too many."

"And down to the last Harlowe who isn't dead or imprisoned. But you won't see *that*." She gave him a slow shake of her head. "I was right not to clear you."

He got the impression that was supposed to bait him. Maybe she wanted him to hate her more than he did Luther, give him a new object for his anger. Man, she was smart. But it wasn't going to work.

What she didn't realize, he felt at peace with what he was doing.

It would come down to a couple of split-second decisions that he was already preparing to make. Could he get Luther, or would Luther get him? And would he pull the trigger, given the opportunity? Amy wouldn't approve if he did. The marshals wouldn't either.

She was watching him again, waiting to see if he'd argue and fall into her trap, give her more words to analyze.

Instead, he stood. "Last chance. You want a slice or no?"

\* \* \*

AMY TRIED AGAIN in the car ride back to the house. Asking him what the outlook was for his mother, could she get out on bail, had he gone to see her.

He gave simple, infuriating replies. The outlook was the best he'd ever seen in a homicide case, on account of everyone, including the judge, understood how bad this vic had been. Yes, she could get out, but it would take a lot more money than he had. And, sure, he'd visited the jail, and she was doing fine, considering.

Shay was more determined than ever, like their appointments and conversations had amounted to nothing. He was willing to risk everything, all for a warped sense of justice that seemed to run in the family.

When they arrived, he shut off the car and moved to get out. She touched his arm, stopping him.

"Wait, you never asked where I'm staying."

"No, I didn't."

He stepped onto the quiet residential street and shut the door.

She followed him to the porch and said, "What if I have a hotel?"

"Do you?"

He turned the key in the lock and went inside without another word, flipping on lights while she went to her own car and retrieved her suitcase. The truth was, she hadn't yet decided where she'd spend the night. Or where she *wanted* to, a horrible, wonderful possibility that she was ashamed of. She wheeled her bag into the foyer, taking time to study his childhood home and picture how the Harlowes had been before their tragedies. The house was quaint, with three different paths to the kitchen, a true southern floor plan.

She didn't see him anywhere.

"Shay?"

His voice said from upstairs, "You need a hand with your things?"

"They'd give me one at a hotel."

He came down in his black suit that seemed out of place here, where he'd grown up. A dark shadow of the boy who had looked forward to a different future. Who deserved so much more. It had been taken from him, and she understood why he wanted revenge. But, whether he realized it or not, he had a lot left to lose, and she wouldn't allow that to happen.

She cared for him. She'd become involved.

How many more professional and moral lines would she cross?

Shay led her into a short upstairs hallway and hesitated in the space between two doors. Then took the one on the left, the guest bedroom, and set her case down by the dresser.

Saying, "This'll be fine?"

"Yes, thanks. Only two bedrooms in the house. Was this yours?"

He nodded. "Used to be, I had Dale Earnhardt posters and diecasts all over. Had my trophies in a case we hung there, on the far wall."

"Where is all that stuff now?"

"Ma's got some of it in the attic. I took the rest with me."

Then they were quiet, looking at each other.

"You've seen everything," he said. "I've let you in. And you haven't run."

"What made you think I would?"

"People usually do."

"I thought you liked that, being intimidating."

"Not this time."

If they were going to make a move, now was the perfect moment.

"Well," she said, "you don't scare me."

"You terrify *me*."

Stop talking and go to him.

But she couldn't.

"Why is that, Shay?"

He put his hands on his hips and looked disappointed, then relieved. For a second, it seemed he might come to her, but instead he stood in the threshold and grabbed the doorknob.

"That's enough of my psyche for one evening," he said. "You want anything else, I'm right across from you."

He closed the door behind him.

## CHAPTER TWENTY-SIX

LUTHER TOOK THE NISSAN OFF-ROAD, ONTO A DIRT trail that wound deep into the hills, not far from the Ashe line. The sedan's front end was dented and scraped where it had pushed Clint and his redheaded bitch over the ledge.

He had one working headlight, making it a harrowing trip through the forest. When this was over, he'd dump the car and find another ride, something with the power of his SS. But, first, he needed a new second to help him start over. Find a fresh area to dominate, a better market. Take it over and create his own legacy for the name of Deegan, without the stain of his father's sins.

At the end of the road was a trailer, on top of a rise. It was in good shape, fresh paint, a manicured row of bushes in front, a gravel drive framed by neat rows of cement pavers. The light at the front door shined into the dark, a beacon welcoming him. Luther knew the owner took pride in keeping a tidy home. And the prick brought that same dedication to wet work.

Luther parked the Nissan and went around the back of the trailer. Descended the far side of the hill until he came to a small dip before a second rise, this one shallower.

The man he was here to see stood behind a plywood table and held a Smith & Wesson revolver. Metal targets in the forms of various farm animals dotted the hillside ahead. They were spaced out at different distances, some more challenging than others. Tall spotlights illuminated the entire shooting range. He fired fast and loud on the cow, pig, and chicken, two bullets each. Six metallic clangs replied.

Then he popped the cylinder and emptied it. Set the revolver on the table and replaced the red hat on his head, before getting to work reloading from a box of cartridges.

Luther said, "You make them count."

Bellamy Keith spun around, the Smith & Wesson half-loaded and fully raised. "Shit, boy, you know better'n to surprise an armed man."

"Quite the compound you've built here."

Bellamy lowered the gun. "I'm fucking rich, thanks to your dad. And I ain't got no other hobbies. This one turned out to be a stable career, how you like that?"

"You looking to keep it up?"

"Joseph's dead." Bellamy gave him a pitiful look, like he assumed Luther hadn't heard.

Luther said, "I'm aware. And that wasn't my question."

"I figured I'd enter competitions. *Win* my money, 'stead of killing for it."

"I'd bet on you."

"You know something, your dad, he loved you. And all you did was disrespect him."

"I didn't come all the way out here to discuss my old man."

Bellamy turned back to his box of ammo. "Then get to it. I'm trying to have some fun tonight, forget that my boss, my oldest friend, got fucking smoked. His own son don't give two shits. But me? I'm out here blowing off my guns in the dark, 'cause what else have I got to do now?"

"Come and work for me."

The man laughed from under his red hat. "You're a pipsqueak next to him."

"Yeah, I don't like you either. But you don't have to *like* a man to make a fortune with him."

Bellamy took up his position and stance again, aiming for the farthest target, a round gong. "You finally grew a pair of balls, that it?" He fired six more, missing two, four making contact, the gong emitting a low ring each time. "Or, what I see, you can't make it happen on your own. You need a number two."

"You were my old man's second, why not mine?"

"I remember what you did to your last guy—Derek? The Atlanta man from prison, thought people'd think that was cool. How I know you won't repeat history?"

"You don't," Luther said in his bored tone, his owl eyes studying this button man, out here in the woods at night.

That got Bellamy to snort. "Aside from this *fortune*, why should I still be listening to you?"

"Your brother, Byron Keith, is still locked up in Charlotte. Shot by the U.S. marshal who was guarding Earl Tucker Lee, when my old man sent Byron to tie up that loose end."

"What's this got to do with Byron?"

"I can get you a shot at that marshal."

"Harlowe," Bellamy said, facing Luther now, interested.

"That's right."

"I been threatening his mama, so he'd back off of you. That was Joe's idea, looking out for your ass all the time. Then she turns around and shoots *him*. That whole family's a plague, always has been. Look what they cost us. I mean, they killed your fucking father, Luther."

"You don't know the half of my trouble with the Harlowes. How about we *both* settle our scores?"

Bellamy spun the revolver's cylinder, something to do with his hands as he contemplated his options. Luther almost had him.

"Toe to toe with a marshal?"

Luther frowned. "And you said *I* don't have the balls."

"I got them, boy, I got a pair like you wouldn't believe."

"Then what's the fucking problem?"

Bellamy cleared his throat, recovering his pride. "How we getting this money you talked about?"

"Reefer. A whole hell of a lot of it in one spot, just waiting for us to go and take it."

"There's reefer and *reefer*."

"This is the latter. We're about to raid Purdy Farms. Tonight."

"Clint's place? Ain't he your supplier?"

"Dead like my old man, like Derek. This county? It's tapped out, all our people gone. I'm looking to be a pioneer. Be the head dog somewhere more profitable. And I'm giving you that same chance."

Bellamy licked his upper teeth and spat. "You killed him, too."

"It's a burden to know everything. To those who can, I advise staying ignorant."

The button man removed his red hat, as if paying respects. "Your dad told me a similar thing, when he gave me each and every job."

"Then you'll feel right at home with me."

\* \* \*

VICKIE HAD SPENT the twenty-four hours since Clint's death in a numb state, lying on the sleeper sofa and watching past NASCAR races on his TV.

More than once, she'd considered calling the marshal and pleading for his assistance. Each time, the selfish part of her said not to. Luther believed she was dead, too. She should leave and forget about Clint and everything they'd done.

Survive.

Except she didn't have the will to do that, either. So she stayed put. Didn't turn tail and didn't call Harlowe. Just shut down.

Tonight her anxiety over Clint's passing was at its worst. She felt a pain in her chest and an overwhelming sense of imminent danger, signs of a panic attack.

Okay, deep breaths. It irritated her that she could diagnose herself with logic yet not relieve the symptoms. Her fight-or-flight response was triggered and wouldn't listen to reason. Her body remained tense, like she was in danger sitting on the sofa.

Maybe some of Clint's weed would do the trick. Then she remembered: No, it would do the opposite. Get her excited. He was famous for cultivating herb that got your motor humming.

*Had been* famous.

She went to the window, opened it, and let the cool air and tranquil dark ease her nerves.

More.

Outside.

She walked through the front door and dropped onto one of the park benches, wondering how he'd managed to steal two of them. A story he'd never told her, and she hadn't thought to ask about it. There had been so much time.

The cold wind felt good, and she began to decompress.

See? She didn't need Harlowe.

When she spotted flashlights in the distance, at the main drying shed among the Christmas trees, she changed her mind.

* * *

AMY WOKE up and listened to the noises that had roused her from across the hall.

Shay was talking to somebody on the phone. She couldn't make out what he was saying, but his voice would get louder and more animated every few seconds, like he was concerned. Or excited.

Was it his mother?

She slipped out of bed and put on a pair of blue jeans and a long-sleeve T-shirt, sensing he was about to go somewhere. It wouldn't be without her.

Now he had hung up, she was pretty sure. Amy went into the hallway and put an ear to his door. Heard the clicks of a deputy marshal checking magazines and slides in his handguns. No, this wasn't about his mother. He was going for Luther Deegan. She was out of time to change his mind.

Was he ready to do this right? Was she ready, in case he wasn't?

Then they were face to face, Amy with her arms crossed, Shay holding a bag and looking at her with the same skeptical glare from their first appointment. Confrontational, intimidating. Then he seemed to remember she was there to support him.

"It'll be dangerous," he said.

He was quick to recognize why she'd gotten dressed.

She nodded. "You love that."

"It's the job."

"But this is personal. Don't hide behind your badge."

"You see a star on me? What's going on, Luther's about to kill somebody else. Unless *I* stop him."

"Call the police."

"They'll take too long. He'll do his damage and run, like always."

"Make up your mind," she said, "are you a hero or not?"

"Luther better hope so."

She moved to the stairs and waited for him to come along. He kept his eyes on her the whole time.

"I do not have vests," he said. "No Kevlar to protect us."

"There are holes in your *house*. How safe would I really be, alone and asleep? I'd rather go with you. Make sure you don't do anything foolish."

He hit the side of the bag and gave her his Cheshire cat grin. "What makes you think I plan to?"

## CHAPTER TWENTY-SEVEN

AMY HELD ON TO THE SIDE OF HER DOOR, AS STOCK CAR champion Shay Harlowe took the winding roads to the northwestern corner of the county at well over the limit.

"Are you able to speed like this?"

He didn't shift his gaze from the double yellow lines ahead. "I know how, if that's what you're asking."

"I mean, as a marshal."

"We get pulled, I guess we'll find out."

He would take a curve by going straight on, for a couple of yards farther than she would ever consider safe, like he didn't intend to turn at all. Then, just before they would've crossed into the oncoming lane, he'd make a smooth pull on the wheel, cutting toward the apex of the corner, which was what he said the official term was. At the same time, he'd lift his foot and let the engine braking—another bit of racing jargon—slow the Tahoe to make the turn. On exit, he'd plant his foot, and the back end of the SUV would step out. Not as much, he said, as a sports or muscle car would, and a hell of a lot less than a late-model on slick asphalt. He'd jerk the wheel left and right to settle the car down again on the straightaway and repeat the whole process at the next bend.

"You only drove on circular tracks?"

"They're ovals," he said, "and that doesn't mean I can't handle a street sprint."

Each corner made her grip the door handle harder. She looked to their left, out over the guardrail and the valley below.

Shay caught her nervous expression and said, "Luther pushed a man off a hill like this one. The wreck, the collision with a boulder at the bottom, it killed the poor bastard."

"The woman we're going to see told you that?"

"She was with him and lived through the crash. Banged up, but not dead. Why she thinks Luther's coming back for her tonight."

"Have you called it in?"

He hesitated. "No time."

"It's a simple phone call. That's why they kept 911 to three digits. Just takes a second to dial."

He didn't answer her.

"Fine. How much farther?"

"We're close," he said. "Which is good, because Luther's already there."

* * *

LUTHER HAD INSTRUCTED his new second to use the service entrance that allowed trucks easy access to the area where Clint Purdy stored his trees when they were ready for shipping. It was also closer to the main drying shed, where he and Bellamy had already packed as much of the dried reefer as they could into the back of Bellamy's F-250, a massive green pick-up with extra-wide, double rear wheels.

Purdy's latest harvest was sizable, worth a lot of money if Luther could get it to his dealers before it went bad. And without being arrested by any number of cops and feds who were looking for him.

"This is it," Bellamy said, and chucked the final black trash bag onto the pile.

Luther pointed to the grass trail that climbed the hill to Purdy's farmhouse. They couldn't see it from this far into the fields, but he knew the way.

"We raid his place next. He'll have had a personal supply and who knows what else."

"You want to break in?"

"It's a dead man's fucking home. You afraid of ghosts?"

"Ain't afraid of nothing. Including you. *Boss.*"

He said it in a snarky tone full of resentment. Luther stared at the prick, then looked over the garbage bags stuffed with his fortune, then back to Bellamy. Now that the heavy lifting was done, why did he need somebody who'd want a cut of the profits?

"Tie those down," Luther said.

"I got a tarp, I'll put it over the whole bed, nobody'll see our shit."

"Don't *tell* me."

Bellamy put on a real show, walking slow as hell to the back seat of his four-door cab, retrieving a blue plastic tarp, and now securing it to the truck in no hurry at all.

It didn't anger Luther. It annoyed him.

His number two finished his task and said from the other side of the F-250, "How's that, boss?"

The same slimy tone of voice, revealing, like the fool he was, that he was up to something.

Luther had plenty of time to get ready for Bellamy to come back around.

When the prick did, he was holding that Smith & Wesson revolver. Almost managed to raise it before Luther shot him at close range, sending Bellamy's body careening backward, knocked off its feet by the blast, until it crashed down and stayed still.

Luther stood over the man. He retrieved the revolver and a box of ammo from Bellamy's pocket.

"Say hi to Joe for me."

* * *

THE FIRST THING Shay noticed about Vickie Beaumont,

she had a Springfield rifle and seemed to be comfortable with it, the way she held it toward the floor, her finger extended and not resting on the trigger, no risk of an accidental pull before she was ready. The second thing, she walked with a limp, an injury to her left leg, no doubt caused by the wreck.

Amy offered to examine it for her.

"Thanks, but I already treated it," Vickie said. "You see, I work in healthcare." Paused and said, "I didn't expect anyone to come with the marshal."

"I'm his doctor," Amy said.

She moved to sit on the sleeper sofa mattress, but Vickie reached out to stop her. "Sorry, do you mind not touching that?"

Amy gave her an apologetic nod and a look of surprise, before standing beside Shay. He couldn't help but smile, how strange this Vickie Beaumont seemed to be. Still, he knew Marty's U.S. Attorney friend would love to meet her, get her in front of the grand jury and hear what she knew about Luther Deegan's many crimes. She could be as odd as she wanted, long as she was willing to testify.

Vickie saying now, "Luther's in the fields somewhere. I spotted flashlights in the trees, way, way out there."

"I expect he believes you're dead," Shay said. "Although that'll change, he catches a glimpse of activity at the house."

"Why else would he come, except to ... finish me off?"

"To raid Clint's reefer. Get the last of the supply before clearing out of the county. That much product, it would earn a hefty sum on the street. Enough to make starting over somewhere else a whole lot easier."

"What do we do?"

Shay put his hands on his hips. "Working in health-care, do you find much occasion to use that rifle?"

"It was Clint's. He showed me how."

Amy stepped between them. "Shay, you can't seriously want to shoot it out with Luther Deegan."

"Well, I wouldn't do it jokingly," Shay said.

"You're going to run out into the dark and chase him through those Christmas trees? *High Noon* it in the middle of the night?"

"No," Shay said, moving to the window and peering out at the quiet farm, no signs of trouble between the firs for now. "I plan to let him come to me. He will. He can't let *her* live," he said, hooking a thumb at Vickie.

"So we sit and wait for a homicidal fugitive to find us?"

"Same thing I did when Joseph Deegan sent that killer to silence Tucker Lee. Set a trap for the man thinks *he's* setting one. Then allow him to spring it."

"That strategy got you suspended," Amy said. "A prisoner in your custody died."

"But I didn't."

\* \* \*

LUTHER STARTED the truck and rolled it up the trail, through the lines of Christmas trees.

Finally, the farmhouse came into view. Shit, why were the lights on? Was someone in there? Could it be Purdy? But how? That crash should've done him in, but maybe he and the redhead had gotten away.

Luther got out and approached on foot, keeping to the firs for cover.

Couldn't believe what he saw—Shay Harlowe's Tahoe parked out front of the home.

He looked down at his two weapons, the shotgun and the Smith & Wesson. Neither would be able to hit the marshal at this distance. No, he'd have to find a way to bring Harlowe out here to him. It wouldn't be hard. The lawman wouldn't pass up a chance to bring him in. Hadn't that been Harlowe's whole purpose for coming back to Wilkes County?

With Bellamy gone, there was one last part of his old man's legacy to erase—the war with the Harlowes.

Luther aimed the revolver at the front windows on the first floor of the house and let off all six rounds. He let the sound of the shots settle over the hills before emptying the cylinder and reloading it from the box.

A minute passed. Then came the report of the same rifle they'd used against him at the speedway, the night of the fake drop. He recognized its distinctive *crack* and took cover behind a tree, watching for the muzzle flashes. There they were, in the upstairs window on the far-right end of the house.

The bullets impacted the ground twenty yards to his left.

Good, they didn't know where he was.

\* \* \*

THEY WERE in the master bedroom, Vickie returning fire with the rifle, Shay and Amy by the door.

He gave Amy the SIG Sauer and said, "Just in case."

"I'm not shooting anyone."

"You will if you have to."

"How is this so easy for you?"

"I never said it was."

Vickie turned to them. "I can't see him. He's somewhere in the trees. They're spaced out enough that I thought I'd spotted him, but now I'm not sure."

Shay slipped the Glock into a carry holster at his hip. Then took the Judge in both hands, the big gun's weight feeling powerful, but not comforting.

"I'll flush him out," he said.

Amy held up a hand. "He'll see you coming."

"I'll slip out the back, scoot around to the other side of the road, and flank him from behind. Push him into the rifle fire."

"Unless he gets you first."

"He won't."

"You can't control that."

Vickie said, "Yes we can." Then held the Springfield out to Amy, saying, "I need you to cover me while I get to the cabin, the one on the trailer? And while the marshal gets into position."

Amy's eyes widened at the prospect of using the gun, and she didn't move to take it.

Shay put his hands on his hips. "What is it you intend to do?"

"Light the Christmas trees," Vickie said. "Like Clint would've wanted."

# CHAPTER TWENTY-EIGHT

AMY HAD A CHANCE TO HOLD THE RIFLE AND PRACTICE aiming it, something she had never imagined doing in her life.

Everything she'd done in the last day was a blur, one event rushing into the next without a break. What would Mark think when she told him? Yes, dear, I helped catch a fugitive. Nearly slept with a patient, too, in his childhood home. We had it to ourselves, because his mother was in jail for murder.

God, who was she? The same person she'd been before, the composed psychiatrist who had always acted based on logic and intelligence, not the raw emotions that she had indulged lately? With Shay, she was somebody else. And she liked it, which scared her the most. She felt ridiculous holding this gun, but not unhappy.

"We don't know his position," Shay said. "Just focus

on getting off shots quick as you can, don't worry about accuracy. We only need you to pin him down in those trees, not hit him."

"What are you going to do? Chase him around in there?"

"I'll keep him distracted while Vickie goes for the cabin."

"What if he has one of these?" she said, holding up the Springfield.

"Then I'd better move faster than he can shoot."

She scowled at him. "I'm serious. I hope I *do* get him, so you won't have to. Your mother gave everything to keep you out of a situation like this, and here I am helping you rush into it."

Shay squinted at her, ever the tough guy in his black suit, the country man in his element out here. "I'd prefer you didn't."

"It could save you more trouble with the marshals."

He put a hand on her shoulder, and she liked his touch. It made her wonder about what could've happened earlier in the night, had they lost their self-control.

She said, "Is it that you think I can't take it?"

"You can, but you shouldn't have to. I do."

"You're saying you *deserve* this?"

He pulled back his hand. "Listen, I'm just ready to be done with him, his whole family, the sorry business we've had for so long. It ends now."

"Will you kill him?"

"My conscious mind," he said, "tells me not to. Let him rot in prison, the feds and staties can fight over him. All the charges against the man, they'll choose which court of law would see him put away for longer." He held the grip of the holstered pistol at his waist. "But who knows what my subconscious mind will do?"

LUTHER COULDN'T DECIDE which weapon would be better for his idea—sneak around to the rear of the farm-house, smash a window, and find Harlowe inside. Both guns would do well in tight quarters. The shotgun was suited for crowd control, something about it more threatening than a lone revolver. You pointed the barrels at somebody, like whoever was in there with Harlowe, and they'd back down. The Smith & Wesson might get the same reaction, but he didn't think it made as much of a statement.

Plus, the shotty had served him well. Derek, Bellamy, and now the marshal. For years, it had protected his restaurant, his pill and weed operation. Wasn't it just poetic that he was using it to destroy all that now? The kind of ending somebody like him, who wanted his story to play out like a great novel, would want.

All he had to do? Defeat the villain of his story. The

man in black, who had come into his world and fucked it. Had incited him to take action and change.

Question was, had all his trials prepared him to face the marshal?

The rifle cracked again from the upstairs window, one shot after another.

It was time to find out.

\* \* \*

VICKIE STAYED low in the shadow of the house and made her way through the bushes and across the far side of the dirt road to the barn. The emptiness of it gave her pause. She pictured Clint's van at the bottom of that slope, Clint still inside. This was all she could do for him, at least until Luther was gone.

She searched the walls and floor for the industrial jerry cans Clint had mentioned using to burn the bulldozer as a kid. His father had kept them full, and she hoped Clint's sentimentality and commitment to tradition had inclined him to do the same.

There they were, with two smaller cans resting alongside, all four heavy. A good sign. They still had their price stickers from the historic hardware store in North Wilkesboro. Clint hadn't bought them for this purpose, but he would've approved anyway.

Vickie lifted the smaller pair, one can in each hand.

Her ankle protested under the additional weight, but she ignored the pain and limped from the barn.

Like that, she retraced her path, the shots from the Springfield filling the otherwise quiet woods around her. She slipped behind the house and now crept across the other side of the drive, until she reached the little cabin on the trailer, its wheels locked for now. With a final look at the jerry cans and a moment to ask herself if she was really going to do this, she splashed the wooden exterior of the portable building in gas. Made sure to douse the dried-out holiday decorations too, the cloth bows and the worn wreaths that the sun had faded.

Almost done.

She reached into her pocket for her Zippo.

* * *

LUTHER COULD TELL the shooter didn't know how to handle the gun. Or couldn't find him in the sights. Even still, running into the open toward the house would be potential suicide. He still had the upper hand, so why risk it?

Then he heard rustling in the Christmas trees behind him. Seconds later, a much louder shot boomed from a few yards away, though he couldn't tell the direction.

It was a heavy caliber, and it was close.

Luther got onto his belly and lunged for the next fir

over. He could hear the marshal—he was sure of it—shifting to a new spot as well.

He said, "Harlowe, I'm giving you fair warning to leave me fucking be."

The marshal fired again, the bullet slicing off a tree branch two firs to Luther's right, Harlowe's voice saying, "There's yours."

"You should be thanking me. I destroyed everything my old man built. Isn't that what you wanted?"

Another shot, this one hitting the tree to Luther's immediate left. He dropped to his stomach once more and moved toward the house.

Shit, he couldn't go much farther, not without backing into the rifle.

"Harlowe," he said, breathing hard, "how about let's see this for what it is. The good guys have won."

"You're including yourself in that?"

The marshal's voice was closer now. Luther thought he had a general idea of the lawman's position. He started slinking in that direction, the shotgun leading the way.

Harlowe said, "I don't think it's me, either. But I *know* it ain't you."

Got him.

Luther raised up fast, aimed the shotty, and fired without looking to see if he was correct. But the buckshot hadn't hit a damn thing, except the grass in a dark space between two Christmas trees.

Harlowe answered the attempt on his life with

another bullet of his own. It missed by ten feet this time, and Luther hit the dirt, not willing to risk it. His owl eyes scanned under the low branches for feet moving between trunks, Luther sweating now, his heart racing.

Afraid.

But it was all right. Heroes *had* to experience this kind of fear. To vanquish a terrifying villain made the hero worthy of the happy ending. Otherwise, the victory wasn't earned, wasn't satisfying. This, he decided, was his "hero at the mercy of the villain scene," something every epic protagonist had to endure.

Just a little longer.

Harlowe saying, "I don't want to kill you, you under-stand? Too many people've died already, thanks to us. *Our* people."

"How else do you see this resolving?"

"You could drop your weapon and come on out."

Luther laughed and then shook his head. Follow the voice, hands and knees until you get there. Let the marshal talk. Villains always rambled on, and it gave the hero time to think of a way to cheat death.

Harlowe saying, "We can put an end to the blood-shed. You want to be the good guy in this? Go on ahead. Do the right thing and turn yourself in. I'll see you're given credit for it with the judge."

Almost there. He was only a couple of firs away now. Almost fucking there.

"Granted," Harlowe said, "the marshals ain't even the

ones in charge. DEA, county sheriff, state police, they'll decide. My word may not amount to much, but I'll do my best, I promise you that."

Luther saw him. The black silhouette of Shay Harlowe was crouched behind a Christmas tree and staring at Luther's previous location.

The marshal didn't see Luther take up a shooting stance. Didn't see him aim the shotgun, finger over the double triggers.

Luther couldn't believe he'd really done it, cornered the son of a bitch.

He would've pulled, but a burning log cabin on a trailer crashed through the trees behind them, setting the entire field alight as it came for him.

SHAY HAD BRACED himself to sprint out of the field before it was too late. Heard trunks and branches snapping under the building's weight and momentum, as it careened down the hill, then saw it, flames licking out its windows, smoke billowing from every opening.

He launched from his hiding spot and ran parallel to the house for several yards, trying to outpace the spreading fire that was already overtaking the firs to his left. When he felt he'd gone far enough, he cut back toward the dirt drive, zigzagging between the trees, just in case Luther got off a final blast of his shotgun. All around him, the oddly pleasant smell of burning firs, a choking haze of smoke, and the crackling of half an acre becoming kindling in a matter of minutes.

He cleared the field and made it to the porch steps.

Vickie came up beside him and said, "Where is he?"

Shay nodded at the inferno. "Call 911, get the fire department. And check on Amy for me."

She left him and went inside.

Then, from the edge of the nearest line of firs, Shay heard desperate coughing. Luther Deegan dragged himself to the dirt drive on all fours, the son of the most infamous pest in the county unable to breathe.

When he was clear of the smoke and flames, he rolled over on his back, sucking in air.

Shay set down the Judge and stood.

Pulled the Glock instead. He was more comfortable with the 27, after all the times he'd carried it as a marshal.

Walked over to Luther, the man's face covered in a layer of soot. "You about done?"

Luther coughed again and said, "You know what, Harlowe? No one's fast enough to outrun history."

Shay flashed his Cheshire cat grin from behind the Glock. "You never saw me race, huh?"

## CHAPTER TWENTY-NINE

ONE WEEK LATER, SHAY WAS BACK IN AMY BAROLO'S office for the final session before his reinstatement. She had his file, her notebook, and that pen she liked to fiddle with.

It was the first time they'd seen each other since leaving his ma's place on D Street the morning after he'd caught Luther Deegan.

Amy said, "You must be excited to return to work."

"I am."

"Will you be participating in Luther's case?"

She spoke in a stilted manner that worried him.

"No," he said. "Martellus, my friend at Highway, I called him to pick Luther up that night at the farm? He and the task force got credit for the arrest. They're dealing with the AUSA, the grand jury. Marshals don't have any skin in the game. Never did, which I guess turned out to be a blessing for me. All *I'm* gonna have to do, me and Vickie Beaumont will testify. Thanks to her, they found Clint Purdy's body and she buried him. Man had no family left. Luther will go down for that death, too." Shay hesitated, trying to read her unchanging expression. "We've kept you out of it. Luther never saw you, and I don't feel you need to upend your life to help sort my mess."

"Thank you," she said. "But if I had to, I would. You know that, don't you?"

"I figured. Luther's going away for a long time, regardless. Drugs, attempted murder, murder one..."

"And your mother?"

Amy's cold, awkward tone was gone now, replaced by the warm concern he'd gotten used to since becoming her patient.

"Out on bond. The town came through and raised sixty grand, fifty to spring her, ten to start on her legal bills. We're already talking to this defense attorney who's ruined a couple of *my* cases here in Charlotte. He's optimistic. She's a first-time offender, claiming self-defense, and then there's the reputation of the victim. She won't get life. Hell, may not even do time. Could be house arrest, which she tells me she wouldn't mind. Work on the renovations she wants to do."

He expected Amy to scribble all kinds of thoughts about their conversation. But she didn't. Just sat there and looked at him with uneasy eyes.

"Did you and Mandy reconnect?"

Shay rubbed the back of his head. "That's over. Too many secrets, not that I realized I was concealing those things. What it came down to, I just never felt like telling her. That make sense? Anyway, that'll be one more regret."

Now Amy bounced her pen against the file. Did it twice, paused, and then once more.

Amy saying, "Where do you and I stand?"

"How do you mean?"

"We're both aware of what we were tempted to do."

"Only tempted."

"True."

He smiled, trying to set her mind at ease. "Because *you* ruined the moment."

There was another long silence between them. Shay was tired of it. He wanted to return to how it had been before their trip to Wilkesboro.

"Listen," he said, "when I was standing over Luther, had him at gunpoint? Part of me wanted to pull the trigger."

She wrote something in her notebook, and he was grateful for it.

"Do you want to explore that further? Even though you're cleared, we could continue our sessions."

He said, "You know, I think we'd better."

## THANKS FOR READING!

If you enjoyed the story and have time, please leave a **review**! It's the best way to support an author.

**Subscribe** to Michael's author newsletter for updates on his next novel, behind-the-scenes information, and more crime fiction content: www. michaelsantosauthor.com/newsletter

# ALSO BY MICHAEL SANTOS

Want more Queen City Crime thrillers?

Read the full series at:

www.michaelsantosauthor.com/books

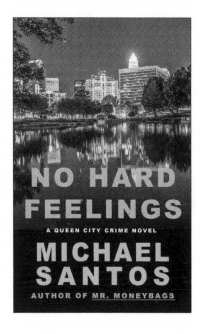

Book 1: No Hard Feelings

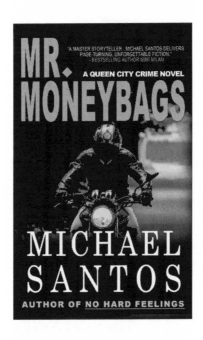

A "A MASTER STORYTELLER...MICHAEL SANTOS DELIVERS
PAGE-TURNING, UNFORGETTABLE FICTION."
- BESTSELLING AUTHOR MIMI MILAN

A QUEEN CITY CRIME NOVEL

MR.
MONEYBAGS

MICHAEL
SANTOS

AUTHOR OF NO HARD FEELINGS

Book 2: Mr. Moneybags

And turn the page for a special Q&A with Michael about *Mean Bones*.

## Q&A WITH MICHAEL SANTOS

*Mean Bones* **is your third novel. What is the biggest lesson you've learned about the writing process since you began your author journey?**

This book got off to a slow start. I wrote the first 20,000 words and wasn't satisfied. The original idea for the novel was too much like other stories I'd encountered, so I scrapped that material. Then I wrote another 20,000 words, but felt that I was contriving a tedious plot, instead of letting the characters direct the story. The truth was, my characters weren't working yet. So, I scrapped those words as well. The third time was the charm. The characters became real to me, and the story flowed from there. After three books, the biggest lesson I've learned about the writing process is that if the characters don't feel right to me, nothing else will. I've always said that they tell me what to write, and it's true.

\* \* \*

**What were your goals for this novel?**

In *No Hard Feelings* and *Mr. Moneybags*, I felt that the characters and dialogue were my biggest strengths. I wanted to take those elements and push them even further in this novel. The dialogue drives the storytelling in *Mean Bones*, whereas the narration plays a larger role in *No Hard Feelings*, for instance. The characters in this book are also more complex, because I made an effort to focus more on their psychology and their pasts. At the same time, I didn't want the book to lose the sense of fun, humor, and style that I like to infuse into these stories of crime, murder, and mayhem. My goal was really to elevate all the aspects that *I* like as a reader.

\* \* \*

**Shay Harlowe is a cool customer. The black suit, the attitude, the intimidating persona ... how did the idea for Shay present itself?**

With this third novel, I wanted to pay tribute to my

influences, which aren't limited to the literary world. I first became interested in crime stories as a kid, when I religiously watched *Batman: The Animated Series*, a cartoon based on the 1989 Batman movie. It was drawn on black paper and the creators then added light, which was an innovative way of approaching animation. The result was a cartoon that looked like film noir. It was perfect for Batman, a hard-boiled detective at heart. Shay pays homage to that character with his black clothing and the way he rides the line between justice and revenge.

I've always been a huge fan of motorsports, so I introduced the racing connection with Dale Earnhardt and Shay's late model career. Racing is also a cultural staple and part of the history of North Carolina, especially the settings in this novel.

Finally, my favorite author, Elmore Leonard, created a U.S. Marshal character named Raylan Givens. I've learned a tremendous amount about writing from reading Leonard's work. *Mean Bones* is my thank you note to him.

All of that combined to form the idea for Shay Harlowe. It's also a story about how our upbringing plays a massive role in shaping the people we eventually become as adults. Shay, Luther, Clint, Vickie—they all face challenges that directly stem from their childhoods, from *their* influences.

\* \* \*

**What do you think are the biggest consistencies across your first three novels? Put another way, what do you hope to be known for?**

I'd like to be known for my writing style and for the way I write the characters. I write stories by taking them scene by scene. I'll place the reader in the perspective—the consciousness—of a character for the duration of a scene. During that time, the narration will sound like that person's rhythms of speech, which is the source of my style. Then, in the next scene, we'll switch characters and the narration will take on *that* person's speech patterns. The goal is to make the entire book sound like my characters' dialogue, without allowing my own narrative voice to pollute it. I feel this is the best way to immerse readers and to bring them closer to the fictional people they'll spend 350 pages getting to know.

**This novel has two major settings: Charlotte and Wilkes County, North Carolina. Why did you decide to expand the Queen City Crime Series to a new location?**

It made sense, given that Shay needed to confront the demons of his past. To do that, he had to return to his hometown, where his tough-guy persona isn't as effective.

When there, he can't hide behind his nickname and his badge, which opened up many possibilities for exploring his characterization. The contrast between urban Charlotte and small-town Wilkesboro set the stage not only for the plot events, but also for Shay's psychological storyline. I enjoy stories in which the author can use the setting to reflect what's happening with the character. Plus, as a U.S. Marshal, Shay's jurisdiction isn't tied to the city. If I write another Shay Harlowe book, I could send him anywhere in the western side of North Carolina.

\* \* \*

**Is that a hint that we'll see Shay again?**

Yep.

\* \* \*

**You always have a romantic sub-plot in your crime novels. In this case, Shay and his married psychiatrist, Amy. Are you a romance fan?**

Romance and crime are two genres that go well together, because they're both founded on values that society strives to achieve. For romance, it's love. For crime, it's justice. You'd be hard-pressed to find someone who doesn't want more love or more justice in their life. In these two genres, we see fictional characters tackle fictional circumstances that are more challenging, more dangerous, and more extreme than anything most people encounter in daily life. So, if the characters can obtain love and justice under such severe pressure, surely, anyone can do the same. It's why these two genres easily blend with one another, and with any other type of fiction.

Love is such a primal need for humans that it's also a necessary factor to explore when developing a character. How does somebody like Shay Harlowe feel about romance? It was a question I had to answer in order to write a complete person.

Finally, it's just plain fun to write a romantic story. What's not to like about an attractive couple thrown together by dire circumstances? In this book, I wanted to play around with a forbidden romance—the protagonist and a married woman. Will they or won't they? The conflict of that question is compounded when Shay learns that his father stepped out on his mother. How much of his father's son is he? Like I said, it opens up possibilities to push these characters using their strongest and most basic human desires.

**What are you reading right now?**

I'm reading heist novels at the moment. It's a sub-genre of crime that I've always enjoyed, so I decided to study them and analyze how they work. Who knows? Soon, you might see a Queen City Crime Series novel about a thrilling heist.

# ACKNOWLEDGMENTS

To Mr. Flinn, the kind of teacher every student needs. Thank you for inspiring and for always supporting my goal of being a writer.

To writer Kara Hagan, thank you for beta-reading and for being a fantastic collaborator on this writing journey.

To Pinckney Benedict, for being a great mentor and for your excitement about my writing.

To Phyllis DeBlanche, for all of your support and hard work!

To Addison Honeycutt, for taking the perfect author photo, and for your constant encouragement and entrepreneurial spirit.

To my writing group, for having my (and each other's) back, day in, day out, on this author journey.

To Angela Santucci, Russell Vacanti, and Jason Sharp:

Thank you for an amazing drama program, an example of how hard work can pay off in the arts. Your lessons on performing scenes taught me how to write them.

Lastly and most importantly, to my parents, who have supported my creative endeavors since my 2nd grade book about dinosaurs, and who have encouraged me to pursue my dreams. They are the first readers of all my drafts, even as they wince at the language my characters use, eventually acquiescing to the nature of the genre because they realize criminals don't say, "Aw shucks!"

69476013R00214

Made in the USA
Columbia, SC
15 August 2019